Earl, Honey

Earl, Honey

D.S. GETSON

Matador
Unit E2 Airfield Business Park,
Harrison Road, Market Harborough,
Leicestershire. LE16 7UL
Tel: 0116 2792299
Email: books@troubador.co.uk
Web: www.troubador.co.uk/matador
Twitter: @matadorbooks

ISBN 978 1803131 696

British Library Cataloguing in Publication Data.
A catalogue record for this book is available from the British Library.

Printed and bound in Great Britain by 4edge Limited
Typeset in 11pt Minion Pro by Troubador Publishing Ltd, Leicester, UK

Matador is an imprint of Troubador Publishing Ltd

Caution: This story includes references to incest and physical and sexual abuse, which may be triggering for some readers.

Although inspired by true events, this is a work of fiction. Timelines have been condensed, and names and other identifying details have been changed to protect the privacy of individuals.

For Earl, who lived it,
and for Elaine, who urged that it be written.

EARL, HONEY

"Blessed is he who plants trees under
whose shade he will never sit."

Indian Proverb

PART I:

COMMON CHICKWEED

STELLARIA MEDIA: A low weed common along roadsides and fields, often consumed by chickens and wild birds. Although it possesses numerous benefits, chickweed is considered undesirable within horticultural landscapes and great effort is expended to eradicate it.

ONE

Summer 1970 / Summer 1921

Ever since Pa hit him in the head with the two-by-four, Earl had lived with blinders on. Not real blinders, of course, because that would be foolish. It was his own brain that blinkered him.

When he was a boy, his ma told him carriage horses wore blinders to keep from panicking on account of all the dangerous things they had surrounding 'em. That made sense to Earl. The world could be a terrifying place. Like a cart horse trotting a well-worn path, he preferred to keep his eyes down, looking neither right nor left to see what might be lurking in the shadows. That didn't mean he couldn't learn from his history. A letter from his sister Lucy could tug on his memory in unexpected ways and send him peeking, squinty-eyed, into the past.

'I've bought you a plot,' she writes in her spidery cursive. *'It's in the Piney Plains Cemetery, next to Ma. I think she would want you there, close to her heart. (Or whatever is left of her.)'*

He snorts then chokes, leading to a coughing fit that brings tears to his eyes. Dang, that girl can make him laugh. Chuckling, he removes a tattered blue handkerchief from his pocket and blows his nose. His sister Rose used to say Lucy had no couth. Lucy spoke what was on her mind and to hell with folks who judged her for it. Ma preferred other words. She told him once the Hahns were not a squeamish people. They were constructed of mud and straw and, like the earth, unrefined. At the time, he hadn't known that word. He knows it now. 'Unrefined' is April 22nd in the word-of-the-day calendar Harold give to him on his last birthday. He'd read the word and the definition that come with it and knew it to be a description of him and all his kin.

Setting the letter aside, Earl lights the flame beneath a burner and puts a pot of water on to boil. While he waits for the water to bubble, he pours himself an iced tea and stands at the window overlooking the garden. Maybe he's of the earth, too, he thinks. There's nothing he likes better than putting his hands into the dirt, burying a seed in a tiny pocket of soil and watching it grow. There's no question in his mind that if he and Lucy are unrefined, it's on account of their pa. He prays every day it's the only thing that man passed down.

The day his pa went on trial, Earl hadn't known many words. He'd barely understood a thing the attorney men were saying. One word in particular buzzed around his head in search of a meaning. He tried using his imagination. Even now, years later, he could picture his pa, mouth wrenched in a grimace, a swarm of black beetles spilling onto Carolina clay. As a boy, the vision scared him and he'd squinched his eyes shut to block it. Which is why, when Pa slammed his fist to the table, Earl hadn't been prepared. His eyes flew open, a startled yelp erupting from his mouth.

Heads swiveled to stare, then pivoted back so as not to miss a single second of courtroom drama.

"I di'nt fornicate with no donkey. Es ist eine dirty lie!"

From the back of the darkly paneled room, he feels his pa's rage like a ground tremor rippling its way through the crowd to the spot where he sits, surrounded by family. Well, except for Rose. She's up front in a special seat. Oh, and Welcome and Faith, who Ma sent away after Rose got knocked up. But Wilhelm, Frieda, Kurt and Orbry fill one end of the pew. No, not a pew, he decides, cause they ain't in church. A bench. A plain ol' bench. Next is his ma. And beside him, his little sister fidgets like a jumping bean. Lucy gets anxious when Pa loses his temper. Besides which, they's all hot as blister bugs. He can feel sweat tears trickling down his ribs. He gazes longingly at the closed window. Judge ordered for windows to stay shut on account of neighbors and newspapermen malingering outside, hoping to hear a bit of juice.

"And what about the other charge, Mr. Hahn? Is it true your daughter, Rose, is carrying your child?"

His pa never looks at Rose. He keeps his eyes hard on the man seated in the high box. Earl looks at his sister and notices the way her fingers tremble every time she lifts them from her lap. She's grown large since he saw her last. Her belly enters the room before she does, making her seem strange to him. She's always been a tiny thing. She looks different in other ways, too. She's replaced her overalls with a proper dress. *Where'd she get the dress?* he wonders. Maybe the solicitor got it for her.

"Vat's my rights, Judge?" His pa points at the man in the black robe then seems to think better of it. The German accent he never lost after arriving in the country thickens each word. "Venn I get sent to da penitentiary, vat vill 'appen to mein property?"

"While you're away, someone can be appointed to take charge of your affairs."

His pa paces the courtroom, the little finger on his right hand twitching in a rhythm you could set a watch by. Usually, that's a sign he's getting ready to punch someone. Earl glances around to see who's within striking distance. No one he knows. He isn't sure his pa would hit a stranger.

Then again, he isn't sure he wouldn't.

The night before, Earl visited him in the jailhouse, delivering a clean shirt and a plate of ham and pinto beans. He found his pa ranting to the officers. The topics were endless but boiled down to one thing: the world had conspired against him. He couldn't pay the money for his bond. He couldn't afford an attorney to represent him in court. Earl had stepped back from the bars of the cage, glad his pa's ire wasn't directed at him. He stayed silent when his pa began mumbling darkly to himself. Finally, the man calmed, noticing the plate of food set before him and attacking the meal with animal appetite.

In no hurry to be elsewhere, Earl lingered at the jailhouse so he could return the empty plate to his ma, knowing she needed every dish to feed their family. He may not have been able to put his thoughts into words, but deep down was an instinctive awareness of something his pa wasn't saying. Something everyone but Pa seemed to know. There wasn't a man within a hundred miles of Sampson County who would stand up for Reinhardt Hahn.

Returning his attention to the action before him, he watches his pa grip the edge of the judge's bench.

"Und ven I plead guilty, mein kinder – dey… dey vill not haf to listen to a trial. Ist das korrekt?"

For one swift second, Earl believes something like compassion flashes across the judge's face. Perhaps he imagines the look, for it comes and goes so quickly, and he's seated at the back of the room where tiny details can be mistaken.

"Mr. Hahn, you've been charged with four counts of buggery. In addition, you've been accused of forcefully and feloniously having carnal relations with your daughter. I have sworn affidavits from your wife and three of your children attesting to these accusations. Even if you plead guilty, I'll need to learn more regarding the nature of the case in order to determine the extent of the punishment. However," the judge scans the courtroom as though daring anyone to disagree, "in light of the delicate nature of these accusations, I could be persuaded to hold the penalty hearing privately in my chambers."

"In dat case, Your Honor, I vill sacrifice myself for the sake of mein kin."

The judge turns to an elderly woman seated at the table below him. "Mrs. Watson, please note for the record the defendant has entered a plea of guilty." He looks at Pa and motions toward the table across the room. "Since you have forsworn representation, you may take your seat, Mr. Hahn."

"Your Honor?"

Major Butler, who's seated between his sister and the solicitor, stands and clears his throat. "Before adjourning the court, I would like to have entered into the record the testimony of Mr. Hahn's neighbors. They can speak to the accused's general character and behavior. I think it's important for their statements to be heard before the penalty phase."

Earl scratches his nose, leaning forward to see which neighbors have come to speak against Pa. He doesn't see Farmer Tate. It would take a lot to pull him away from his daily labor. But he observes with interest as a tall, string bean man named Stanley Strickland makes his way to a seat at the front of the room. Earl has a bad feeling about this, on account of his pa poisoning Mr. Stan's well last year. Earl was with him when he done it, taken a rotted chicken carcass and thrown it into the water with an audible splash.

A few days later, Mr. Stan's family took sick, one daughter dangerously so.

Healthy now, and full of ire, their former neighbor glances toward the back row. Earl responds with a smile and lifts his arm to wave. His ma, catching the movement, presses his hand back to his side and holds it there. He turns to see what's on her mind, but she continues to face forward, her expression impossible to read.

One of the attorneys makes his way to the front and pauses beside Mr. Stan. Earl doesn't know the man and watches curiously as he rocks back on his heels, thumbs hooked through tan suspenders. He hears Frieda whisper about how this man is from Raleigh, brought in to help with the case.

"Can you tell me how you know the accused?" the man asks.

"I lived within a hundred yards of Hahn during his first year in Sampson County. I asked him how he came to be in the area. He told me he answered an advertisement posted in a newspaper up north. He took a train down to work for Mr. Sam Tate and lived in one of the sharecropper cabins. Mr. Tate let him work a small piece of land in exchange for tending to the farm."

"And what were your observations of Mr. Hahn during this time?"

"It was concerning, Your Honor. The man clearly didn't know anything about farming. He couldn't hitch a horse or set a plow." He stares at Pa, who hangs on every word, his eyes spitting black fury at the man witnessing against him.

"I was trying to be neighborly," Mr. Stan continues. "I showed him what to do and had opportunity to observe his manner of life."

"And did he demonstrate an ability to learn?" the attorney man asks. "At any time, did he appear to be crazy?"

"Oh, Hahn has plenty of sense of some kind, but not a bit of another kind."

"I'm not sure I'm following. Can you be more specific?"

"Well, he's got good sense about some things, but he don't have common sense, see? Like, Hahn bought these two mules at auction, but he didn't know how to feed his stock to keep 'em hale. He lost both animals cause of careless handling, plain and simple. He worked 'em till they plumb gave out. Then he shot 'em in the head and took the skirt off."

"I beg your pardon?"

"He skinned them and sold their hides."

"I see."

"Hahn told me he canned the meat. Only the meat spoiled. His boy back there tried to eat it and vomited it out every time."

Earl's eyes widen when Mr. Stan points his way. His stomach flips in remembrance and a sour taste fills his mouth. That had been some bad meat.

"Hahn threw the rest of it in the dirt. I guess he thought it would be good for his garden. Some dogs must have smelled it 'cause they dug up every piece."

"And how would you say the man treated his family?"

"He was harsh, sir, very harsh. I recollect a time his wife, Lizzie Belle, she came to the tobacco barn one morning and I was in there with Hahn. She asked if she might spend the Sabbath. Hahn swore something at her in German. I don't speak German, sir, but I could tell it was something ugly. And he said… these are his exact words… he said, 'you can spend it, woman, but spend it tilling new ground'. Later, I saw her going out to the cropper's field with a hoe and shovel. Also, he showed no regard or affection for the presence of his daughters. He's a hard man and that's a fact. Mr. Tate sacked him before he'd worked there a year."

Earl nods his head in agreement. He may not recall much but he remembers that day. When Pa got sacked, everyone took the brunt of his anger. His violence was sweeping and irreversible. He glances down as Ma covers her right hand with the left, hiding her own reminder of that day: a jagged line that connects her pointing finger to a puckered spot on her wrist.

Sensing his attention, she gives him a look he can't decipher. Neither says a word.

TWO

Earl is surprised at how many stories Mr. Stan knows about Pa. When their neighbor finally falls silent, the judge stares at Pa where he sits at the long wood table, his body vibrating with emotion.

"Mr. Hahn, since you are representing yourself, you have the right to cross-examine."

"Ist my turn to speak?"

His pa's voice contains a tone Earl recognizes. Danger-danger. His heartbeat picks up speed. Time to duck and hide. Or run. Run and run. He casts his eyes around the unfamiliar room seeking a way out. Panic tightens his belly. Reflexively, he grabs hold of his ma and scooches closer. She gives his hand a pat.

"You may stand and address the witness," the judge says, his tones measured, his eye sharp on Pa.

Lucy pokes Earl in the ribs and he leans down to hear her words. "I want to go home," she says, clearly agitated. She heard the same tone.

Earl pulls on his ma's sleeve until she tips her head, her eyes never leaving the action at the front of the room. "Lucy wants to go home," he says. He doesn't say 'me, too' but he's thinkin' it. He knows his pa's explosions. If one's coming, he don't want to be anywhere near.

"Later. Not yet. You need to hear this. You both do." She turns to look at him, her eyes full of feelings he's unsure how to read. She lowers her voice so only Earl can hear. "You're safe here, hon, but you need to pay attention. Someday, you may want to remember this."

"Yes ma'am." He glances at Lucy and gives his head a shake. She releases a puff of breath and sits back on the bench with her head pressed against the wood. Her face has the same long-suffering expression she wears in church. Like all the grown-ups in the world exist simply to thwart her.

Earl gathers his attention and focuses on Pa. He's dressed in his overalls with the oil stain on the bib, but the shirt is clean. Ma insisted her husband shouldn't shame her further than he already had. The least he could do was show up in court looking presentable. Earl isn't sure a clean shirt could make his pa presentable. Still, it's hard to look away from the wiry man as he strides to where Mr. Stan sits in the witness box. Even from a distance, the rage he carries inside shimmers the air around him. He wastes no time lightin' into his former neighbor.

"Sir, you haf perjured yourself. I di'nt fornicate vith no jackass. You're a damn liar."

"I saw you with my own eyes. So did your boy."

"You lie!"

"Then why were you chasing him through the cornfield with your ass hanging out of your britches?"

Several men break into coughing fits. Hahn's face flushes like a scalded tomato.

Eyes never wavering from his pa, Earl chews one finger, remembering his narrow escape. He'd seen something he weren't s'posed to see, somethin' that made his skin crawl. He'd tried to back out of the barn without makin' a noise. He failed. He decided to break for it when he realized Pa had heard his footstep, his head swiveling to pin him with a furious stare. He outran his pa that day – he could outrun just about anyone – but it only delayed the punishment. His pa was waitin' with a fresh switch when Earl slipped into the house later. He never did tell his ma what that whipping was for and one look at her husband's face had discouraged questions.

Now he watches closely as Pa goes nose-to-nose with Mr. Stan. Earl continues to worry his finger, silently assessing the strength of the slender wood barrier separating the two men.

"I'm gonna shoot you twixt the eyes." Pa's voice is low and mean.

"Judge, did you hear that? Did you hear? Hahn threatened me." Stanley Strickland gestures toward the packed room. "Y'all heard it."

"Kvatch! So ein misthaufen! You're a lily-livered chicken shit!" shouts Pa, delivering a sharp kick to the witness stand.

"We'll take this outside and settle it once and for all," Mr. Stan growls back, matching his volume. He rises to his feet with hands fisted.

"I'll vip you vere you stand," Pa snarls. He lifts both arms and crouches into his favorite fighting stance, his right fist and right foot forward. As folks in the courtroom inch toward the edge of their seats, Earl sinks back into his, waiting for Pa to launch his left cross right hook.

The judge motions to an officer by the wall, who reaches his pa in four strides, gripping the man's shoulder like he means business. Feeling the ambush behind him, his pa swirls with an automatic jab to the officer's midsection. The man expels a loud *whoof* then wraps strong arms around Pa.

"That's enough!" The judge gives Pa a stern look then faces the witness. "Mr. Strickland, sit down. Mr. Hahn, you're supposed to cross-examine the witness, not hurl threats and accusations. I won't have you making a mockery of this courtroom."

"I don't know vat you mean," his pa mutters sullenly, squirming in the officer's embrace. His eyes are hot.

"Can you control your temper?" the judge demands. "And I'll thank you not to abuse county property. Not unless you're prepared to make reparations."

After a minute, his pa shrugs off the guard and wipes a hand down his face. He drops his head, staring hard at the floor. Earl knows the man can be wily. He might be readying for another attack.

The judge waits a beat to ensure order has been restored. When it seems as though further violence will not be forthcoming, he motions the officer back to his position beside the flag. "Now, Mr. Hahn, would you like to ask the witness questions regarding his testimony?"

Pa wags his head. His movements appear slow and halting as though he's making his way through mud. "Vat's da use, Your Honor? I'm not a lawyer. Vat's da use?"

Noting the slumped shoulders, it occurs to Earl he's never seen his pa like this, beat down and uncertain. If folks are to be believed, his pa is something called *a moral.* That's another word he doesn't know. What he does know is that it takes a lot to break a Hahn.

His next thought is about heat and the misery of sitting still in such a place. The trial's takin' a long time. Sharp light coming through the near window is hard to bear. It will ease his listening if he rests his eyes, only for a second.

He doesn't stir until he feels a sharp elbow in the ribs. Struggling to come awake, he stares about with confusion. "Wh… what's goin' on?"

"Take Lucy," his ma says briskly. "Go outside. Wait for us."

Yawning, he wipes the grit from his eyes and stares bemusedly at the bank of windows. He can tell from the altered slant of sunbeam that a considerable amount of time has passed. *That was a good nap,* he thinks with satisfaction. He notices Lucy. She's on her feet, watching him expectantly.

"Where're we going?" he mumbles.

"Take your sister outside. The rest of us are going to speak with the judge."

As he processes the words, his brows draw together in a scowl. He doesn't like the idea of her goin' off without him. "I need to speak with the judge, too."

"Go on, now. Look after your sister like I asked. Take her hand."

Lower lip jutting, he opens his hand. Lucy slips hers into it.

"If the judge wants to speak with you, I'll come fetch you myself."

"What are you going to do?" he asks. "Why can't I come?"

She places rough hands on either side of his face and makes him look at her directly.

"What do you ask me every night before you go to bed?"

He doesn't have to think about it. "Am I safe?" he whispers.

"And since your pa's been in the jailhouse, what's my answer?"

"Yes." And it was true. He'd felt safe for the first time in his life. Safe from ugly words and harsh blows; safe from the need to be invisible.

"You and Rose are going to get justice," she says softly. "Ladies and children got rights now. It's the law. It won't make up for what he did. But it's a start. Your pa's going to get what he has coming."

"Like a present?"

She nods. "Like a present for you and me and for your sisters."

"For Lucy, too?"

"Most definitely for Lucy." A look comes over her face that he recognizes. It signals a step back in time, a visible shift from the damp, Southern summer to another century and an old-world upbringing she'd never shaken. "Leviticus says, 'none of you shall approach to any that is kin, to uncover their nakedness.'" She stares him hard in the eyes. "Do you understand?"

He doesn't but nods anyway.

"'Neither shalt thou lie with any beast to defile thyself.' It's a perversion. Your pa is a perversion".

“Yes ma’am.”

“Now, watch your sister. Mind yourself, hear?”

“Yes ma’am.”

She motions to his brothers and to Frieda and they head toward the front of the room, where the judge stands waiting with Rose. Earl glances down at his sister.

“Come on then.”

THREE

Sampson County is known for three things: flue-cured tobacco, grand champion hogs and epic heat and humidity. Even late in the day, the air glimmers with a veil of moisture. Earlier, Earl had craved a bit of breeze. Now that he's outside the courthouse, he feels submerged in the air. He wants to peel his shirt and race for the river.

Loitering in the shade of a brick side porch, he peeks at his sister. Tiny droplets bead on her forehead and above her lip.

"I'm heat-struck," she whispers.

"Pooh. This is nothin'. Last summer was hotter."

"I'm gonna melt right here in a puddle of Lucy, you watch."

"Want me to fan you?"

"Yeah."

He flaps his hands around her head till she shoos him off, giggling.

"Come on." Wrapping his large hand around Lucy's delicate one, he steps down to the sidewalk. At the corner, three kids play a tagging game. He glances their way then tugs on his sister to follow him. He tries to figure the best place to wait for Ma and finally heads across Main Street to the five-and-dime. He doesn't have a penny for candy but the two of them can take a slice of shade beneath the awning and maybe catch up on gossip.

"Hi there, Mr. Purvis," he says, stepping up to the storefront. Mr. Purvis has his head down, looking thoughtful as he walks home from the office. He's a deacon at the church, and he's kind to their ma. As the children approach, he lifts his head and gives them a smile that is reassuring in its sincerity.

"Good afternoon, Earl. The trial still going on?"

"No sir. But the judge needed to speak with Ma, so Lucy and I are to wait outside."

The man reaches into his waistcoat pocket and removes a coin. "Here, son. Why don't you take your sister into the store and share a soda? It'll cool you down in this heat."

"Golly. Thank you, Mr. Purvis." He grins at his sister. They hardly ever get soda. Occasionally a lemon drop or a piece of peppermint. But a whole pop to themselves? This is cause for celebration.

"The missus and I will be praying for your family."

"Thank you, sir."

Lucy's on her toes with excitement, but he restrains her until Mr. Purvis walks away. He knows Ma wouldn't want him to appear disrespectful. Still, he can't hold back a soft whoop as he steps inside the dark interior of the store. There's a photograph of an old war chief on the wall behind the cash register. The face looking out of the photo is fierce and sad and something else Earl can't decipher. It troubles him. He looks away and straight into the eyes of the grocer.

Mr. Wilkins glowers at them from behind the counter. Earl knows why. His pa has stolen from this store many times. The only reason Earl and Lucy are allowed through the front door is because of folks takin' pity on his ma. He holds up the five-cent piece so the man can see he has money to pay. Then he and Lucy walk to the ice chest and remove a bottle from the freezer. The curve of the frosty glass fits his hand like it was crafted solely for this purpose.

"Let me," says Lucy.

He hands over the bottle so she can use the steel opener to pop the top. Then he hands the coin to Mr. Wilkins, who deposits it into an ornate till.

"Take it outside," the man says shortly.

The two return to the store's front porch. Earl takes a swig from the bottle and smacks his lips before handing it to his sister. She takes a long drink then burps, smiling at the sound. Earl's answering grin evaporates when he sees a trio of boys headed their way.

He sends Lucy a glance that means 'look out', but she's seen them too. She watches warily as they approach.

"Hey, moron."

He doesn't respond. Mr. Purvis might be a decent man but his son, James, is a hooligan. Everyone knows it but Mr. Purvis.

"Whatcha got there, moron?"

Earl tightens his lips. He knows it don't matter what he does or what he says. These boys are gonna torment him for their own pleasure. He can take a hit if it comes, but his ma told him to look after his sister. He steals a quick glance at Lucy from the corner of his eye. She stands frozen, her hand clamped around the cold glass.

"Here, give that to me," snaps James.

The Purvis boy steps toward Lucy. She sends Earl a quick look then hands over the bottle. He tips it up to take a sip then spews the soda out of his mouth, gagging dramatically. "I got Hahn skank!" Eyes gleeful, he turns the bottle upside down so the cola pours onto the dirt. "Say, Lucy – that's your name, right?"

She pushes a dark strand of hair out of her eyes but stays silent.

"How old are you?"

Maybe she decides they'll lose interest if she delivers what they're asking for because, after a moment, she replies. "Seven."

An unpleasant look enters his eye. "I bet your pa's gonna come after you next, soon as he gets out of the State Pen. You'll be ripe then. Three years and it'll be your word against his. Maybe you can visit him for one of those… what are they called?… connubial visits."

Another boy snickers. "Shit. One of us'll have her 'fore she's ten, James."

The Purvis boy joins in the laughter and Earl feels a twinge in his gut, something ugly that sets him on edge.

"If your pa hadn't poisoned your sister's belly, I bet he'd o' never got caught." Narrowing his eyes as he looks Lucy up and down, James tips his head thoughtfully. "Maybe he's already been in your bloomers, eh? Or maybe your sisters keep him busy. Your sister Faith is a peach." He shifts his attention to Earl. "Your pa likes donkeys and daughters. Does he bugger his sons, too?"

There's that word again. He's pretty sure it's something naughty. He's unsure how to answer. He's not sure he should answer. These boys are talkin' nasty. And he knows why. He wishes he didn't. He wishes he'd never seen his pa in the barn; that he'd never seen his pa with Rose. Earl always seemed to be in the wrong place. He'd been hidin' in the rafters that day, afraid Orbry was gonna come after him for smilin' when his brother smashed his thumb with the hammer. He should have stayed and taken the punch.

He could never unsee what his pa done, but he hadn't said nothin'. Not then. It was Rose who got up the gumption to visit the sheriff. Later, the sheriff asked Earl to tell, so he did. But not at first. Nibbling his lip, he casts another glance at his little sister. He doesn't think his pa touched her like he did Rose.

Her eyes are wide now, fixed on the taunting boys. He doesn't know what to do. He can't run away on account of Lucy won't be able to keep up. If James and his pals try to hurt her, he'll have to do something.

"You boys get on now before I pay a call on your parents."

At the sound of a deep voice, Earl spins to see who's come up behind him. He's never met the man, but everyone in town knows who he is. Mr. Edwards is Clinton's Superintendent of Public Welfare. Rose works in his home as a housemaid. He's the one who helped her after she run away from Pa.

The tall man gives James Purvis and his friends a long, quiet look. Beside him, the county welfare officer points at the boys. "I'm taking names. Don't think I won't knock on your door, Master Purvis! Loitering, disrupting the peace, being a public nuisance. What else can I add to the list?" He holds a sharpened pencil poised over his writing tablet.

The boys whirl on their heels and run off, hurling the empty soda bottle to the ground. Earl moves to fetch it, knowing he can turn it in at the store for a penny. Maybe he and Lucy can split a peppermint stick. He stops when Mr. Edwards pins him with a look.

"I saw you two in the courtroom. You're Rose's family."

Lucy's cheeks are pink from her encounter with the boys. She steps forward, tight fists on her hips. "That boy said it'd be my turn in three years. What happens when I turn ten?"

"Those boys are misinformed," the man says. "Don't give it another thought." Eyes that had been hard before now look kindly at the two children.

"Tell me," she insists.

Mr. Edwards lifts his face to the sky and Earl has the impression he might be praying. After a long moment, he makes a grunt then turns his gaze on Lucy. "Until recently, ten was the age of consent in the state of North Carolina. It wasn't a crime for a man to…." He clears his throat. "Well, for a man to be, ah…" He looks sideways at his companion and Lucy speaks up.

"Earl and me, we live on a farm. And we know our pa. There's nothing you can say we haven't heard, and worse."

He blows out a long breath. "Fine. Then I'll tell it to you straight. Until recently, if a man was intimate with a girl of ten and she brought a claim of sexual assault against him, he could say she granted him consent and it would be his word against hers in a court of law. Any younger, and it would be a crime. The law states that anyone below a minimum age is legally the victim since they're too young to grant consent. Last year, women got the vote. Slowly but surely, they're changing things. The age of consent in North Carolina *was* ten. Now, any sexual relations with a minor younger than sixteen is a crime."

"Rose is fifteen," she says. "So that's why..."

"Rose may be fifteen, but it doesn't matter about her age, because it's always a crime when it involves a father and daughter."

"Will our pa go to prison?" Earl asks.

"The maximum penalty for incest in this state is fifteen years. Because he pled guilty, and considering the other charges against him, I suspect he'll get at least that."

"How come you know so much?" his sister asks.

"It's my job," he responds matter-of-factly. He leans forward until his face is inches away from the two children. Earl admires the gray hairs mixed among dark whiskers. "Now, I want to say something to both of you and I want you to listen and listen carefully, do you understand?"

Without speaking, the pair nod their agreement.

"Your pa is a son-of-a-bitch. The trashiest of poor white trash."

Lucy frowns, but she doesn't look shocked. These are words they understand.

"I know this is a hard thing to hear about your kin," the man continues, "but I expect you know it's true better than most. That doesn't mean you have to follow in his footsteps. You have a choice. It may not feel like it now, but you do. There's no disgrace in being poor. You can be poor and hold up your head in this town – in any town. You can choose a different way to be. Do you understand what I'm saying?"

Earl doesn't fully take the man's meaning. But his words, his expression, even the tone of his voice – it stirs something inside him.

"Your father came to this country to make a better life for himself. He squandered it. Don't make the same mistake. Every day, life will give you opportunities to be better. Be better."

Be better. Earl ponders the two simple words, his foot kicking absently at a half-buried stone in the ground. The man makes it sound easy.

FOUR

Rose gives birth to a girl and names the child Matilde. Earl's fascinated by the tiny creature and runs the three miles to town as often as Ma will let him go. He bends over the child's cradle, happy as a June bug, to watch the fleeting expressions on her face. "She looks like a little old man," he says, tickling her belly. "Like she's got a secret."

"She's got gas," his sister says tiredly.

He lifts his eyes to watch Rose. She rests in the center of an iron bed, her gaze unfocused on the window. On the sill, a tin coffee pot holds three white gardenia blossoms. After a minute, she yawns and closes her eyes.

That's his cue to reach out and rub the baby's head, searching for the soft spot. When his sister's eyes are sharp on him, she always wants him to be 'gentle, gentle'. But he *is* gentle. He whispers to Matilde, grinning when she squints right at him. Her lips quirk like she's laughing.

It's been explained to him that this is his sister's lying-in period and, boy, does she do a lot of that. Often when he comes to visit, her eyes are rimmed in red and he knows she's been crying. He told Ma this and she said it was on account of Rose's friends hadn't come to visit to fuss over her and the baby.

Maybe that's the reason she gets fed up with bed rest and fed up with the baby.

Earl's coming out of the chicken shed when Mr. Edwards' hired man trots his buggy up to the house with Rose in it. She climbs down then reaches into the buggy and lifts out a plain straw basket. He peeks inside, surprised to see Matilde wrapped in a strip of muslin and narrowing her eyes crossly at the sun.

"Where's Ma?" Rose asks.

"Kitchen."

He starts to follow her into the house, but she turns and gives him a look. Feelin' put out, he parks himself on a cinder block step and tips his head toward the screen door.

Voices are muffled but he hears some.

"I can't carry out my duties with an infant demanding to be fed or changed or burped every other minute," his sister says. "If you'd been a proper mother, I wouldn't have to."

There is long silence that seems full of words unsaid, but Earl believes they're there, invisible messages being conveyed by hot eyes and pressed lips.

"I'm sure Mrs. Edwards understands the demands of motherhood, Rose." Ma's voice sounds strained. "Surely you can work out a way to contribute to the running of the household without neglecting your child."

"I… I don't want to."

There are more words he can't make out and he inches closer to the door, prepared to dash if he hears someone coming. He hopes Rose will leave her baby here. He's never felt so safe in his life as he does now with Pa at the prison. Having a baby in the house will make everything more fun.

Ears peeled, he hears Rose raise her voice angrily. It must upset the baby because she lets out a cry then he hears shushing sounds. He understands it's selfish of him to want the baby here when she rightly belongs with his sister. A part of him is troubled that Rose doesn't want her own child. He figures Matilde is an unwelcome reminder of their pa. Earl isn't bright about many things. But he's seen a stressed sow push away its own flesh and blood, the runt that's unwelcome, unfed. Maybe Rose feels like that mama pig.

Fortunately for his sister, Ma knows all about babies. With fifteen births, and ten children who survived beyond their first year, there's little in the way of child-rearing she can't manage. That's not all of it, of course. His ma is tender-hearted. More than one neighbor had observed it was Ma's tender heart that allowed her to put up with Pa as long as she did; that and God. A devout woman, Lizzie Belle Hahn made a promise to obey her lawfully wedded husband. She'd mostly done it – through beatings and petty thievery and, once Prohibition came, the occasional moonshining. She'd be with him still if he hadn't gone after her own children, who she was also obliged to protect.

With Pa gone, she'd begun selling eggs and washing laundry and taking in sewing to keep food on the table.

She'd sold their little piece of land to pay for taxes but Farmer Tate said they could stay in the old cropper house if they pitched in around the place. Now, Ma helps Missus Tate with cooking and cleaning while Orbry works in the tabacca fields. Farmer Tate asked Orbry if he wanted to go to the farm school half-days, but his brother said no. Schooling had never been important to him and he'd rather have the work.

Earl works too, mostly to keep busy. He tends the chickens, collecting eggs and making sure the hens get fed. And when his wish is granted and Baby Mattie comes to stay, well, he looks after her, too – whenever Ma has her hands full. He doesn't mind a lick.

With Pa gone, his brothers and sisters, one by one, depart also. At first, they write letters. Ma reads the letters out loud, telling those left behind about new lives in new places. For a while, Wilhelm lives with his eldest brother in New Jersey, but when he and Emil fail to get along, Wilhelm enlists in the Army. Kurt, Earl's favorite, writes about his new job in a watch factory and then about a girl he's met. The letters slow. Then they stop.

"I'm never gonna leave you, Ma," Earl says, leaning his head against her skirt.

She's silent, knitting quietly. He lifts his head to see if he can figure her thoughts, then casts a questioning glance toward Lucy, who shrugs.

"I expect Kurt and Wilhelm thought Emil could help them get a start in the world," his sister says. "That's why they left."

"I don't remember him," he mutters, frustrated not to recollect his oldest brother.

"That might be a true idea you have, Lucy. But I also expect your brothers left because they decided I didn't need looking after now that your pa is gone."

"They should buy a farm and we could all live there," Earl says. "Family should stick together. I can look after the livestock. I don't mind. I can run the mule team through the fields. I'll make the straightest rows you ever seen. And when crops come in, well, I'll help in the fields with the pickin'." He says it and means it, but deep in his heart, he hates working in the fields. Bending over all day hurts his back. And pickin' time is when it's the hottest. One time, he nearly drowned from how much sweat poured down his face picking field peas.

His ma becomes still, the knitting forgotten in her lap. Earl detects a sadness in the lines of her face. "Your brothers never cared for farming," she says softly. "Factory work or soldiering suits them better. It's more secure right now than having to depend on the land or weather or crop prices. I'm happy for them. You should be, too. It's okay to miss them. But as long as they can look after themselves and their families. That's what matters."

"Ain't we got factories in North Carolina?" he asks.

"P'rhaps they don't want to be found after Pa gets out of prison," says Lucy. "That's why they moved so far."

"Your pa won't be getting out for a long time. He'll be an old man then. I expect wages are better up north. It was always your pa who wanted to move south, not your brothers."

Of course, it's not only the boys who leave. After Wilhelm and Kurt pack their belongings, Frieda moves, too. She catches a ride with a friend to someplace called

Camp Bragg. The government is building an army base there and Frieda decides that means opportunity. "Orbry said Frieda's liftin' her skirt for the soldiers now," Earl says, wanting to contribute to the conversation.

"You hush."

His ma's harsh tone cuts him, brings tears to his eyes.

"I don't want to hear you say that ever again, you understand me?"

"Yes ma'am." He drops his head, staring sullenly at the floor. He suspects there's something he don't understand. He thinks it's nice Frieda gets to be a dancer. She and Faith was always twirling around the house when Pa weren't around.

He's been hopin' Welcome and Faith will come home after the trial, but they decide to stay where they are. Ma explains her absent girls are gettin' a chance at a better life. And that makes Earl think about what Mr. Edwards said, about being better. He's not sure how to be better. His life is already so much better without Pa here to beat him. It seems greedy to want more.

And things are better. But as Christmas approaches, there's precious little to put toward any kind of festivity. Ma goes to her special trunk and brings out a lace doily she inherited from her mother. With care, she places a small carving of the Baby Jesus on it, centered between a prayerful Joseph and Mary. Lucy loves to hold the tiny carvings in her hand, stroking the smooth olive wood. Earl curls beneath the evergreen branches Ma places about the house, inhaling the sharp scent of pine as he listens to stories from the old country.

Some nights, they sing. "*The holly and the ivy, when*

they're both full grown; Of all the trees that are in the wood, the holly bears the crown."

One night during the countdown to Christmas, Ma tells them how in Germany on Christmas Eve, the rivers turn to wine and animals talk to each other just like folks. The mountains open up to reveal caves full of hidden treasure and church bells ring throughout the towns.

The day before his own Christmas, after trekking through backroads and hollers, Earl trudges home, stomping loudly through the front door.

"Earl Hahn, where have you been? I called and called for you."

He faces his ma, unable to hold back his frustration. "All day, I been up and down Six Run Creek. It's plain and brown and the water tastes like shit."

"Don't say 'shit', Earl. That's an ugly word."

"Why don't we have any Christmas magic?"

His ma sets down her piecework and motions for him to come closer. "Earl, honey, it's been a hard year for our family and that's a fact. But don't lose your belief. If you've been a good boy this year, put your shoe by the fire before you go to bed. Saint Nicholas may find his way even to our poor home."

"Can I tell you my Christmas wish?" he asks, kneeling beside her. He reaches with his fingertips and strokes the soft yarn in her lap.

"Tell me your wish," she says, speaking slowly. "There are no guarantees, but sometimes a Christmas miracle happens, and we may be due."

He whispers into her ear and she nods somberly. She presses one hand against his cheek, full of tenderness.

“Are we safe now?” he asks, quietly so he doesn’t wake Lucy and the baby.

“Do you feel safe?”

He thinks for a moment, nods.

“Good.” She kisses his brow and bids him goodnight.

Earl goes to the room he shares only with Orbry now. Beds belonging to Wilhelm and Kurt have been taken apart and stowed in Farmer Tate’s shed. It’s lonely without the tussle and energy of his big brothers. Colder, too. Newly exposed gaps between planks invite winter air inside. He’s tried stuffing cracks with the *Sampson Democrat*, but the weekly newspaper is a mite thin to keep out the chill.

He pulls one of his old brogans from beneath the bed. When temperatures dropped, he found two pieces of paperboard behind the general store. He poured melted candlewax across the surface of each and slipped them into his shoes to weatherproof them for winter. Now he checks the tattered sole and gives it a sniff. He removes the waxed insole so it won’t melt. Later, when his ma leaves the front room to give Mattie her bottle, he sets the shoe beside the cast-iron stove and says a small prayer to Saint Nicholas. Lucy has already set out her slipper and he wonders what her Christmas wish might be.

A sharp knock startles him. They don’t get visitors after dark.

“Ma!”

“I heard it. Stay where you are.” She exits the bedroom with a frayed shawl over her nightgown and opens the front door. Disregarding her instruction, he follows close behind, peering over her shoulder.

He sees a round, red light and the dark outline of a Ford Model T leaving the yard. It turns onto the dirt road that winds through Farmer Tate's fallow field. The tail light briefly illuminates a swirl of red dust kicked into the air by the rear tire.

"Look, Earl."

Ma points to a grass basket resting on the topmost cinder block step. He grabs it and carries it inside. "It's heavy!" He lifts the gingham cloth covering the basket and peeks inside before letting the cloth fall. "Ma, it's full of things for the larder."

"Place it on the table."

Lucy hears the commotion. With twice-darned socks covering her feet and a thin winter coat on top of her nightgown, she tiptoes out to investigate. "What is it?"

Careful not to jostle the contents, Earl places the basket on the kitchen table. Ma pulls one corner of the cloth aside and begins removing items: cornmeal and a can of lard, even a small bag of sugar. His sister takes a carton from the basket. She sounds out the words on the box. "C… corn… f… flakes," she says, reading aloud.

Earl's impressed. Ma's been workin' with Lucy on her counting and her letters. He expects his little sister is the first person in the family to show an interest.

"What do we do with… cornflakes?" he asks.

"I think you eat it like oatmeal," Ma says, "but cold. Mr. Wilkins just started carrying it in the store."

"I'll get bowls!" says Lucy.

He takes a seat at the table, scraping the chair across the floor in his haste, and watches as his sister gathers dishes and spoons from the cupboard. Ma fetches a bottle of milk from the icebox and pours it over the toasted flakes his sister deposits into each bowl. He grabs a spoon and shovels a hefty portion into his mouth.

"It's good," he mumbles around a mouthful of crunch. "I like it."

Lucy, eyes alight, nods in agreement. "Who do you think left the basket, Ma? Was it Saint Nicholas?"

She gazes at each of them, brow furrowed. "I expect someone from the church wanted to do a good deed," she says. "They understand that with your pa gone, times are leaner than usual." A fleeting smile crosses her lips and is gone. "When you say your prayers tonight, thank God for this blessing and the person who delivered it."

"We will, Ma. And I'll say an extra thank you for corn flakes."

"Me, too," Lucy says quickly.

"Thank you, dear."

"What else is in the basket?"

"You'll see in the morning," Ma says, her expression lighter than it's been for days. "Now, finish your treat and put your bowls in the wash tub. I'll clean them before I go to bed. You need to get a good night's sleep before Saint Nicholas visits."

"Orbry's not home," Lucy says, her chin quivering in distress. "He has to be in bed, too!"

"He's helping Missus Tate with last-minute holiday preparations. He'll be home soon. Don't you worry."

Back in his room, Earl strips to his long johns before sliding beneath the faded quilt. He doesn't know how he can possibly fall asleep. He's too excited. They have more food in the house than he's seen in a long time. Tomorrow, Ma will walk to the Tates' house and help prepare Christmas dinner, but first, she'll wake them in the morning to have hot breakfast. Maybe, just maybe, Saint Nick will leave a surprise in his old brogan.

With the bedroom door open to catch the heat, he's comforted by the sound of his ma banking the fire before going to the room she shares with Mattie. He's wearing two pairs of socks and he's thrown his coat on top of the quilt for an extra layer of warmth. Cloaked in semi-darkness, he pulls the cover up to his chin.

As his body warms beneath the covers, he thinks back on Ma's story of Christmas in the old country. Eyes closed, he tries to imagine a river of wine. Pa made elderberry wine once and even Ma took a sip. He hadn't cared for it, finding it bitter and nothing like the elderberry jam his ma made in summertime. He decides to think about cold cola instead. A river of fizzy soda would be a fine thing. His tongue tingles with anticipation as he drifts into slumber.

The following morning, it's Earl's nose that wakes first, twitching from the yeasty smell of baking bread. A drowsy smile crosses his lips. Enjoying a few lazy moments wrapped in warmth, he tries to distinguish the morning smells. Salt pork pops and sizzles on the stovetop, making his mouth water. This is followed by the aroma of roasted chicory root. He opens his eyes.

Christmas!

Too eager to run to the privy, he removes the chamber pot from beneath the bed and takes care of business. He buttons himself then checks to make sure Orbry is still snoring. He didn't hear him come in during the night.

Tiptoeing, he makes his way out of the bedroom, pulling the door shut behind him.

A fire blazes in the wood stove and the room is filled with warmth and light. He glances at three shoes by the hearth and discovers each one contains a new pair of knitted socks. A drawstring bag tucked into the opening holds a half-dozen peppermint sticks. Saint Nicholas hasn't forgotten them. Even Orbry's work boot is filled, and his brother hasn't been good at all this year.

He looks up as his ma presses a kiss to each cheek. "*Fröhe Weihnachten euch*. Happy Christmas."

"Happy Christmas, Ma."

"You're the first one awake this morning."

"Saint Nicholas came," he says, smiling broadly.

"He did."

"Is that yeast bread I smell?"

"Wasn't that your Christmas wish?"

He nods happily. She moves to the stove and returns with a hot loaf wrapped in a flour sack towel.

"For me?"

"It's all yours."

"And I don't have to share it?"

"Not with anyone."

Earl presses his cheek to the towel, inhaling the smell of warm bread. The realization that he can have a slice now and another slice later fills him so full of emotion, he fears he'll fly apart from sheer joy.

"Do we have butter?" he asks.

"There was a cake of butter in the Christmas basket."

"Let's cut thick slices of bread. One for you and me, and for Lucy and Orbry. Let's melt butter on top of each slice and... and we'll have each person's plate with hot bread and butter waiting when they wake up. They'll be so surprised."

She tilts her head, regarding him closely. "Are you sure?"

"I'm sure." He can't remember the last time he felt this happy. He wants to share it with everyone.

FIVE

Orbry flicks Earl in the head for the third time that morning.

"Quit!" Earl swats at his brother's arm. "Leave me alone."

"Whatcha doin', Wilbur?"

"My name's not Wilbur!" He glares at his brother, unsettled by the glint of malice in Orbry's eyes. Sticking out his tongue, Earl can't help noticing his brother's mousy hair, grown long around a thin white neck. For a moment, he pictures wrapping his hands around that neck and squeezing till his brother can't call him no more names. Agitated at his thoughts, he drops his head, gazing absently at his breakfast. Fried cornbread and onions. Again.

"What're you staring at, Wilbur? Huh? Huh?" Orbry flicks him again.

It's a month past Christmas and the joy of the holiday has given way to cold, dreary days framed by thin meals and meager warmth. Everyone is on edge from the shortage of labor or money coming into the home.

"You need a haircut," he says matter-of-factly.

Lucy steps through the doorway dressed for the day. She's wearing the socks she received from Saint Nick. After a month of wearing, hers still look new. Earl's socks have a hole in the toe.

"Luce, that dress is so thin, I can see your nips." Orbry waggles his brows suggestively. Earl gives him a dark look.

Ma enters the kitchen with Mattie slung over one shoulder. Simultaneously trying to burp the baby and tuck in a strand of loose hair that's fallen into her eyes, she swings around to face her daughter. Looking Lucy over head to toe, she makes a soft clucking sound, her expression disapproving. With a tilt of her head, she motions toward a row of hooks on the wall. "Wear your apron or see if you have a jumper that fits. Your brother's right. That dress isn't decent. I'll visit Mr. Wilkins this week and get fabric for a new one."

"With what?" Orbry asks, his expression doubtful. "Since the weather's turned, folks ain't sendin out their wash. The hens are barely laying. We ain't got no money."

"I'll speak with Mr. Wilkins about extending store credit. When the weather warms, I can pay him back." She sends her son a sharp glance. "Don't you have somewhere you need to be?"

He leans back, lacing hands behind his head. "Farmer Tate drove the missus over to Piney Grove. He don't have nothin' for me to do today."

The tension in Ma's shoulders ratchets up a notch. There's a watchful flicker in her gaze. She stares at nothing for a spell, but when her lips firm, Earl knows she's made up her mind about somethin'.

"Orbry, will Farmer Tate mind if you borrow one of his mules and a chain?"

"He won't care."

"There's a fallen hickory in the woods. Take your brother and haul that tree to the house. Since Farmer Tate doesn't need you today, you can split firewood."

Orbry scowls.

"It's not like you have anything better to do. We need the firewood and I'm tired of listening to you two go after each other."

"We got wood," Earl points out. "There's half a cord on the porch and more stacked beside the house."

"That wood is for this winter." His ma walks into the boys' bedroom and returns with two coats slung over her arm. "You boys put these on. The two of you can split and stack now so the wood has time to dry for next year."

"I don't need Earl's help," Orbry insists. "He'll just be in the way."

"It's a two-man job," she says tiredly.

"Yeah, it's a two-man job," Earl says, parroting his mother. Then he processes the words and clamps his mouth shut. He doesn't want to work with Orbry any more than his brother wants to work with him.

Orbry flicks him in the head.

"Ma!"

"Orbry!" she snaps, her face flushed.

He stiffens then stands, grabbing his coat. "Fine. I'll fetch Virgil. He can help me haul the tree into the yard. He's handy with the mules."

"You know the tree I mean? The one near that thicket of rhododendron."

"I know."

"When you're done, I'll bring the tub inside. You need a bath and a haircut." Ma turns her attention to Lucy and Earl. "Come on, you two. We're not sitting inside all day. I'll put Mattie in the sling. Y'all can help me collect turkey tail."

Minutes later, Orbry stomps out the door, releasing the screen so it slaps back with a loud *pap*!

"One day, that door's gonna fall off its hinges," Earl mutters.

"Not today," his ma answers. She pulls on her winter coat and wraps a knitted scarf around her neck. She collects the baby and straps her into a papoose bound across her chest. Finally, with a gentle hand, she holds the door open and motions for him and Lucy to join her, handing him a burlap sack as they step outside.

Forcing cheer, she leads them across bare fields lightly covered with frost. Lucy hops and skips across the cold, hard ground while Earl looks on with a grin. He wants to skip, too, but worries it might not set a good example. With Pa gone, he figures it's time for him to be more growed up. Someday, Orbry will be gone too. His brother's been hinting about it for weeks. Then Earl will be man of the house. He figures he can do anything Orbry can do, as long as he's not bein' rushed. He doesn't like to be rushed.

Once they leave Farmer Tate's field and enter the woods, the children move closer to their ma, staying together in the dim shelter of the trees. The baby coos, wrapped snugly against the chill air.

"I don't know about this," he whispers.

"Shh, we're fine. Stay close and you may learn something." When they come to a fallen tree loaded with thick scallops of brown and tan mushrooms, his ma bends to inspect the growth. The mushrooms spread along the mossy trunk and he watches as she plucks each scallop from its base, one at a time, and places them into the burlap bag.

"Remember to look for this white tip along the outside edge of each scallop." She cradles the fanned shape in one hand and draws a finger along its rim. "That's how you know it's ripe for harvest." She holds it out. "Feel how soft it is."

He rubs his finger down the center. "It *is* soft."

"As soft as…" she prompts.

"As soft as… a mushroom," he responds.

"As soft as velvet!" Lucy shouts. Her fingers flutter over the layers of dark color. "It looks like a turkey tail, but it's stiffer than feathers."

He tips his head one way, then the other. "It don't look like turkey feathers to me."

"Don't look at one. Look at all of them together. See how the colors fan out from the tree here?" His ma points out each layer. "Imagine if the tree was upright and not down on the ground. Each scallop layers over the one below it like feathers on a bird. Remember that wild turkey Orbry shot last month?"

"That was good turkey," he says, his nose filling with the remembered scent of roasted meat. "I wish he'd get us another one just like it. I like the gizzard most. And the neck bone. There's good eatin' on a neck bone."

"But can you see it?" Lucy huffs.

"See what?"

"The turkey tail!"

"Oh." He gives the tree another look, steps back, and stares at it sideways. "I sure can," he agrees wonderingly. "The way those mushrooms clump together looks just like a turkey tail."

"That's what we been saying!" Lucy walks off, kicking at dead leaves and muttering to herself.

Ma gives him a gentle smile. "Tonight, I'll cook the mushrooms in lard for supper and serve them with hush puppies. I've got pork fat, too. It ought to be filling enough for the four of us, don't you think?"

Earl, who's never not hungry, isn't sure. He recognizes a familiar rumble deep inside and presses his belly to calm it.

"I bet your brother will have an appetite after splitting wood all day." She pauses for a moment to scout out their location, then points deeper into the woods. "I used to have luck down in that gully."

Because the brown and tan of the mushrooms blend with the bark of the trees in the shadowed wood, Ma asks Earl and Lucy to be her spotters. Casting his eyes from one tree to the next, Earl's surprised to discover this place feels familiar to him. He can't pinpoint a specific memory, but the deeper they go into the holler, the greater his sense of recognition. He stops so he can concentrate. He pictures giant raindrops plopping on fall leaves, red and yellow. He recollects a smell in the air – wood smoke – and gazes upward, marking the pattern of the tree branches.

"I been here," he whispers.

His ma turns, her eyes questioning. “Sure, honey. You’ve been here. You and Kurt used to come here and set rabbit snares. Are you remembering?”

He nibbles his lip, watching her uncertainly. He hates when he can’t remember. “I don’t know.”

“You loved coming to the woods with your big brother.”

An image flashes into his mind then is gone – his brother’s fingers looping a delicate wire. It’s accompanied by a vaguely remembered sense of ease because they’d been out of sight of their pa. “Do you know how to set a snare?” he asks.

“That’s not a bad idea, Earl. Tomorrow, we’ll come back with wire and an ax. If we’re lucky, we can have a rabbit stew this week. We’ll gather wild onion grass and add the mushrooms.”

“I like stew.”

“Me, too!” his sister adds.

“Then you better get busy.” Ma’s tone is brisk. “Put those sharp eyes of yours to use. Whoever finds the most mushrooms gets a penny.”

The children whoop and run in opposite directions, determined to find enough to eat on for the week. When the burlap bag is filled to the brim, each is promised a penny for their hard work.

Lucy looks at Earl meaningfully, her brows lifted. “Horehound,” she says.

“Lemon drop,” he replies. His mouth juices up in anticipation of the tart candy, just as another growl erupts from his belly.

A few feet away, his mother places a hand against the small of her back and arches slowly to stretch. Earl pays attention, sensing there's something on her mind. Why else would she bring all of them to the woods to do something she could easily manage on her own?

"The baby's asleep," whispers Lucy, peeking into her ma's sling.

"And getting heavier every day." Ma reaches for Lucy's hand and guides her to a tree root arcing out of the ground like an otter's back. "Sit with me. I want to rest before we head back."

Earl remains standing, a jitteriness teasing the hairs along his skin. "I'm not tired a bit," he says.

When there's no further comment, he steps closer. His ma has a serious look that makes him feel serious, too. She laces fingers with Lucy and pulls her close.

"Lucy, has Orbry ever touched you in a way he shouldn't?"

"He flicks me," says Earl. "It hurts."

"I know, honey. And I'll speak to him about it. But right now, I need to hear from Lucy." Her tone sounds no-nonsense but also… careful.

For a long moment, his little sister keeps her eyes locked on something she finds fascinating near the forest floor. Earl squints toward the spot where she's staring then wrinkles his nose. *Just damp leaves and pinecones,* he thinks disgustedly.

When she speaks, her voice is so soft he has to lean closer to hear. "He says things he knows will upset me. Naughty things. Last week, he spied on me in the privy. He thinks I don't know but I knew it was him. Only… he ain't ever touched me like you mean."

A ripple of emotion flashes across his ma's face then is gone.

"From now on, I want you to stay near me or Earl. Try not to be alone with Orbry. Especially, don't be alone with Orbry and Virgil and any of the boys he runs around with. Do you understand me?"

His sister looks up, a tiny wrinkle pinched between her brows. Her gaze conveys something he doesn't fully grasp. "Yes ma'am."

Feeling distressed but unsure why, Earl drops to the ground and scooches close to Lucy. He reaches for her other hand and she gives it willingly. His ma sends him a stern glance.

"What?"

"Earl, I don't want you to speak about this to anyone, but I need to know you're looking out for your little sister. From now on, if she wants you to walk with her to the privy, you do it, no complaining – hear? And stay close by till she's finished."

He pauses for a moment, thinking hard about everything he's heard. He decides his mother is entrusting him with an important duty. He mustn't let her down. "I'll make sure there's no snakes and no Orbry."

"Lucy, starting tonight, you'll sleep in the big bed with me. Now that your pa's gone, it doesn't make sense for me to have all that space to myself. We can keep each other warm."

"My bedroom's lonely since Frieda and Rose left," she admits. "I hear noises."

"I'm sorry I didn't think of it sooner. Your room can be my sewing and folding room. Maybe when Mattie's older, the two of you can have it back."

"Is Orbry in trouble?" Earl whispers.

He wants to ask if he can take Lucy's room and then he won't have to share space with Orbry, but something in his ma's face convinces him this isn't the time.

"He's not in trouble and I mean to keep it that way. Right now, he's got hostility in him and pent-up energy. When your pa got sent to the penitentiary, Orbry was the only one who grieved the absence. And when your brothers struck out and left him behind, it hurt his feelings. Maybe he wanted them to invite him, too. I don't know. Earl, I know he takes it out on you the most. I want to make sure he doesn't take it out on Lucy, too."

"I'll fight back," she says, her voice hitching slightly. "I'll bite and scratch and punch. Orbry don't scare me."

Ma places one arm around her daughter. "You might want to be a little scared, Lucy. Without his big brothers around to keep him in check… well, there's no good can come of you being reckless. As long as you don't give him opportunity, maybe his better nature will prevail."

Earl finds this funny. "Better nature," he grunts, rolling his eyes.

Lucy giggles.

"Yeah. Maybe his better nature will prevail." At that, she laughs so hard, she topples over the tree root. "Ow." She reaches beneath her bottom and pulls up a giant pinecone. All three break into new peals of laughter.

"Okay," Ma wipes at wet eyes, "that's enough silliness."

"You should send him to live with Kurt," says Earl. "If he wants to be gone, we could help him."

His ma gives him a thoughtful look. "You might be onto something. I know Farmer Tate appreciates Orbry's contribution to the farm – he's a hard worker – but knowing he's feeling restless, it might be worth an enquiry. I'll write to your brothers and see what they say." The baby stirs and his ma stands, signaling it's time to move. "I'm trying to learn from my mistakes, children. But maybe my imagination is getting the best of me. I could be worrying over nothing."

Feeling subdued, Earl falls into step beside his ma and sister as they head home. A pale winter light finds its way through the branches of bare trees and in-between dark evergreens, adding a touch of magic to the scene. There are places beneath his feet that crunch. Water has pooled beneath damp leaves and turned to ice. They come out of the trees and, across the field, he sees his brother and another boy guiding one of the mules over hard ground, a tree trunk dragging behind them.

"Ma, why on earth does Orbry call me Wilbur?"

"Oh, Earl, why on earth do you care?"

SIX

"I don't feel so good."

His mother places the back of her hand against Earl's forehead. "Maybe you're coming down with something."

"I prob'ly need honey."

"Does your throat hurt?"

He thinks about it and comes to the conclusion that one answer is more likely to get him what he wants. "Yes ma'am."

"Come with me."

He follows her to the kitchen and watches as she opens a small door in the icebox. She removes a Mason jar filled with cloudy liquid. He shivers, feeling the temperature drop thanks to a frosty new block the iceman brung the day before.

"You don't keep honey in the icebox!" he says, suspecting a trick.

"I'm not giving you honey. I'm giving you kraut juice."

"Yuck."

"If you're ailing, this is the stuff that can help you get better."

He pinches his nose between two fingers and watches her silently.

She watches him back, not blinking. "I can either pour some of this sauerkraut liquid for you to drink or I can slice an onion for you. Your choice."

"Honey," he says, in a flat, nasal voice.

"That's not one of your choices."

He releases his nose and crosses his arms against his chest, waiting for her to offer him another choice.

His ma sets the jar on the table, but she doesn't release it. "Does your throat hurt or not?"

He considers his options. "I might wait and see if it gets better on its own."

"Uh huh." She returns the jar to the icebox.

At the sound of a soft tap, two heads turn toward the doorway.

"Anybody home?" The deep voice carries easily through the screen.

Earl follows his ma, surprised to discover Rose's employer standing on the front porch.

"Mr. Edwards, is Rose okay?" Wiping both hands on her apron, Lizzie Belle ushers him into the house.

"Rose is fine. I'm here for myself today. Official business. Do you have a moment?"

Flustered by the unexpected visitor, she lifts a hand to her hair and smooths the flyaway strands. "Of course. Come in and have a seat. Can I offer you a glass of iced tea? I have a pitcher in the icebox. Earl, why don't you pour Mr. Edwards a glass of tea?"

The tall man steps inside, removing his hat as he enters. His eyes casually survey the sparsely furnished room. Earl tries to see what he's seeing. A threadbare sofa is shoved against the far wall, and two ladderback chairs stand caddy-cornered near the woodstove, unused today as the weather has warmed. A cushioned rocker where Ma likes to rest at the end of the day is clearly the most comfortable seat in the house.

"Take the rocker, Mr. Edwards."

He grabs one of the ladderbacks from beside the hearth and moves it closer to the rocking chair. He pauses, hat in hand, and motions for her to take a seat. "I'm fine here, Mrs. Hahn, if you'll sit with me a moment?"

She takes her seat and Mr. Edwards takes his, resting the hat on his lap. She glances at Earl who hasn't moved. "The iced tea, please."

"Don't bother yourself, son. I'm fine." The gentleman bestows an easy smile then returns his attention to Ma. "Mrs. Hahn, I've come with news I thought might interest you and your little girl."

"Lucy?"

"The county has decided to close the farm school and invite rural children into town to receive their education."

Earl shifts to get a better look at his ma's face. Instantly, he's on alert, concerned by her pinched look.

"Mr. Edwards, I cannot possibly get Lucy to school in town."

"You have no need to worry, madam. The town's going to take care of everything."

"What do you mean?"

"If you'll permit me a few minutes to explain…"

She nods cautiously, shifting in her seat.

"Since the end of the war, the state's become invested in compulsory education and enforcing truancy laws. With women voting now, there's a new regard for the education of young people. It's believed the country – certainly Sampson County – would benefit from educating its citizens, even the females."

Lizzie Belle frowns but doesn't say anything.

"This year, the county received funds to purchase a motorized school car. We'll be sending this vehicle around in the mornings to local farms to collect children and bring them to town. We'll return the children after they've completed their classes for the day."

He glances up as Lucy barrels into the house, the screen door smacking the wood frame in her wake. "Ma, there's a buggy…"

"Settle down, Lucy. You remember Mr. Edwards. He's come to talk to us about your school attendance."

Eyes fixed on the man's face, Lucy takes the second ladderback and pushes it where she can face their visitor.

"Ma's been working with me on my letters," she tells him eagerly. "I can read all kinds of things. Like labels on soup cans. And sometimes there's letters from my brothers. I can read whole sentences."

"I'm pleased to hear it." He gives her an encouraging smile. "How about books? Do you have books to read?"

Ma's eyes turn cool. "We have a Bible, Mr. Edwards. That's the only book we need in our home."

"Mrs. Hahn, it would please me to bring a few small chapter books for your little girl to read – stories with good morals. You'd be familiar with these stories, like Jonah and the whale, but simplified for a child's vocabulary. Perhaps young Lucy could read them aloud to you and to Earl. Recitation is highly valued by the town teachers and it would be good practice for her."

She shakes her head. "We don't need—"

"Mrs. Hahn…" he interrupts gently, his smile making it seem like he knows what she's going to say. Earl doesn't know and struggles to follow.

"These books can be provided to Lucy on loan," he continues. "She's welcome to keep them as long as she's enjoying them, then she can return them when she's done. My Susan is a few years older than your girl and has books she's outgrown. These would be quality books that might help Lucy be better prepared for school in the fall."

"That's kind of you. I… I don't know." She sends a sideways glance toward Lucy, who's hanging on every word, her eyes filled with unspoken desire. Ma rubs a finger between her brows. "I suppose she might borrow one or two books from your girl, as long as you don't think she'd mind."

"She won't mind."

"She's a good learner, Lucy is." The words don't sound prideful coming from Lizzie Belle Hahn. If anything, she sounds slightly surprised. "I expect she'll advance in no time."

"I don't doubt it."

"And this school car…" She lifts her gaze, her eyes asking a question. "You're sure it's safe?"

"We haven't taken delivery yet, but I'm assured the vehicles have a safe driving record. Each one can carry over twenty students. The sides are iron-reinforced wood panels. Many districts have already adopted this mode of transportation and are seeing great success. Why, Pamlico County's offered transportation to their rural students for three years already."

Lucy grabs hold of her mother's arm, squeezing tightly in her excitement. "Just think, Ma. I won't have to race through the pasture when it's icy or muddy. And on rainy days, I can stay dry. This school car, it's got a cover, right?" She glances at Mr. Edwards.

"The vehicle is fully enclosed."

"See, Ma, it'll be fine. And the other kids will be doing it, too. It won't only be me."

Mr. Edwards leans forward, his expression earnest. "Can we count on seeing Lucy at school next year?"

Ma puffs out a breath, her eyes locked on her daughter. "I imagine you won't be able to keep her away."

"Thank you, thank you!" She bounces up and down, threatening to bust through the cane seat. "I wish school was starting tomorrow."

The gentleman rises to his feet. "You've got a lot to do between now and the start of school, Miss Lucy. Someone will stop by later this week with the chapter books. Begin practicing right away."

"I will. I promise."

"Mrs. Hahn, I'll let my assistant know Lucy's name can be added to the list of incoming students. If you have any questions at all, please don't hesitate to visit the office. My door is always open."

She stays by his side as they walk to the front door. "Thank you for coming, Mr. Edwards. It's kind of you to take an interest." She looks like she has more to say but presses her lips together instead.

"Was there anything else?" he asks.

She searches the eyes of the tall man and seems to find reassurance to speak. "I was interested to know how Rose is getting along, sir. The children and I attend the Baptist Church on Sundays. I look for her…"

"Miss Rose has been attending Black River Presbyterian with my wife and me. She keeps an eye on the younger children. She's a good worker, Mrs. Hahn. She's become invaluable to us."

"That's good then." Her lips lift briefly. "I appreciate the news."

"I'll mention to her that you'd enjoy a visit."

"If it happens to come up naturally, in conversation. There's no need to make a fuss."

"Of course."

Pushing the door closed, Ma stands behind the screen, watching as the man clucks to his mare and turns the buggy down the dirt path.

"Do you want to visit Rose?" Lucy slips a hand into her mother's. "I know right where Mr. Edwards lives. It's that white house on the corner by the band shell. He has pretty bunting on the porch. Red, white and blue."

Ma turns away from the door. "I wouldn't want to show up when Rose is working. I expect she needs to concentrate on her duties." She rests a hand on her daughter's head. "That was nice of Mr. Edwards to come himself and explain about the school car. Are you excited?"

"If I'm going to school with town children, Ma, we need to get busy." Lucy lifts her mother's hand off her head. "No more easy words."

SEVEN

"Ma?" Earl steps from the shadows, shuffles his feet.

"What, honey?"

"Can I go to school, too?"

The room grows quiet as the two females turn. He looks at his ma. He looks at Lucy, her face gone blank.

"Earl, come sit by me." His ma returns to the rocker and motions him forward.

He takes the seat Mr. Edwards was using, perches on the edge.

"You went to school once, do you remember? To the farm school down the road. You and Rose were in the same class. When Faith and Welcome got old enough, y'all would walk together."

He frowns at her. "Are you sure?"

"After your… injury, we pulled you out of school."

"Why did you make me leave?"

"Whenever you tried to read or do your sums, you'd

press your hands against your eyes. You said it made your head hurt. You couldn't remember things you used to know. We went to see the doctor. He's the one who suggested we remove you from school."

"Oh."

"You don't remember any of this?"

He huffs a breath, feeling put out. "Ma, I don't remember what you're saying. I don't remember gettin' hit. Or what come after. Orbry told me one time. He said we was buildin'."

"You and your brothers were helping your pa build a new chicken shed. It was after the big storm. Do you remember the storm? The winds were so strong they blew down the coop."

"When?"

"Right before your pa moved us to the other house, the one in Clinton."

Lucy places a gentle hand on his shoulder. "Does it hurt when you try and remember?"

He thinks about this. "Backward feels dark, like there's no way for me to get there. Orbry says I was different then, before Pa hit me." His voice shakes slightly. "Was I like Orbry?"

"No, honey. You were different than you are now, but you weren't like Orbry. You weren't like any of your brothers. You had a personality that was all your own."

"Was I smart?"

She clasps her hands together, a smile breaking across her face. "Oh, my goodness – so smart! You were always full of sass. Always cracking a joke. Always asking questions."

"Did I make Pa mad?"

"Hon, your pa was never not mad. It didn't take much to set him off. That day, your sisters and I were in the yard cleaning up after the storm."

"Right here?"

"Yes, in the chicken yard. Broken boards and shingles were scattered everywhere. We lost two chickens. Your pa was afraid we'd lose more. He had to get a shed up quickly so dogs couldn't get them."

"What dogs?"

"Oh, any dogs. Farmer Tate's dog. Dogs from neighboring farms. Wild dogs, maybe."

He nods in understanding. A lot of folks have dogs.

"Your pa asked you to hold two boards together while he nailed them. I think that's right. I don't remember exactly. You sassed him. You were trying to be funny. Then you laughed. I remember that part because when your pa swung the board and hit you, the laugh choked off. Instantly. And I knew..." Her voice breaks and she stops, taking a moment to gather herself. "I snapped my head around because I knew somethin' awful had happened. One of the boys shouted at your pa and I watched you drop to your knees. You looked so surprised and then..." She presses her lips together and Earl is startled to see tears have sprung to her eyes. She slides from the rocking chair and kneels in front of him, gripping his hands.

"What happened?"

A raw scraping sound escapes from her throat. It hurts him to hear it, but he needs to know. More than anything, he wants to understand why he isn't as smart as his little sister. He wants to know why his own brother calls him a moron.

"Was there blood?" he whispers.

"There was blood from your head and your ears. I screamed. Kurt, he ran over and grabbed your pa and shoved him to the ground. One of the boys went to town to fetch the doc. After that you were… you slept for a long time and I was so scared you might never wake up. When you finally opened your eyes, you vomited, and your words were hard to understand. We knew you'd been hurt bad. But the doctor, he said… he said the brain was a funny thing and you might get better in time."

"I did get better. I speak fine now, don't I?"

She gives his hands a squeeze. "You're so much better. For a while after, you had seizures. You'd twitch so hard we thought your teeth would break. We'd moved to Clinton by then so your pa could get a fresh start. He'd leave each morning for the waterworks and your brothers would perform odd jobs around town. Some days, it was just you and me and Lucy. Y'all would be outside playing and you'd drop for no reason, just collapse to the ground like a sack of potatoes. And when I picked you up, you had no memory of any of it. So, you understand, don't you, why we didn't think you should do school?"

"What about Kurt and Wilhelm? Did they do school?" he asks.

She gives a kind of laugh that isn't happy. "Your pa saw to it that none of his boys took school too seriously. He wanted them working all the time. Kurt tried to do school for a while, but he spent a fair amount of time standing in corners."

"Why did he stand in the corner?" Earl asks, puzzled by the image it conjures. "Did he get stuck?"

"I think the teachers put him there so he wouldn't cause trouble."

"Kurt can write. He wrote us letters," says Lucy. She presses against her ma's side. Their mother releases one of Earl's hands to slip an arm around her daughter.

"I guess most of them learned enough to read and write, not that you'd know it from their lack of correspondence." Releasing her children, she stands, her eyes fixed on something he can't see. He hears cooing sounds coming from the bedroom. Mattie's awake from her nap.

His ma gives him a serious look. "Earl, let's try this. If you want to learn your letters, you can sit with me and Lucy while we're having our lessons. See if it sticks. How about that? If you're able to hold onto it, then maybe we can talk about school."

He chews his lip and ponders the idea. He's seen Ma testing Lucy with reading cards and there's pictures on 'em like apples and cats. "Yes. Let's do that."

"There's one thing you need to keep in mind."

"What?"

"If you're at the school in town, it's different from the farm school. In town, they put the students in classes based on what they know. You'd be older than the other children in your class, and bigger. It… it would be a hard thing to be so far behind. You might be behind even Lucy's class. Do you understand? You'd be the big kid with all the other kids littler than you."

"I don't care," he insists. "As long as they're not mean to me."

"They might be."

He thinks about this for a moment. "They might not be. I might make a friend."

"Alright then." She pulls him to his feet.

Lucy wiggles between them, looking between her ma and her brother with shining eyes. "If Earl comes to school, I'll help him," she says fiercely. "I'll help him with his lessons and if anyone says boo to him, I'll kick 'em in the shins."

Ma plants a kiss on each of her children. In that spare room, standing between the two people he loves most in the world, an unfamiliar wave of optimism sweeps through Earl. This is a chance to show his ma and Lucy what he's capable of accomplishing. For the first time in his young life, he feels anything is possible.

EIGHT

Earl knows he's not supposed to touch Pa's gun. It's not because of his age. After all, Orbry's been shooting since he was ten. He glances at the rifle where it rests on the ground within arm's reach. He feels bad for misbehavin', but not bad enough to return the gun to where it belongs.

Spring has come and he and Lucy are hidin' beneath the house. They're trying to catch the hens sneaking beneath the porch to lay. The hens do that sometimes, trying to have a chick hatch outside the coop before Earl can collect the egg and deliver it to Ma.

Now that warmer weather is here, their ma is full of bustle and purpose, selling her eggs to the grocer in town, boiling shirts in lye for the local farmers who don't have wives and just generally bein' available for any service that will bring in some coin.

He touches his sister's arm and points. A hen pecks the dirt as it slowly makes its way into the shade beneath the house. Once she thinks she's safe, that bird is bound to settle down into some soft spot and push out an egg.

Suddenly, an unfamiliar aroma sneaks beneath the sour ripeness of the chicken yard. Earl and Lucy inhale, astonished at this sweet deliciousness. For a second, they gape at each other with wide eyes. Then, of one accord, they wiggle skinny bodies into the sun and lift twitching noses into the air. Like moths following the flicker of candlelight, the children track the elusive scent up the porch steps, through the front room and into the kitchen.

Their mother is bent over the open oven, removing two round cake pans. Nearby, Mattie pulls potatoes from a wooden bin and spins them across the floor.

"Whatcha doin'?" Earl asks. Even at Christmas there hadn't been an aroma like this. His ma rarely made cookies, never made pies. The price of sugar was too dear. But here, like a miracle, rest two golden circles of warm cake.

She presses two fingers to the top, testing doneness. "Mr. Tate's boy, Henry, brought me a message from Mr. and Mrs. Randolph," she says, humming softly under her breath.

"Who?"

"They're the retired couple that took in your sisters. Welcome and Faith have asked if they can visit for my birthday. Isn't that fine?" She turns, eyes glowing with pleasure as she shares this news. "Mr. Randolph's going to drive them over this afternoon on his way to Raleigh. He has business to attend to in the city. Your sisters will spend a few days here then he'll collect them upon his return."

Lucy claps her hands. "I can read one of my chapter books to Faith. She'll be so surprised!"

Ignoring his sister, Earl moves close to the oven for a better look. "You're baking?" He takes another sniff, tasting the sweetness in the air as his mouth releases juices that make him want to eat that minute.

"I've been hoarding the sugar from our Christmas basket. One patch of strawberries is ripe so I thought I'd make a shortcake. Maybe I can offer Mr. Randolph a slice before his long drive. It's a small thing to show my appreciation for bringing the girls to visit."

"Can I have a piece? Now, Ma, while it's hot?"

"Later, hon. There are biscuits on the table. Take one to tide you over."

Earl wrinkles his nose. Biscuits are everyday. He wants cake.

Seeing his expression, his ma walks to the table and grabs a biscuit from a plate. She pokes a hole in the doughy center and pours a dab of molasses inside. "Better?" she asks, handing it to him.

He bites into the sticky sweetness. "Better," he says, accepting the substitute with good grace.

"Can I pick strawberries?" Lucy asks.

"Can I trust you to put more in the pail than you put into your mouth?"

"Ma!" Lucy crosses her arms with a huff. She's partial to strawberries.

"How many is one?" His ma peers at Lucy with one eyebrow lifted sharply. It's a look that means she's not takin' any sass.

His sister snorts, trying to hold in a laugh. After a minute, she holds up one finger.

"I'm holding you to it. You can have one strawberry –

not two, not three…"

"Not a hundred!" Earl chimes in.

"You can have one berry to eat and the rest go into the pail. Those strawberries are for our supper."

"Yes ma'am."

"Don't go just yet. I need your help putting Mattie down. She's been underfoot all morning."

Ma pauses, staring blankly inside herself like she's figuring what's next on her list of chores. "Earl, go call Orbry. I need your brother to kill a hen. I'm going to make buttermilk chicken. I won't have time to let the bird rest but it can't be helped. I can soak it in brine before putting it in the icebox."

"Orbry left. Farmer Tate promised him a dollar to help put up the new tabacca barn."

Earl had volunteered to help, too. He wanted to earn a dollar. His brother told him to get lost. Scratching at a scab, he watches as the baby removes the last potato and sends it careening wildly across the wide plank pine. His ma bends to lift Mattie onto her hip.

A thought pops into his head. "I can do it!" he says, stuffing the last bite of biscuit into his mouth. Maybe Ma will let him shoot the gun. Orbry got to shoot the gun. But Orbry wasn't here.

"I don't know, Earl."

He clasps his hands, puts his entire body into the pleading. "Let me shoot Pa's gun. I know how. Honest. I'll shoot that chicken right in the head."

Lucy pinches her brother.

"Ow!" he shouts, rubbing his arm.

"You don't kill chicken with a gun, silly. You wring

the neck then chop its head off." She gives him a look of exasperation. "You don't know nothin'."

His eyes never leaving his ma, Earl reaches one hand to swat his sister. She squeals and pivots out of the way. He discerns a look on his ma's face that means she's wavering. He sends silent prayers to the Baby Jesus that she'll swing in his direction.

"We'll compromise. Kill the chicken the way Orbry does it. Take the hatchet. Toss some corn. Wait till the hen's head is down then grab it and wring its neck. Chop the head and hang it by the shed to drain."

"Yes ma'am!" He turns to sprint out of the kitchen.

"Earl, honey, repeat what I just said."

He pauses impatiently, bouncing from one foot to the other. "Throw down corn. Grab the hen. Chop the head. Hang to drain."

"Fine," she sighs. "Be careful. The minute the hens get riled, you stop. Do you hear me? Agitated hens won't lay properly."

"I hear you."

"Go."

He dashes out, not giving her a chance to change her mind. He's already in the chicken yard with the hatchet when he remembers Pa's rifle is hidden below the house. Maybe he'll fire it, just once. He's watched Orbry shoot all kinds of things… squirrels and rabbits and possums. Little things, but big things too. A fall buck or wild turkey. How hard can it be? Besides, chicken are stupid. Shootin' a hen will be less trouble than trying to catch the bird and wring its neck. His ma can't be mad about the gun if he brings her a chicken.

He shimmies beneath the porch and grabs the rifle, startling the hen who sneaked in earlier. She's had time to lay her egg in the soft dirt. He considers shootin' her there and then but can no longer see the sport in it. "I'm comin' back for that egg," he warns.

He inches backward till he's standing in the sunlight. He remembers the promise Orbry made Pa to always respect his weapon. He uses his shirt tail to wipe a film of dust that's gathered on the stock. Once the wood is clean, he lifts the rifle to his shoulder, sighting down the barrel the way his brother does it.

Treading softly on the balls of his feet, he sidles toward the flock. He keeps his movements casual-like, so the hens won't become suspicious. Lifting one hand from the barrel, he reaches into his pocket and tosses a handful of corn onto the ground. The hens cluster, kicking up dust and pecking at each kernel. Earl spies the chicken he wants, a Rhode Island Red, plump enough to fry up good. As the hen's head goes down, Earl aims, and then fires.

He forgot there'd be a kick and staggers slightly when the recoil knocks him backwards. The crack splits the air and slaps against his eardrums. The smell of gun smoke stings his nostrils. He pinches them together with two fingers as panicked birds squawk and flap awkwardly off the ground.

He stares around the chicken yard, expecting to see a dead bird.

There's no dead bird.

He hears his mother inside the house, her voice raised to reach him where he stands in plain view. "Great day in the morning, Earl! Are you hunting chicken with a rifle?"

He knows he won't get but one more shot before his ma takes the gun away. He spots the hen with the rust-colored feathers perched now on the woodpile. He lifts the rifle to his shoulder, ignoring a blur behind the window. His ma pushes open the casement as he squeezes the trigger. The hen goes airborne in a flurry of frantic flapping. He hears a gasp and sees his mother stagger, grip the windowsill with one hand.

"Lucy, take the baby."

"Ma'am?" His sister sounds confused.

"Take the baby."

Earl stands frozen, the rifle held loosely in his hands. "Ma?"

She sends him an odd look. "Earl, honey. I've changed my mind." She sounds out of breath. Why is she breathless standin' in a window? "Come inside and put the gun away. We won't be having chicken today."

NINE

He's in trouble. He shouldn't o' taken Pa's gun. He shouldn't have shot at that chicken. Ma will be mad. Worse, she'll be disappointed, giving him that look that makes him feel low when all he wants is to please her. Every instinct tells him to run. He scans the fields, green now with new sprouts. He can disappear in a shady holler. He can stay there all day until his ma calms herself. He casts his eyes toward the distant woods.

He's disturbed by a vision so unexpected it stops him mid-step. He pictures Mr. Edwards from town, speaking to him and Lucy on the day of Pa's trial. He closes his eyes, lets the memory wash over him. *"Every day, life will give you opportunities to be better. Be better."*

He wonders if this is one of those moments. Maybe life is giving him an opportunity.

Earl doesn't run away.

His tread purposeful, he climbs the front porch steps and enters the house, propping Pa's rifle against the wall. He can still smell the aroma of warm cake. A shaft of sunlight enters the room with him, illuminating dust motes dancing in the air. It gives him an idea how he can make things better. Ma will want the house cleaned before his sisters arrive. He can help her. He'll sweep and dust and wipe the windows with an old rag to make up for disobeying. Surely his ma won't stay mad with a clean house and her girls on the way.

He hears Mattie being fretful and forces himself to move forward. He finds his ma standing by the open window, her hand white-knuckled on the sill. Her other hand presses against one side and he can see a red stain there that shouldn't be. It spreads in front of his eyes, a dark blot against the faded yellow of her dress.

"Ma?"

She smiles at him. She looks him in the eye, and she smiles… like she's sad about something, but everything will be okay. He feels cold in himself, more frightened than he's ever been. He watches with helpless astonishment as his ma slides to the floor. Lucy, bent with the weight of the baby in her arms, lets out a cry.

"Earl, honey, run to Farmer Tate. Fast as you can." Ma's voice sounds tight to his ears. She stops speaking as a sharp indrawn breath twists her face. It scares him to see it. A second breath gives her the strength to continue. "Make him bring the Ford. Your mama has to go to the doctor right now."

He looks at Lucy once, quickly, and sees her silent fear. Then he turns on his heel and busts through the wood screen door, knocking it lopsided. He runs. He runs until he has no breath. He runs farther and faster than he's ever run – through the fields and up the road to a barn where a half dozen shirtless men hammer shingles into place. Earl might be slow in his brain, but he's fast on his feet.

He sees Farmer Tate and grabs hold of him, holds his hammering arm until the man turns, cussing, his face a mix of anger and exasperation. Finally, the man hears him, hears the words Earl stammers in his haste to get them out. "I sh- shot Ma. Th- there's blood. You have to come. Please come!"

Vaguely, he's aware of shouts to the other men. "Cal, get your truck and head to Doc Honeycutt's. Tell him we're on our way with a gunshot wound."

Earl chases after Farmer Tate when he runs to the Model T. He hops into the passenger seat and holds on as the car lurches down the road toward where his ma lies bleeding. It feels like forever. For a wild, brief moment, Earl imagines their shabby home on cinder blocks is vanishing from sight, moving away from him every bit as fast as the motor car is racing to reach it. Why is it takin' so long?

When the vehicle slams to a stop, Earl dashes inside the house, followed by the farmer. His ma is slumped against a wall. Her eyes are closed. Lucy shivers and sobs, one hand patting the baby. Farmer Tate lifts his ma without a sound, carries her to the automobile and speeds down the road in a cloud of red dust.

"What do we do?" Lucy whispers. Her face is white, her eyes stark with fear. She's never looked at him like this. Like he should have answers.

He hears the screen door ripped off its hinges, hears men from the farm spill into the house. He steps hesitantly toward the front room, sees Orbry push through the crowd. His brother grabs him by his shirt collar and hauls him forward. Earl watches in slow motion as Orbry's arm rears back, fisted. *So much like Pa's,* he thinks absently, then the fist strikes him on the side of his head and he falls back against the wall.

His brother hits him again. And again. "You dumb fuck!" he shouts. "You stupid fucking dumbass."

He cries out in fear. He raises his arms to block the next blow, then lets them fall limp to his side when one of the men seizes Orbry and pulls him off. Earl collapses to the floor, covers his head with his arms and bawls.

"I'll never forgive you for this! Never! You idiot!" His brother's face contorts with rage and something else. Terror and heartbreak.

A neighbor hustles Orbry into the back room as another man helps Earl to his feet, leads him to the sofa and hands him a sweaty handkerchief. Earl tries to calm down. Hiccoughing and unable to get air, he struggles to regain control. He wipes his eyes. Wipes his bloody nose. He studies the faces of the men gawking at him.

"What happened, Earl? Tell us what happened."

"It was an accident," he whispers. "I didn't mean to do it."

A new person enters the room and this time it's Missus Tate. She takes in the scene at a glance and motions to Lucy, who stands frozen in the corner. Mattie clings to her big sister, her face wet with tears of her own, her dimpled chin quivering in distress. Earl can see his sister's arms shaking. She looks like she's going to pass out.

Missus Tate strides over to Lucy. "Here, let me have the baby. Go splash your face and get your brother a drink of water."

When Lucy returns with a cup of well water, Earl gives her a grateful look. He reaches for the cup, but his hands tremble too hard. He can't take the cup without spilling. "It's okay," she says, sitting beside him. "Use both hands."

He wraps his hands around the cup and Lucy steadies them as he drinks. He pauses when his eyes catch someone unfamiliar entering through the doorway.

"Sheriff?"

"Earl Hahn, I need you to come down to the jailhouse with me."

"Sheriff, is that necessary?" Missus Tate's eyes snap. "He's just a boy. He says it was an accident."

"We'll sort it out down at the jail. I was at the doc's when they brought in this boy's mother. My deputy's on his way to take statements." He glances around the room. "Are there witnesses?"

A few heads swivel toward Lucy, causing her eyes to widen in alarm. "Young lady, you stay put until Officer Dewey arrives. I want you to answer his questions, do you understand?"

She nods, doesn't make a sound.

The sheriff turns to Earl, who hasn't moved. "On your feet, son."

Earl shoots Lucy a look of pure panic. He looks at the local men, at the sheriff with flat eyes he doesn't know how to read. Shakily, he hands the cup back to his sister and wipes his nose one more time with the soiled handkerchief. He searches for the owner, holds out the square of blue cloth.

"Keep it."

With jerky movements, he stands, stuffing the handkerchief into his trouser pocket. Then he turns to face the sheriff.

"Hold out your hands."

He watches the man snap the cuffs onto his wrists and feels instantly trapped. He wants them off, off, off. He swivels his head to find Missus Tate. Mattie has laid her head against the woman's shoulder. His baby sister watches Earl solemnly, thumb in her mouth.

He glances at Lucy and her eyes fill with new tears. She lets out a sob and wraps her arms around his waist. He wants to hug her back but can't.

"Missus Tate, ma'am, you'll look after Lucy and Mattie?" His eyes search the woman's, craving reassurance. "Don't let them be alone."

"Don't you worry, hon. You go on with the sheriff. We'll get this straightened out. Your sisters can stay with me."

Orbry re-enters the room, his hands clenched. If the sheriff weren't there, Earl knows he'd be receiving more violence from his brother. Orbry stares at him with hate in his black eyes and hate in his heart.

The sheriff gives a tug and Earl lets the man guide him out of the house and put him into the patrol car. There's a squawk as the vehicle cuts through the chicken yard, scattering hens in its wake.

TEN

"Do you hate your mama, boy?" The police officer stands, hands on hips, squinting through the iron bars of the cell. There's a twist to the man's mouth Earl doesn't like.

He ducks his head and stares at a stain on the floor. It don't look like blood. Upchuck maybe, an old upchuck stain.

"I bet she was mean to you. Did she hit you, boy? I know your pa hit you."

Mute, Earl shakes his head.

Another officer enters the room and stops in front of the cell. "Is that the boy shot his mama?"

"That's him."

"What's your name, boy?"

"Earl, honey." As soon as the words are out of his mouth, he knows they're not right. The man sniggers.

"That there's Earl Hahn," says the first officer. "Reinhardt Hahn's boy."

The other man clears the phlegm from his throat and spits toward a brass spittoon in the corner. His spew misses the rim and hits the wall. Earl notices it isn't the first to do so.

"You know your pa slept in the same cell you're sitting in? I guess the saying's true, huh? Like father, like son."

"I ain't like my pa," Earl says, his voice soft. His pa was mean, quick to anger. Earl is slow, slow to anger, slow to just about everything.

"What'd you say, boy? Speak up."

"I said I AIN'T LIKE MY PA!" He fists his hands in frustration. It upsets him to raise his voice, but these men aren't listening.

"No, I guess you're not," says the officer, making a sucking sound through his teeth. "Your pa was a depraved rat bastard, but even he never aimed a gun at his own family."

"It was an accident," Earl says miserably, dropping his head to his knees. He wants to be left alone, not realizing that left on his own, the images in his head will be worse than the taunts of the officers. Flashes of color and sharp bursts of gunshot skitter through his mind, refusing to obey his desire for peace, for quiet. He fears he might never lose the memory of his ma lying on the floor with the blood, the smear of red on her dress, even on her hands where she tried to stop the hole from draining her empty. Earl has never been good at remembering. Now, he worries he might not be good at forgetting.

He tries to take his thoughts back to the morning, to before things took a turn. His sisters are coming to visit. He hasn't seen them in so long. He feels light-hearted in anticipation, and more grown up, because he's been given a job to do. He's been trusted to kill the chicken Ma will cook for her special birthday dinner. And there's the promise of cake – cake and family, something sweet to close the day.

"Throw down corn. Grab the hen. Chop the head. Hang to drain." He whispers the words, his mother's instructions bouncing around the vast empty spaces inside his head. They seem so simple. "Throw down corn. Grab the hen. Chop the head. Hang to drain. Throw down corn. Grab the hen. Grab the hen. Grab the hen…" A sob breaks through his feeble attempt at self-control. If only he weren't stupid. Stupid Earl. He knows there's one vital instruction he failed to follow. He's heard his pa say the words many times. They echo in his brain, refuse to be silenced. *"Never shoot toward the house."*

He removes the handkerchief from his pocket and blows his nose. "It was an accident," he murmurs vaguely, unaware his audience has drifted away. He wraps his arms around his knees and presses himself small into the corner. Every once in a while, someone, or several someones, enter the corridor. They stare, point, say things. On two occasions, officers sit outside the iron bars with notepads and ask him questions. Did he have a fight with his mother? Did something make him angry? Does he like to harm animals? Does he hear voices in his head telling him to do things? He shouts at them. "No! No and no and no!" He covers his head with his arms. He closes his eyes. He closes his ears.

He thinks about cake. He thinks about the day that should have been, sitting with his ma and his sisters, the soft, sugary sweetness of shortcake melting on his tongue. He's unaware of the tears streaking his face, soaking his trousers, still dusty from the chicken yard.

It's dark when he feels a hand on his shoulder, someone shaking him roughly.

"Get up. The preacher's here. He's going to take you home."

Earl rubs his eyes then slowly stands. He wobbles, braces himself with a hand against the cinder block wall, then follows the officer sent to collect him.

When he sees Pastor Jack, he walks into the man's arms, places his head on the broad chest, and lets the tears flow. The preacher smells like bright leaf tobacco. His breathing is deep and slow, and Earl finds comfort in his presence. After a minute, the man speaks, his voice a low rumble. "I'm taking you home."

"Ain't I bein' arrested?"

"No. After taking statements from Lucy and the neighbors, the sheriff has come to the conclusion the shooting was an unfortunate accident. Even your brother admits you wouldn't have done such a thing on purpose. No one wants to press charges."

He wipes his nose on his sleeve, letting this news sink in. He should prob'ly feel relieved. "Where's Ma?"

"Your mother's been taken to Rex Hospital in Raleigh. The doctors are looking after her."

He steps back, feeling the first glimmer of hope he's known since Farmer Tate put his ma in the Ford and drove away. "Is she going to be alright?"

"The doctors are doing everything they can. It's a good hospital."

He releases a shuddering sigh. The doctors are smart. They hadn't been able to help him, but surely they'll be better at patching up his ma. A hole in the side is something you can see. It'd be easier to fix than a brain. And even he got better over time. Ma said it herself. He didn't fall down no more. So that meant there was hope. The docs would fix his ma. They would fix her right up.

The preacher leads him outside to his automobile. The front seat smells of smoke and sweat. The odors are reassuringly familiar, calming his jangled insides. It's late when they arrive at the house. The sky is a blanket of stars glimmering above the small cabin perched in the middle of a cornfield. Inside, a kerosene lamp radiates a soft glow through the screen door.

Someone has fixed the screen door.

"Your brother's run off and we can't find him," says Pastor Jack. "Ladies from the Salvation Army are going to take turns checking on you and your sister. Lucy insisted on staying here to wait for you. Miss Hazel is inside now. She's a kind woman. You should try and get some sleep."

"What about the baby?"

"Mattie's with Mrs. Tate. Oh, I just remembered. Your other two sisters are at the hospital. Their guardian… um… Mr. Reynolds or Randolph? He drove them to Raleigh straightaway when he heard about the accident. I expect you'll see them later."

Earl rubs a hand over his eyes. So Welcome and Faith knew what he'd done. They'll hate him now. His whole family will hate him. And they should. He hates hisself. He stares blindly through the window. He doesn't want to leave the dark vehicle. He knows Pastor Jack. He doesn't know whoever's keeping watch in his ma's house.

"It's alright, Earl. Go inside."

"Yes sir."

"Wait." The preacher turns in his seat and reaches for Earl's hands. "Can I pray with you?"

He thinks Ma would like that. "Yes sir."

For a long moment, the preacher is silent, gathering his thoughts. When he begins, he keeps his eyes closed, his face somber in the darkness. "Dear Heavenly Father, in your scripture you tell us that when we call out to you, you will give the order to heal and rescue us from certain death. I have read of your miraculous healing and believe you can still heal the same way today. I believe there is no injury you cannot repair in your awesome power. I ask for your healing of Earl's mother, Elizabeth Belle Hahn, who has suffered a severe injury."

Earl thinks this is a fine prayer. It's exactly what he wants, to have his ma healed.

The preacher's not done.

"Lord, I know, in your infinite wisdom, you do not always heal."

"What?" Earl whispers.

The preacher squeezes his hands. "Whatever happens, please help keep Earl's heart soft toward you, to submit to your plan for his life. Please pour your blessings on the doctors and nurses caring for Mrs. Hahn that they may be knowledgeable and compassionate. Guide their hands to instruments of thy purpose. And Lord, please bestow your blessings on Earl, that he may be comforted in his time of anguish.

"Lord, I know you are in control of everything that happens from our first breath to our last sigh, and I submit to your all-loving, all-powerful, eternal being. In the name of Jesus, we say…" He gives Earl's hands another squeeze.

Earl holds his breath, waiting for the final part. The preacher gives another, harder, squeeze and he realizes he's s'posed to say something.

"Amen."

"Amen." Pastor Jack releases him. "Okay, Earl. You go inside. I'll stop by tomorrow and see how you're doing."

Pulling himself together, Earl exits the car and stands silently as the preacher turns the vehicle around in the dirt yard and heads back toward the road. With painstaking slowness, he climbs the steps to the porch and slips inside the front door. He faces the woman seated in Ma's rocker, taking in the dark hair threaded with gray, the round spectacles perched on the end of her nose. *She shouldn't sit there*, he thinks. *That's Ma's rocker*. But he stays silent. The only sound is the click of knitting needles as she works on a half-finished blanket in her lap. She lifts her eyes above the rim of her glasses and peers at him standing in the doorway.

"Are you Earl?" she asks, her eyes steady on his.

He nods.

"See if you can get some sleep. Your sister's already gone to bed. I'll make breakfast when the sun comes up."

Without a word, he heads to the bedroom he shares with his brother. Orbry's not there. His bed is empty.

Earl lays on top of his mattress, eyes wide in the darkness. He wants his ma. He wants to crawl into her arms. He wants her to kiss his forehead and tell him everything is alright. But his ma isn't there, only a strange woman he doesn't know. He sends his own urgent prayer to Heaven. "I done something bad," he whispers. "I didn't mean to, honest, I didn't. Please look after Ma. Please save her. Save her. Save her." He turns his face into the pillow.

Once during the night, rolling over in a dream, he imagines he hears footsteps on the porch and the muffled sound of voices. Then all is quiet. Finally, a thin sliver of light begins to seep into the room, finding its way through cracks and crevices. When he hears the woman moving around in the house, he wipes his eyes, clenching his teeth with sudden pain. He forgot about being punched. And Ma isn't there to tend him. Moving stiffly, he leaves the bed and slips quietly into the kitchen.

"I'm going to collect the eggs, then I'll make breakfast," the woman says. "Are you going to be alright?"

He takes a seat at the table.

After gazing at him for a moment, she makes a clucking sound. Grabbing one of Ma's flour sack towels, she spreads it on the counter. She takes a scraper and shaves ice from the block in the icebox. She deposits the ice shavings in the towel and wraps them inside. She hands the towel to him. "Put this against the side of your face," she says.

He does as he's told.

A few minutes later, his sister enters the room, still in her nightgown. Her feet are bare. Violet shadows hug her eyes, red-rimmed from crying. She puts an arm around his neck and rests her head on his shoulder. "Was it awful?" she asks.

He grabs her hand, clutches it tightly. "Stay with me," he croaks.

She pats his shoulder. "I will."

The woman returns from the coop with her basket. "There weren't many eggs. Are the hens poor layers?"

Lucy glances at her brother then back at the woman. "I expect the hens are riled from yesterday."

For a moment, the woman looks perplexed, then her face clears. "Of course. Right." She walks to the stove. "Breakfast will be ready in a moment."

In short order, she places two tin plates on the table and serves breakfast, an egg over-easy for each of them. "Has the other boy come home? Is it Orbry?"

Earl and Lucy have a silent exchange. Neither one minds if their brother is gone. Eventually, the children realize this woman is waiting for an answer. "Sometimes Orbry stays with a friend," his sister lies.

The woman nods, then pours three small cups of coffee and brings them to the table. She sits with her own cup and sips slowly while the two of them eat. Earl watches her from the corner of his eye, eating with one hand while the other presses the cold towel against the sore side of his face. When the plates have been cleared of every drop of yellow yolk, the woman speaks.

"Children, your mother passed away early this morning."

Earl drops his head to the table, the damp towel slipping from his fingers to the floor. He stays that way as the rest of the woman's words disappear into the whirlwind ripping his world into something unrecognizable.

"There's going to be a burial at the church cemetery. Pastor Jack is reaching out to the immediate family. We need to get in touch with any aunts, uncles or cousins. Do you know how to reach them?"

The woman pushes her chair back and walks around the table. Gently, she lifts Earl by his shoulders and stands there, one arm bracing him up. He doesn't resist but sits numbly, his eyes wandering vaguely to his sister.

She blinks rapidly, struggling to keep away tears. "Ma has addresses for our brothers and sisters. Other than that, it's just us," she says.

"You don't have other kin?"

"Pa came here from Germany before the war. He's got a brother somewhere, but we don't know him."

"How on earth has your mother been surviving all on her own?"

"Since Pa got sent up, she takes in sewing and laundry. And she helps Missus Tate." Her voice sounds wet with unshed tears.

"I see."

Miss Hazel pats Earl's shoulder then walks to the other side of the table. She appears lost in thought.

"What's going to happen to us, ma'am?" asks Lucy.

"If you've got no family willing to take you, the Salvation Army will help you find a place."

"Together?"

"We'll see what happens," she says briskly, discouraging further questions. She collects the plates, stacking them together with forks on top. Before turning to the washtub, she pins the two children with a sharp glance. "Earl, I want you to wash up and put on clean clothes. Lucy, that goes for you, too. Run a comb through your hair. Be ready for visitors. Ladies from the church will be stopping by with food. I expect the two of you to be on your best behavior."

ELEVEN

"First, Pa. Now, Ma. If it's true what folks say and bad luck comes in threes, our family ain't done yet." Welcome stares solemnly around the small group huddled on the bed. Her voice drops an octave. "One of us might be next."

Earl shivers.

"Hush, Welcome. You're not helping." Faith's tone is sharp. "This misfortune affects all of us," she continues. "You, me, Lucy. That's way more than three so let it be someone else's turn for bad luck. We don't need your foolishness making things worse."

"You're not so smart!"

"Welcome, enough!" Faith snaps.

The flickering candle on Ma's nightstand casts shadows across the bickering sisters, making them appear hollow-eyed and ghoulish. Earl watches warily, eyes darting from one sister to the other. In the year since Welcome and Faith have been gone, they've become strangers to him.

When Mr. Randolph brought the girls home from the hospital, they appeared solemn and haggard. Faith was noticeably taller and more grown up since he'd seen her last. After staggering through the front door with a carpet bag in her hands, she'd gone straight to the big bedroom and climbed into Ma's bed. Welcome scurried around the house, snooping to see what was new since she'd been gone, before joining her sister.

Now, the two of them rest beneath rough sheets that smell of Mattie's baby powder and Ma's lavender oil. Earl and Lucy face them from the other end of the bed. He doesn't remember his two younger sisters ever being close, but now he senses a great friction between them. Maybe it has something to do with their new family. Mr. Randolph is in the front room speaking with Pastor Jack and ladies from the church. Snippets of conversation rise, then fall away as someone is shushed.

Orbry steps into the bedroom, his outline a dark silhouette in the doorway. With a heavy tread, he comes forward and slides beneath the sheets next to Faith. Earl watches silently as his brother reaches a beefy hand beneath her nightgown.

"Stop it," she hisses, kicking back at him with one leg.

"I thought you might be missing Pa at a time like this," he says, groping her clumsily in the half-dark. "Let me feel your bubs."

"Stop it, Orbry." Her voice holds a veiled threat.

He removes his hand.

Welcome lifts her head from the pillow. "What'd you find out?" she whispers.

"They're trying to decide what to do with us."

"Do you think they'll let Pa come home early?" she asks.

"Pa's not coming home," Orbry says shortly.

"You don't know that."

"I do."

"He only poisoned a well," says Welcome. "Nobody died. How long does he have to stay in prison for that?"

"Hell's bells. What have you been told? Pa's not in prison for poisoning a well. He's in prison cause of Rose's baby. It's Pa's fault she got knocked-up."

"Maybe Farmer Tate can talk to the warden," she continues, oblivious. "Once he understands our situation…"

"You're such a Dumb Dora," Orbry snaps. "Do I have to spell it out for you?"

"I'm not dumb," Welcome says, her voice quivering. "And you're mean."

"Orbry, keep your voice down. She doesn't need to know everything." Faith sends Earl a quick glance but doesn't speak to him. Neither of the girls have said boo to him since their arrival. He knows why. He considers walkin' out but where could he go? He has to stay and listen. He has to know what will happen next.

Faith shifts so she's leaning against the headboard. She stares at her brother, looking determined. "Orbry, we have to figure out who's going to look after Lucy and Earl. What about Frieda?"

"I heard the church ladies talking. They know Frieda's turning tricks for the soldiers. They said she's not fit."

She seems to understand what Orbry means, but Earl's confused. He thought Frieda was a dancer, not a magician.

Besides, he doesn't want to live with Frieda. He wants to stay here on the farm with Lucy and the baby. They can take care of theirselves.

"What about you, Orbry?" He speaks hesitantly, his muscles tensing in case he has to make a quick escape. Earl has a black eye and split lip to remind him how much damage his brother can do. "You could farm full-time for Mr. Tate. I can do more. I can help in the fields and… and tend to the livestock. Then we can stay in the house."

"I'm not sticking around to look after you babies. I'm headed to the Army recruiter the first chance I get."

"You're too young to join the Army," says Lucy. She reaches over to squeeze Earl's hand. She's the only one bein' nice to him.

"I'm tall for my age. Everyone says so. It's not like anyone's gonna ask to see the family Bible. How do they know how old I am?"

"Orbry, you're selfish," says Faith.

"I'm realistic," he says, his voice hard. He climbs out of the bed and stares at his family in the darkness. "You lot better grow up fast. Things ain't ever goin' to be the same." He turns to Earl, his lip curling with scorn. "Brother, you're going to get what's coming to you. If Welcome's right and misfortune happens in threes, I hope you're next. A stupid moron like you – you're bound to end up in prison or the crazy house, but I won't be around to see it."

Without another word, he clomps out of the room. Earl flinches when he hears the wood screen door slam against its frame. He drops his head into his hands, his mind spinning with grief and fear. The sheriff let him go but what if Orbry's right? What if they're not done with him? What if Ma has kin who come after him? Will he have to go on trial like Pa done? Who will speak for him?

"Faith?"

He lifts his head. Welcome's voice sounds shaky. Is it because of Ma? Or is she feeling picked on cause Orbry called her a Dumb Dora? Shoot, that's nothin'.

Faith chews on a fingernail, her eyes staring vacantly toward the doorway. The grown-ups can be heard talking in muffled voices. "What?"

"Can Lucy go with Orbry? To the Army?"

"No."

"Why not?"

"'Cause she's a girl."

Welcome's silent for a long moment. "They must need girls to do things, too."

"The men do everything."

"Even the cooking and cleaning?"

"Yes. Even the cooking and cleaning. There's only one thing soldiers want from the girls." Faith's voice sounds bitter. "If the Randolphs decide we're too common to be looked after, we may have to move in with Frieda and charge a family rate." She glances at Earl. "I don't know what options the world holds for you, brother. Evidently, you're good at shootin' people. You gonna join the Army, too?"

He suspects she's bein' mean 'cause she's sad, but it still hurts his feelings. There's a tone in his sister's voice he hasn't heard before. He's unsure if it's Ma's dying that done it or if something else put it there. Before she went to live with the Randolphs, she'd been nice to him. Once, when he was beat up on account of Pa, she sat by his bed and sang to him. "*Whatcha gonna do with the baby-o, wrap him up in calico. Wrap him up in calico, send him to his mammy-o. That's what I'll do with the baby-o. That's what I'll do with the baby-o.*"

She's good at singing. But now Faith seems different, hard. He's unsure why.

"Hey, you."

He jolts when Welcome kicks him beneath the sheet.

"What'd you do that for?" he says, shifting out of reach.

She pushes out her lower lip and glares at him.

"I want Ma. And I want a piece of cake. Lucy said there was shortcake."

"Did someone take the cake?" he asks, confused.

Lucy moves closer and leans against his shoulder. Her eyes are focused on her big sister. "Faith, did Pa ever touch you… like that, like he did Rose?"

Earl tries to remember what Mr. Edwards told him about girls and consent and something about their ages. He's not good at remembering dates, but he knows he's thirteen. Lucy just turned eight. That means Welcome is ten and Faith would be nearly twelve. But Mr. Edwards said age doesn't matter when it's a pa and his daughter. He watches as Faith rolls over and punches her pillow. "It's late," she says. "I expect we're going to need our sleep for whatever's coming next." She inhales a quick, sharp breath. "And no. The answer is no."

Lucy crawls on hands and knees to the top of the bed, slipping between her sisters. That's Earl's cue to climb down and head to his own room.

"You know what," Welcome mumbles drowsily, pulling the covers to her chin. "Today is Ma's birthday. Happy birthday, Ma." She hums a few familiar notes then releases a sigh that signals sleep.

Earl hurries from the room and slides into his own bed. Today is Ma's birthday. He forgot. A flood of sorrow washes over him, leaving him shaken and more alone than he's ever felt in his life. Last year, he picked a bouquet of wild flowers for his ma. She put them in a milk bottle and placed them on the table where everybody could see the pretty colors. Even Orbry was on good behavior. He whittled her a dozen new clothes pins. Earl spares a brief glance for the empty bed across the room. He wonders if the Army will take Orbry. Would his brother come to the funeral? Of all Ma's children, he was the one most like Pa. And that was the meanest thing Earl could think about anyone.

He sits up when a small shape flits through the doorway. Lucy leans close to whisper in his ear. "Don't pay attention to Orbry," she says, her voice a balm in the darkness. "Don't pay attention to any of 'em. They're upset now. But they'll come around." She pats his shoulder then hurries from the room.

Lying back down, he's surprised to discover he feels better. He closes his eyes, convinced he won't be able to sleep. In spite of himself, his mind softens and sinks. Soon, he's making his way through a veiled mist, sifting through the fabric of his dream for something… something he doesn't know the word for. It's something lost, lost behind grief and guilt and stark terror.

He's awakened the next morning by the sound of clattering pots and the smell of hot coffee. *Ma must be getting breakfast ready*, he thinks lazily. He pictures her standing at the stove with the morning sun behind her, lighting her up like an angel. For one swift second, he's filled with pleasant anticipation. Then he remembers. Whoever's in the kitchen, it's not his ma. The realization that he'll never see her again as long as he lives punches his lungs, makes him gasp like a drowning man. He wants to pull the covers over his head and hide from the world. Instead, he makes himself swing his legs over the side of the bed. He presses hard against his eyes with both hands before any tears can fall, then whimpers when his swollen eye rebels against the rough treatment. Orbry's fists had only beat his face but it felt like every square inch of him ached, especially the parts inside.

Feeling brittle, he gets himself ready for the day. Once he's presentable, he steps out to see who's here. Rose and Frieda are in the kitchen with Mr. Randolph. Last night, neighbors started dropping off platters of food. There are tins of cornbread and jars of homemade jam. Someone brought a smoked ham and Rose is placing slices of meat in the oven to warm.

"The hospital will deliver the body today," Mr. Randolph says. "There's insufficient space here for visitation, so they're going to take your mother to the church. The ladies' auxiliary will prepare the body. Your neighbor, Mr. Tate, has made arrangements for a simple pine coffin."

Earl bends and clutches each skinny thigh, squeezing as hard as he can to keep from blacking out. He doesn't want to think about his ma in a box. The sounds of the kitchen dim. When he releases his grip, everything returns in bright relief. When he's gotten himself together, he stands, taking his first good look at the tall, bearded man before him. This is Welcome and Faith's new family. He's old. Way older than Pa. He's grandpa old. Earl has never had a grandpa. The man holds out his hand.

"We weren't properly introduced yesterday. I'm Ralph Albert Randolph. Mostly, folks call me Professor. Your sisters live with me and my wife, Mary Alice. I'm sorry she couldn't be here. She's feeling poorly."

Earl shakes the offered hand. Something about the man's eyes unsettle him, the pale intensity of his gaze. "Thank you for bringing my sisters home," he says, his voice sounding scratchy to his ears. "Ma was happy Welcome and Faith found a... a safe place to live after Pa... after Pa."

The man squeezes his shoulder. "Can I get you something? Would you like a ham biscuit? What about a cup of coffee?"

"Yes sir. I guess I could eat."

Rose puts a piece of ham on a plate with a buttermilk biscuit. "Eat this. You'll feel better." Mr. Randolph brings him a cup of hot coffee.

"Thank you." Earl can't remember when he ate last. Had it been breakfast yesterday? A biscuit with molasses. Or had that been the day before? His ma had been alive then. Alive. Then, not alive.

He tries to swallow a piece of biscuit but it gets stuck at the back of his throat. He coughs, tears springing to his eyes.

"Maybe just a sip of coffee to get you going first, what do you think?" Mr. Randolph gives his shoulder another pat then returns to the kitchen to assist the others.

He sips the coffee and watches as his sisters bustle around, chopping and slicing and mixing and frying. Soon, the smell of food lures Welcome, Faith and Lucy to the table. No one asks about Orbry.

"Who's gonna tell Pa?" Welcome asks, reaching for a dish of fruit preserves delivered by a neighbor. "Does Pa know?"

"The preacher's going to the prison today to deliver the news," Frieda replies. "He said he'd swing by the house to check if any of us want to go with him." She gazes around the table. "So. Anyone want to see Pa?"

The room grows quiet as the Hahn children steal glances at one another, then turn to look somewhere else. All of them understand it's dangerous to be present when Pa learns his wife has been shot dead. Pastor Jack is bein' brave. If Earl went, his pa would turn on him for bein' the one who done it. He'd never make it home alive.

"After we eat, I'm taking Matilde's things over to Missus Tate," says Rose. "She's agreed to look after her." She doesn't say 'today', and Earl knows why. Missus Tate is taking the baby for always. He doesn't like to think about it, but he knows the Tates have a good home. There's a hint of something in Rose's voice, something like she's askin' folks to argue with her, but prob'ly everyone around the table agrees it's a fine solution.

"I can help you carry stuff, Rose," says Earl. "I can carry the cradle. Put me to work."

She looks at him and nods. "Yes, I can do that. You'll be a big help."

He can feel the tears pricking the back of his eyes and has to look away. He doesn't deserve kindness.

TWELVE

"Stand by the casket," Pastor Jack says, tugging Earl and shifting him into position. "Your neighbors will want to express their condolences and they shouldn't have to chase you down." He motions for Welcome and Faith to move closer. "Don't huddle together. Give people room to approach you. Allow them to hug you or shake your hand. This grief belongs to the community. It may console you to discover how many people feel blessed to have known your mother. She was a good woman."

Earl feels uneasy. It's a hard thing he's bein' asked to do. It's hard to stand so near to a body that looks like Ma but isn't. He's gratified to see it's not only him who's dismayed. As more people enter the church fellowship hall, Lizzie Belle Hahn's four youngest children inch themselves as far from the plain pine box as they can while still appearing respectable. From this distance, they can't see Ma's face, but they can eavesdrop on what folks are sayin'. Neighbors agree Mrs. Hahn looks lovely in her flowered dress, but her children know the woman in the pine box isn't their ma anymore. The sight of the vacant body simply drives the point home.

Now, struggling to do their duty, the four watch with a collective distrust as Mr. Wilkins approaches, tugging nervously on his mustache. Upon entering their small circle, the grocer works his face into a mournful expression.

The young people stand stiffly. Only Lucy is visibly restless. Earl waits for the man to speak words he's already come to dread. Words like 'she's in a better place now'. Or 'God has a plan for each of us'. Earl rejects this wholeheartedly. His ma's best place was with him and Lucy and Baby Mattie.

Mr. Wilkins is silent for a long moment, his fingers steepled as though deep in thought. "I was sorry to hear about your mother's passing," he says finally. "Your family has been touched by tragedy."

Welcome appears to appreciate this observation and doesn't hesitate with her reply. "We have surely been touched by tragedy. Thank you, sir, for your condolences."

"She acts like she's playing a part," Lucy whispers in his ear.

Earl agrees. Welcome seems to enjoy the attention they've received on account of Ma's death and it rubs on him.

"You're the one called Welcome, aren't you? Such an unusual name."

She fusses with her dress then gazes at the man from beneath her lashes. "Ma told the midwife, 'the last one's as welcome as the first'. That's how she named me."

"But…" He looks confused. "You're not the youngest."

"No sir. I was lucky thirteen. Then Lucy was fourteen and there was another baby that didn't make it. That's fifteen. But then Ma got Mattie – Matilde – she's Rose's child by way of Pa, but Ma was raisin' her. Missus Tate is going to keep Mattie now 'cause she's so young and sweet and all. Faith and I got lucky cause the Randolphs took us in before Ma passed. But I don't know what's gonna happen to Earl and Lucy." She glances sideways and makes a clucking noise. "I'd hate to see them come to a bad end."

The man doesn't appear to know what to do with this information. "I see. Yes, it's quite… quite a dilemma, I'm sure." Looking everywhere but directly at them, he finally lets his eyes rest on Faith. "Did any of your older brothers come for the funeral? Wilhelm or Kurt?"

"No sir. They're working up north. The distance was too great for them to be here on short notice." Her voice is cool. "Was there something you needed?"

He opens his mouth to reply, shuts it, seems to reconsider then plows forward. "Well, I hate to mention it, but there's an outstanding balance, you see, at the store. I wasn't sure who to speak with now that your mother has passed."

His sister's expression darkens.

"See Frieda," she says shortly. "She'll settle any debts."

"Frieda." He glances around the crowded room, spots Lizzie Belle's eldest daughter arranging platters of food on the buffet table. "The one with the, ah, rouge on her cheeks," he says slowly.

"That's right," she says, her voice like ice.

"I'll speak with her directly. Again, my condolences on your loss." He gives a small head bob and hurries away.

"Weasel," mutters Faith. "He's always hated our family."

"Pa stole from him all the time. You can hardly blame him," says Welcome.

Earl stays silent. He's tired. It takes energy to be with his family, let alone neighbors he barely knows. He doesn't want to be here but his sisters have threatened him with violence if he ducks. At least one of Ma's sons needs to pay respects, they said, and it seemed easier to go along than to resist. He wants to slip away but catches a look from Pastor Jack, who appears to suspect his intentions. He decides to hold his spot a mite longer. Finally, when Welcome and Faith start talking about some guy named Valentino who he's not acquainted with, Earl sees his opportunity and spins himself out of the family circle.

He's headed toward the food table when Frieda catches his eye and gives her head a tiny shake. He stops in his tracks, watching as Farmer Tate's eldest boy, Henry, strikes up a conversation with his sister. Frieda smiles and then laughs with the young man. Earl wonders at it, convinced he may never laugh again.

Thwarted, he takes a moment to scan the room. Ladies from the United Daughters of the Confederacy meander around the hall, speaking to their neighbors. "Don't forget to purchase a ticket to the gala, Mr. Williams. The funds will be put toward a statue to honor the glorious dead." The women dole out modest smiles and reach daintily to touch an arm or press a powdered cheek in comfort, all the while reminding folks of their upcoming fundraiser. Faith observes that Ma's viewing is an opportunity for them to campaign for their latest cause. Not one of those ladies approaches the grieving family.

He pivots and finds himself face to face with the Bennett sisters: Ona, Nona, Lona, and Dona May. The town gossips, they're here for the spectacle and nothing more. With twitching noses, they step around him like he isn't a boy who just lost his mother. His lip trembles at the meanness of it. Then he catches the eye of James Purvis, huddled in a corner and whispering into the ear of another boy.

Without further thought, Earl dashes for the door, craving fresh air and daylight. He's going home. Away from folks talkin' about him behind their hands. Away from the husk of pale skin and blue muslin that looks like his ma but isn't. Halfway down the street, he realizes James Purvis and his pal have him in their sights and trail a few yards behind.

He hasn't gone two steps further when he catches a hiss behind him. "Murderer!" Then another hateful word reaches his ears. "Moron." Then a flood of them. "White trash, redneck, retard, rube." The boys are relentless, wild dogs tearing at an open wound.

Earl picks up speed, tears whipping his cheeks as he veers down the street. The boys make a half-hearted attempt at pursuit but quickly give up, realizing he can't be caught. He runs and runs. Not home, but to the old tabacca barn, weathered and abandoned. Farmer Tate hasn't torn it down yet, even though his new, better barn is almost complete.

Nearly undone by the sobs racking his body, he fumbles for the ladder that leads to the rafters. He's watched men hang tabacca leaves here in the summertime, their skin slick with sweat. Now, blinded by tears, he feels his way to the top, his hands gripping old wood. Inch by precarious inch, he makes his way to the darkest corner and wedges himself in-between two beams. He could stay up here all day and no one would find him.

He has the handkerchief with him, the one a neighbor give to him after Orbry's beating. It's a mess, stiff from dried blood and snot. He uses it now to wipe his cheeks. Inhaling a shaky breath, he tucks the square of cloth back into his pocket. Later, he'll draw a bucket of water from the well. He'll rinse the handkerchief and let it dry on the line. He wraps an arm around one of the beams and stares through the vast, empty barn. He relaxes for the first time since pressing the trigger on Pa's gun. His mind finally, blissfully empty, Earl counts white spatters where birds have crapped on the beams. He can't count high, but it doesn't matter for he's asleep in seconds. When he wakes, he's wobbling precariously on his perch, late afternoon light slanting through the eaves.

Reluctant to face folks, he nonetheless climbs down and makes his way behind fields covered with green shoots of corn. He goes the long way, sneaking behind the faded dwelling that represents home and safety. He finds a spot behind the coop where he can hide from view. He sits cross-legged on the soft dirt and watches the action. Neighbors come and go in their black Model Ts, on horseback or by mule. One family walks up the dirt road, stands in the yard eating pie, speaks to the pastor then departs. He doesn't want to face them. He doesn't want to see the accusation in their eyes.

As pale streaks of pink fade from the sky, the last of the guests make their way down the front porch steps and head to their homes. It's mostly family now. He stands and dusts off his trousers before approaching the house.

"Hey, stranger." Rose is seated in a black buggy.

He walks over to give the pretty bay a pat on the neck. "Are you leaving?" he asks.

"As soon as Mr. Edwards finishes saying goodbye."

"Can I climb up?"

"Suit yourself."

He swings up in the buggy beside her. Frieda appears behind the screen door and stands quietly, her eyes on Welcome. His younger sister has climbed into Mr. Randolph's lap where he's seated in one of the porch rockers. She pats his pockets, probing with nimble fingers while he chuckles.

"Earl?" Rose pokes him in the ribs.

"What?" he says, pulling his attention from the front porch.

"Go tell your sister to get off that old man's lap."

"He's her new daddy."

"I bet he is." She narrows her eyes at the pair, much the same way Frieda glares at them through the mesh screen. "What's she about anyway?"

"He hides horehound candies in his pockets for her to find."

"That's one way to do it, I suppose."

"Do what?"

"Maybe it's a good thing Ma's not here to see this. Out of the frying pan and into the fire…"

"Are you mad at Welcome?" he asks.

"Am I mad? Am I mad Ma sent Welcome away so Pa couldn't touch her? Ma knew, you know. Since Frieda, she knew. She didn't send me away, did she? Why is that do you think?"

Earl glances sideways at his sister, sitting tensely beside him. Two bright spots of pink bloom across her cheeks. He watches as she tightens her hands into fists, staring down at her lap before slashing hot eyes his way. "Well? Why?"

He speaks aloud the first thing that pops into his brain. "If Pa was busy with you, maybe it meant he was leavin' Ma alone."

She lets out a sob, her eyes welling with tears. "Yeah. That's what I think. I'm so angry I could scream. And she's… she's not here to defend herself. And that makes me angry, too. I'll never get to confront her. She'll never get to ask my forgiveness and…" her voice breaks, "I'll never get to give it to her." She takes a trembling breath, swiping angrily at damp cheeks.

"She dressed you in overalls."

"What?" She gapes at him.

"She dressed you in overalls so you wouldn't look pretty."

Rose lets out a half laugh, then shakes her head. "Good Lord, Earl. She put me in overalls because they were hand-me-downs from Kurt, and we couldn't afford fabric for dresses."

He thinks for a moment. "She took Mattie. That's something. Right?" He doesn't want his sister to be mad at their ma, not now, not when it's too late.

For a moment, she looks lost. "Yes. That's something," she whispers. She turns to him with a desperate motion and he gets his first good look at her eyes. She's broken, he realizes. Something inside her has torn away and might never be repaired. He can't comprehend the deep well of emotion he sees there and shifts his eyes uncomfortably to look anywhere else.

After a moment, she pulls herself together. "Now Matilde's going to have yet another mother. I wonder what her new name will be."

Earl doesn't say anything.

"Go get Welcome," she snaps.

Relieved to escape, he hops from the buggy and approaches the front porch. "Welcome, Rose is gettin' ready to leave. Do you want to say goodbye?"

"I'm tired of her puttin on airs," Welcome says, directing a dark look toward the buggy.

Mr. Randolph pats her arm. "Go on, girlie. There's no telling when you'll see your sister again. It will give me a chance to speak with Earl."

"Oh, alright," she grumbles. She climbs from his lap and flounces over to the buggy. Earl fixes his gaze on Mr. Randolph and waits.

"How would you feel about coming to stay at my place?" the old man asks. "I've got one boy now who helps me on the farm. Frank. He's a couple years older than you. He handles the plowing. He performs small repairs. I'm unable to pitch in as much as I used to. It puts a strain on him. An extra set of hands would ease things."

Earl nods his head slightly. He's unsure why, maybe to appear agreeable.

"Frank sleeps in the tack room. We'd have to make your own space in the barn. That won't be hard. We can set up a camp bed in one of the stalls till the end of summer. I suppose the two of you can share the tack room once the weather cools. There's a small wood stove. Of course, you'd be sharing space with the livestock, two mules plus Roberta, she's our dairy cow. One barn cat. The pigs have their own pen. You'd work hard. From sunup to sundown. But you'd get three square meals a day and you'd get to spend time with your sisters, mostly on the Sabbath. We keep the Sabbath religiously. That day is yours to relax and worship how you see fit."

"Can Lucy come?"

"No, Earl. I'm sorry. Another home will need to be found for Lucy. I spoke with your neighbor, the woman from the Salvation Army. She's going to help your sister find a good situation. The Salvation Army made the arrangements for Welcome and Faith, you know. They have connections all over the state."

"Lucy should be with family."

"I don't disagree, son, but you'd need to speak with your brothers about that." The man's gaze is straightforward. "I'm leaving with Welcome and Faith tomorrow, directly after the burial. There's space in the Model T for one more. This is your decision, Earl. You have until tomorrow to make it."

THIRTEEN

Earl takes a cautious step into the house, trying to be invisible. The kitchen table's covered in plates of picked-over food: sausage rolls, pork cracklings, last fall's canned jam and half a rhubarb pie. Flies flit from plate to plate. He checks the coffee pot and wrinkles his nose in distaste. The dregs have gone cold. His stomach growls. He hasn't eaten since a few bites of biscuit at breakfast. Some bread and jam would take the edge off his hunger.

"Earl."

Pastor Jack sits in one of Ma's ladderback chairs. He pats the cane seat of a chair beside him. "Come join me."

Earl casts a wistful look at the food but takes the offered seat. Bowing his head, he waits to be scolded for runnin' off and leavin' Ma's special reception.

"Earl, I know today was hard. And there are hard days ahead, but continue to say your prayers. God looks after the less fortunate."

He wonders about this. It hasn't been his particular experience but it hurts to think after the day he's had, so he releases the thought. He wants his head empty.

"I went to see your father at the prison, to inform him of your mother's passing. I hadn't intended to reveal the full details – by that I mean your involvement." The preacher's gaze is compassionate. "It seems someone in town had already given him the news."

A tightness grips Earl's chest. He doesn't want to picture his pa's reaction. He knows too well the man's rages, the lightning-fast reflexes. He examines the man's face, looking for a black eye or split lip. He appears uninjured. The preacher might be faster than he looks.

"I can reassure you that your father won't be pressing charges."

Earl's eyes widen. "I don't understand."

"He doesn't have the resources to procure an attorney even if facts supported him taking such a step. The county has no desire to prosecute and all agree the passing of your mother is a tragic accident. God rest her soul."

"Is that…" He rubs a spot between his eyes. "I don't understand."

"You don't have to. The point is, there's insufficient motive for a criminal trial and you have no assets for a civil one."

"So… I don't have to go on trial like Pa did?" he asks, feeling both relieved and somewhat unconvinced.

"That's the situation as it currently stands." The preacher inclines his head toward the window screen, indicating front porch conversations drifting inside the room. "I overheard your discussion with Mr. Randolph.

It's good he's offered to take you into his employ. You can have a fresh start, Earl, somewhere folks don't know you."

"I guess."

"One thing you need to understand..." Pastor Jack pauses, glances around the room. "By any chance did your mother keep paper in the house?"

"Ma has notepaper."

"Can you bring me a piece of paper? And a pencil, please, if one can be found."

"Ma prefers pencils for Lucy's lessons but she has a fountain pen. She writes letters to Kurt with the fountain pen."

"A pencil will do fine."

Earl rises and rifles through a drawer in the kitchen. Inside, he finds Lucy's flash cards and papers with her practice letters. He removes a pad of lined notepaper and a pencil and delivers them to the preacher. "Ma used this paper for her dry goods list."

"This will do." With a bold hand, he writes something on the paper and hands it to Earl. "Can you read?"

"Not so well." He looks at the page. "What is it?"

"That's the month and year your father is scheduled to be released from prison."

"Oh."

"Keep this in a safe place. Your father has fourteen years to serve on his sentence. A lot can happen in that time. He may forget the injury to his wife. Or, the wound may fester, become toxic with time. It's impossible to tell. The point is... he... well, he might..."

Gravely, Earl meets the man's eyes. "So I'm to keep this paper safe so's I'll know when he's comin' to kill me?" This is what he was afraid of. He knows his pa will never forgive him for what he done. Deep inside, he believes this future punishment is no less than he deserves.

"It's futile to speculate about what your father's state of mind will be when he's released from prison. The wound is fresh now. Over time, he may forget all about it. Nevertheless, if you ever see him coming down the road, Earl, you need to get yourself to safety as quick as you can. Do you understand me?"

He understands. His ma and pa married till death do us part. When his pa gets out of prison there'll be no one obliged to take the man in, to feed him and see to his care. His children will not want him. Earl knows this. He had not meant to kill his ma. It was an accident. But his pa will pursue him to the ends of the earth to punish him for it.

The preacher stands, places a hand on his shoulder. "God keep you, Earl."

Feeling subdued, Earl returns the writing materials to their rightful place then enters his bedroom. Going to the bureau he shares with his brother, he opens a drawer, unsurprised to find Orbry's clothes gone. All that's left is one ratty sock and a discarded aspirin tin. He folds the piece of paper Pastor Jack gave him until it's small enough to insert into the tiny container. He snaps the tin shut and tucks it into his pocket.

Heart heavy, he listens to the creak of the front door, to the footsteps of departing guests. He meant to do something. Oh yeah. Bypassing clusters of folks saying hushed goodbyes, he peeks into doorways. In Ma's bedroom, he discovers Frieda seated on the bed, head in her hands.

"Frieda?"

She lifts red-rimmed eyes. "Do you know what this is?" she asks hoarsely. She lifts a hand to his gaze. It takes him a moment to realize she's wearing Ma's gold ring.

"You can't wear that till you're married," he says.

She chuckles roughly. "Ma removed her wedding band when Pa went to the jailhouse. It's why she wasn't wearin' it in the coffin. I figured if she hasn't worn it this whole year, she wouldn't want to take it with her."

His sister's words make sense to him.

"The thing is, Earl, I'm not thinking of keeping it. I'm thinking of selling it. I don't even know what I could get for this." There's a quality in her gaze that asks something of him. "It's gold, right? It must be worth something." She strokes the slender band.

"You should take it. Ma didn't wear that ring no more. She prob'ly only kept it so's she could give it to one of you girls."

"Yeah," she whispers. "Maybe."

"Have you seen Lucy?" he asks.

"What? No. Not since we got back from church."

He concentrates, listening for a familiar voice. Not hearing it, he leaves Frieda and continues outside. Arriving at the back of the house, he stoops to peer into the darkness below the floorboards. "There you are."

Lucy lies stretched on her belly beneath the house. Her head rests in the crook of her elbow.

"Whatcha doin'?"

"Nothin'." Her voice is barely audible.

He drops to the ground and scooches forward until he's lying beside her in the soft dirt. He can hear Rose's employer, Mr. Edwards, speaking to Mr. Randolph, still seated in the porch rocker, his movement sending rhythmic squeaks to the children below. Earl watches as the bottom half of legs clad in black trousers make their way toward the buggy. The pretty bay stamps a hoof, impatient to be off. As the buggy turns down the path, he squints at Lucy, frowning at the shadows beneath her eyes, a pale cheek that gleams ghostly in dim light.

"I heard you talkin' to that man," she says. "You gonna go live with Welcome and Faith?"

"I asked him to take you with us."

"I heard."

"I guess you heard his answer."

She stays silent.

"What if you was to go live with Kurt? He's got a job at the watch factory, don't he?"

"Pastor Jack telephoned the place where he works and told him about Ma, asked if he could take you and me so we'd be looked after by family. Kurt said he's got himself a girl knocked up and he don't know how to pay for the kid he's gonna have, let alone more kin dropped on his doorstep."

"What about—"

"Wilhelm's soldiering and Emil can't be found. The preacher sent a telegram to Emil's old address and wrote a letter, too. Kurt doesn't know how to reach him."

"Oh."

"Nobody wants me, Earl. My own kin don't. Missus Tate only wants Mattie." Her voice breaks. "I heard Frieda and Miss Hazel talkin' about givin' me to the Salvation Army."

He pats her shoulder awkwardly, leaving a trail of gray dust on her dress. "If I had any say, I'd keep you with me,

Lucy. Shoot, you could go in my place with that old fella. I don't mind."

"You heard him. He wants a boy to work his farm."

"Yeah." His breath stirs tiny swirls of dust into the air. "I guess I'll be workin' pretty hard from now on."

Hearing a soft *tuk tuk*, he turns to investigate. He watches as a red hen lifts one sharp-toed claw then sets it down gingerly, skulking her way beneath the house. In an instant, he's consumed with a choking rage. "Git!" Digging his fingers into the dirt, he finds a stone and hurls it, smacking the hen in the breast. "Git, I said!" He finds another stone and throws it after the hen as it scrambles clumsily toward open air and safety.

Grabbing hold of his throwing arm, Lucy wraps the other arm around his shoulders. "Shh. It's gone now," she says, tears making stark tracks down her cheeks.

"I want to kill all of 'em," he says. "I want to wring the neck of every bird out there. I want to take the hatchet and chop them to pieces."

"I know," she says. "I know."

Spent, his anger disappears as quickly as it erupted.

"Farmer Tate's taking the hens over t' his place," Lucy tells him in a practical voice. "You know he's got better layers than we do. Every single one of Ma's hens will be chicken dinner before the year's out."

"Good."

The two shift their gaze when a new person starts down the cinder block steps. Red T-strap pumps are a dead giveaway. Earl and Lucy stare transfixed, unable to look away from the bold color.

"Where'd Frieda get them shoes?" he whispers.

"I asked. She said her friend John gave them to her for a present."

"I never seen shoes so bright."

Upon reaching the yard, the shoes turn one way, stop, then turn and face the opposite direction.

The man in the porch rocker clears his throat. "Miss Frieda, may I be of assistance?"

"Mr. Randolph, I'm trying to find Earl and Lucy. I need them to gather their things." The shoes shift again, move closer to the porch. "Sir, I'm afraid I haven't been able to locate a proper tote for Earl."

"A burlap sack will do fine. Or a pail if you have one large enough. The boy doesn't have much, does he?"

"Not much, no. A few items of clothing."

There's a pause then the shoes start forward. Lucy brings one finger to her lips but Earl fears it's too late. Has the old man given away their location? He imagines a gnarled finger pointing beneath the floorboards. The shoes stop. Frieda's face appears upside down before them.

"Whatcha y'all doin? Come outta there. You need to clean up and get yourselves packed."

He shimmies through the dirt, following his sister until both stand upright in the now-empty yard.

"Lord have mercy! Look at you two."

Earl looks at Lucy, sees nothing out of the ordinary, and shrugs. Frieda didn't used to be so fussy.

"I don't have time for this foolishness," she says, her voice tired. "Lucy, fill the washtub. After you're clean, rinse your dress and hang it on the line to dry. When you're done, Earl can take his turn. Afterward, the two of you come inside. I need to know what you want from Ma's chifforobe."

"What?" Lucy frowns in confusion.

"Rose didn't want anything except a pink powder box Ma kept on her dressing table. I found that pretty knit scarf she used to wear when it got cold outside. I thought you might want it, something to remember her by."

Lucy drops her head without replying and trudges around the house to do her sister's bidding. He gazes after her.

"I'm packing Pa's things too, Earl." Frieda claps to get his attention. "Hey, are you listening to me?"

"I'm listening."

"Pastor Jack is going to store Pa's things at the parsonage until he gets out of prison but there's no reason for you not to take something. You're too tall for his overalls but some of his undershirts might fit you. Once you're clean, try on whatever you want."

"Golly."

"It has to be done. Farmer Tate needs the house clear for his next tenants." She returns inside.

Earl stares at the old man on the porch. "Where's Welcome and Faith? Don't they want some of Ma's things?"

"Missus Tate took the girls to the farm so they could spend time with the baby before they leave. When they return, I imagine they'll each find a keepsake."

"Yes sir."

He rubs his head, shaking soft dust all around him. Feeling dejected, he drags himself to the rear of the house. He finds his sister standing beside the handpump.

"Don't save any water for me, Lucy. I'm gonna take a dunk in the creek. If Frieda wants to know where I am, tell her I'll gather my things once I'm done."

"Alright."

He steps close and lowers his voice so only she can hear. "Lucy, you should take Ma's manger scene from the trunk."

"What?"

"Tell Frieda to let you have that. Ma knew how much you loved the Baby Jesus."

Her lower lip trembles as she processes his words. "I'll be sad every time I touch it, Earl. That was her most special thing."

"Maybe it won't always be sad. Maybe someday it will be a happy memory, how Ma made Christmas for us even when we didn't have nothin'."

She wipes her nose on a dusty sleeve. "Alright. I'll tell Frieda." She sniffs wetly and gives him a forlorn look. "What are you going to take?"

"I don't want nothin' of Pa's, not one blessed thing."

"What about Ma?"

He sucks the inside of his cheek. There's nothing he can think of to take, no articles of clothing or items from her dressing table. Then it comes to him. "There used to be a small picture of Ma. She kept it in the trunk. Do you remember?"

"I'll put it somewhere safe for you, Earl. I won't let Welcome or Faith have it."

"Okay."

Without warning, he's undone by a sob that wracks his entire body. He gazes around with desperate eyes then extends one arm blindly toward his sister. Lucy clutches his hand, her eyes wide with pain. After a moment, he lets his fingers slip free and takes off running toward the woods. He's lost his ma. Now he's losing Lucy. He needs a place where no one can hear his grief.

PART II:

SOURWOOD

OXYDENDRUM ARBOREUM: A small tree native to North Carolina. It grows in acidic soil and does best when protected by other trees. This tree does not like to be relocated so transplant only young plants. Coveted by bees, sourwood honey is one of the most singular and sought-after honeys in the world.

FOURTEEN

Spring–Early Summer 1922

Earl crouches beneath an open window, swatting at gnats swarming his head in the twilight air. Inside, Mary Alice Randolph is having evening Bible Study with Welcome and Faith. Boys aren't allowed. Since arriving at the Randolph farm a week earlier, Earl has relied on Faith to prop open the window so he can listen. The other field hand – Frank – has no interest in Bible stories. After a long day in the fields, all he wants is to lay on his bunk in peace. But Earl gets lonely in the barn with only Frank and the animals for company. He's taken to sneaking over to the farmhouse after supper, in order to eavesdrop.

"Girls, we've finished the second chapter of the Book of John. What are your thoughts?"

Welcome always speaks first.

"It's interestin', Miss Mary Alice. So, the first miracle Jesus did was to turn water into wine?"

"That's correct, Welcome. I'm glad to see you're paying attention."

"Didn't they have Prohibition in Cana?"

There's a long pause. Earl shifts closer to the window, careful to make no sound that might alert Missus Randolph to his presence.

"What an unusual question."

The old woman sounds cautious, like she's feeling her way to someplace new. "I suppose Prohibition hadn't been invented yet."

"Your Bible verse says it was superior wine that Jesus made, huh, the really good stuff. I bet everyone wanted a drink of that good wine! Miss Mary Alice, do you drink wine?"

"No, Welcome. We're Baptists. Why? Did your parents drink?"

"Oh, yes ma'am. We're German."

Below the window, Earl nods his head vigorously. His pa loved his beer and his shine. He could make moonshine out of anything: corn, potatoes, even yams. That yam shine hadn't taste like much. But there had been a batch of peach moonshine… *whooee.* It burned a hole straight down to the gullet but left a hint of sweetness in its wake that made you thirsty for more.

Faith clears her throat. "Welcome, I think we should say the Lord's Prayer and let Miss Mary Alice get some rest."

"Thank you, dear. Welcome, why don't you get us started?"

"Our Father who art in Heaven, hallowed be Thy name…" Welcome's strong contralto carries in the night air, quickly followed by Faith's smooth alto and the high, tremulous tones contributed by Missus Randolph. Earl hasn't decided what he thinks about this ghost of a woman who supervises his new household. He hasn't seen enough to form an impression.

"…for Thine is the kingdom, the power and the glory, for ever and ever. Amen."

Taking his cue, Earl turns silently in the gathering darkness and makes his way back to the barn. He steps through the doorway to find Dick and Dock reaching their heads over the stall door for a scratch. He approaches the first mule and runs a hand down the long, supple neck. He likes the beasts. He likes livestock and barns and the sweet smell of fermented hay. The only disappointin' thing about living with the two mules is how protective Frank is. He watches every move Earl makes like he's waitin' for something hurtful to happen.

He pokes his head out of the tack room now and gives Earl a stony look. "They got plowin' to do tomorrow. Better let 'em rest."

"Alright then," he says, shrugging. "Guess I'll go to bed."

Three stall doors down the barn is his space, a narrow camp bed that sleeps worse than the sagging mattress in the room he'd shared with Orbry. He dreads the moment he has to close his eyes. That's when stuff rushes in – the crack of a rifle and squawks from angry hens and an outpouring of blood that won't be stilled. Night after night, he wakes gasping for breath, whimpering for his ma, for Lucy, for his life before.

He tries to work hard so he won't dream. So far, the only chore Earl has done for Mr. Randolph is to take rocks from the field and pile them. According to his new boss, they'll be used to build a second pen for the hogs. It's boring work, but Earl does it with vigor, pushing himself to move more stones and faster, whatever it takes to wear down his body.

Hearing Dick chuff, he sits up on his cot. He tugs his ear, trying to decide what to do. After a minute, he gets to his feet and shuffles back to the animals. "It weren't fair of me to scratch Dock and not give you a rub, was it?" He croons softly to the sleepy-eyed mule.

With a final tickle on Dick's soft nose, he steps around where he can see Frank in the tack room sitting on a wood trunk. A lantern on the floor brings light and heat and ghostly moths to the small space. "Whatcha doin'?"

"Fixin' this harness."

"Can I help?"

"Do you know how?" Frank is slouched, casual-like, eyes intent on his task. He doesn't look up but works the leather in his lap.

Earl stays silent.

"What *do* you know how to do?"

He presses his lips together, feeling a ball of pressure expand in his chest. He's pretty sure he knows how to do things but the question puts him on the spot. "I know how to collect eggs," he says, finally.

"Well, hell, anyone can collect eggs."

He continues to stand in the doorway, swaying slightly. He's unsure if he should stay or go. Frank isn't chasin' him off so maybe it's okay if he visits a spell. "Mr. and Missus Randolph sure seem smart," he remarks.

"Oh, sure. They used to teach at a college out in the Midwest somewhere. Iowa or Illinois, one of those 'I' states. Anyway, they're retired now. Mr. Randolph keeps the farm to have something to do."

"Is it a lot of land?"

"Three hundred acres. But he doesn't farm all of it. He just works a few fields each season."

"Don't they have children t' help?"

"I guess they wanted 'em, but it never took. He blames the missus. She blames him. Anyway, that's what the boy before me said."

"There was another boy?"

"Hell, yeah. There used to be two. Alton and, um, Paul Vernon. I guess Mr. Randolph got them boys from the charity home over in Raleigh, same as me. Once they come of age, he moved 'em somewhere and brought me in."

Earl hadn't considered there might be a time limit on his stay. This is unsettling news. "Where'd they go?"

"One of the boys got into a school. He was going to be a preacher. I hear the other one's working a cigarette line in Durham."

"Is it hard, do you think, working a… a cigarette line?"

"Nah. I bet there's nothing to it. The machines do all the work."

Earl's brows knit together. He's not too good with machinery.

"Don't let it worry you," Frank says matter-of-factly. "I figure when my time comes, I'll take the new job and be glad for it. It's hard work plowing under the hot sun all day."

"I like being outside," he responds, bouncing lightly on his toes. "I don't know if I could get an inside job."

"How old are you anyway?"

"Thirteen."

"You got time. Maybe old man Randolph will let you stay till your sisters leave."

His sisters were leaving, too? "Where are they going?"

The other boy lifts one shoulder, lets it drop. "I expect they'll get married or keep house for somebody. Maybe you can live with them in their new home. Unless their husbands don't want you. That'd be tough luck."

Golly. He'd only been here a short time and suddenly he was learnin' he had all manner of moves still to make. Why couldn't a fella just find a good place and stay there? Was that too much to ask?

A small breeze wafts through the doorway, stirring loose hay that eddies along the barn floor. The animals stamp their hooves and Earl walks to the large sliding door and peers into the darkness. He can't see many stars. Must be cloudy. "Feels like rain," he murmurs.

"Mr. Randolph won't like that. Either there's not enough rain or there's too much. This spring, it's hardly let up. We're already behind puttin' corn in the second field." At that moment, there's a flicker of light, followed seconds later by the roll of thunder.

Frank gives Earl a cheery wink. "On the other hand, if it rains, maybe I'll get a day off. I don't mind that."

Earl isn't sure if rain means he gets a day off, too.

The older boy pauses in his task to give him a once-over. "Why don't you go to bed? It's late. If the rain passes, you're going to wish you was rested."

Earl glances toward his stall with distaste, reluctant to end the day. Turning back, he spots a light moving through the farmhouse. The barn is a fair ways from the house, but he can tell when the back door opens. Mr. Randolph steps onto the screened porch with a kerosene lamp held aloft.

"Does Welcome always sleep on the back porch?" he asks.

"Spring and summer, she does. When it turns cool, Mrs. Randolph says everyone has to be in the house. Well, 'cept us."

"Does Mr. Randolph often visit in the evening?"

Frank sets the harness aside and gives Earl a look he can't decipher. "I expect he's just making sure she's brushed her teeth."

"Welcome always was lazy 'bout tendin' to her teeth," he agrees. "Ma used to tell her she was goin' to end up toothless in her old age." He falls silent at the thought of his ma. He's struck by a memory so vivid he can feel the weight of the air on the day it happened. It had been bright and sunny with hardly a cloud in the sky. A man and woman came by the house in the middle of the afternoon and gave ev'rybody toothbrushes. The woman showed them how to dip the brush in baking soda then move it all over their teeth and gums. Ma had been a real stickler for brushing teeth after that. He glances back at the farmhouse, but the light is gone. It's prob'ly too late to knock on the door and speak with the missus. He brought every stitch of clothes he owns, but he forgot his toothbrush.

FIFTEEN

He awakes in a panic, instantly aware he overslept. Paralyzed by fear of the consequences, he grasps hold of his camp bed and listens intently to the sounds of the farm. No one is yelling for him. That's good. The sound of soft rain may explain why he hadn't been shaken awake at sunrise – and why he hadn't heard Frank leave the barn.

Pushing his senses out into the space around him, he realizes the tack room is empty. He has the barn to himself. Well, not entirely. He hears Dick and Dock shifting in their stalls. One of 'em, Dock prob'ly, chews the top of his stall door while the other takes a long piss. From the wood line, he hears a morning bird that sounds like a cat. Then he hears a cat too, hunting in the hay room. A mouse most likely, late getting back to its nest. Caught.

It's time to be up and about his day. There are stones to be moved. Mr. Randolph showed him what to do. See a rock. Lift the rock. Place it in the wheelbarrow. If a stone is wedged too deeply in the ground, he uses the pick to loosen it. It's work he can do.

This first rain shower in his new home introduces unfamiliar aromas. Saturated clay releases something bitter into the air, where it blends with damp wood and grass. He breathes in deeply, letting his belly fall flat with the exhale. If the sun comes out, it will be sticky today, no question about it. It's a good thing he has his handkerchief to keep the sweat from his eyes.

He tenses at the sound of running feet, knowing who it will be before Welcome pops her head over the dividing wall. "Shake a leg!" she cries. "Daddy's takin' Mary Alice to the doctor. Faith is goin with 'em to be helpful, so you and I get to spend the day together."

"Don't he need me to move rocks so Frank can plow the new field?"

"It'll be easier when the ground is dry. Come on, slowpoke!"

"Where's Frank?"

"Daddy leant him to Mr. Jeffries today on account of he's got a project needs an extra hand. Later, when it's harvest, Mr. Jeffries will send his boy over here to help out."

Earl swings his legs over the bed and stands, stretching his arms as high as they'll go. It feels good to get the kinks out. He sucks on his cheek and stares through the open doorway to daylight. He detects a break in the clouds and the rain is already starting to peter out. It doesn't feel right takin' a day off when Frank has to work. "You're sure it's okay if I don't move rocks?"

"I said so, didn't I?" She leans forward to hand him something wrapped in wax paper. "I brought you a piece of salt pork."

"Thanks." He points down the barn where one of the mules has stuck his head over the stall door. "Go pet Dock while I get dressed."

She trots off to greet the animals. He wonders if they'll be pleased they're not pulling a plow today. Once he's dressed, he pitches a forkful of hay to each mule. He checks the buckets to make sure they have water.

"Does the missus go to the doctor a lot?" he asks.

"She's always complainin' of a pain."

"She's old." He pictures the slight woman, tiny but upright. Silvery, crimped hair is pinned close to her head. She possesses a sharp chin and cornflower blue eyes behind her glasses. He's never seen her in the barn. And he's never been invited into the house. His meals are always delivered by one of his sisters. "Old people are s'posed to have pains," he says, deciding to stick up for the woman who's taken him in sight unseen.

"I guess." She sticks a piece of straw into her mouth. "Just 'cause they have 'em doesn't mean they have to talk about 'em all day long."

Welcome follows as he wanders to check on Roberta. She's in her paddock, grazing quietly. She lifts her head and stares at the two of them with soft cow eyes. A fly hovers over her eyelashes. Her tail flicks back and forth. Not much excites Roberta.

"Mr. Randolph milked her this morning."

"I wonder why I didn't hear him."

"Maybe 'cause of the rain. He said you was snoring like

a freight train." She tugs his arm. "Come on. Time's wastin'. I fed the hens and Puss has a fat mouse. I saw her."

"Fine." He steps outside to confirm the rain has slacked off. It might turn out to be a nice day, after all. "What do you want to do?"

"Let's go fishing!"

"It poured last night, Welcome. The fish'll be stuffed from gorging on what the rain stirred up. It's better to go fishing when it's dry and they's hungry."

"I'm tired of all the rain," she grumbles. "It rained ev'ry day before Ma's birthday. That's why we was begging to make a visit. It'd give us something to do besides bein' cooped up here." She picks a stone from the ground and hurls it as far as she can. She throws like a Hahn. Far.

He gives her a disgusted look. "You just throwed that rock in the new field. Now I got to go get it out again."

"Shoot. That's your job, ain't it?"

He points to large piles of rocks stacked at one end of the lower field. "If you want to throw rocks, throw 'em right there. You can throw all the stones you want, as long as they go right where those other rocks are."

"Don't you try and boss me," she huffs. "I get enough of that from Faith."

"Why do you two squabble all the time?"

"Faith's too big for her britches. She thinks she knows everythin' and she don't know nothin'."

He's quiet after this remark, trying to remember if he's seen Faith in britches. Rose, for sure. Even Ma, on occasion, would put on Pa's trousers or a pair of overalls to work in the fields. But Faith, she was a different kind of Hahn. She liked to primp.

"How far is it to the creek?" he asks, hoping to put Welcome into a pleasing mood. Earl is partial to creeks. He likes the sound the water makes when it tumbles over stones. He likes the critters that come to the edge to drink. And he likes the way sunlight makes the water look like it's hidin' jewels deep beneath the surface. He'd spent many hours at the creek back home. There was one spot in particular, beside a grassy bank that overflowed with pods of wild peas in summertime. His ma would collect 'em in a bowl then sit on the front porch and shell peas to eat for supper.

With a hurried wave to follow her, Welcome sets off toward the outer boundary of the farm. "The creek's this way," she says. "Yonder, behind those trees."

As they make their way side by side across the wet ground, Earl ponders how to speak to her about something weighin' on him. He coughs once or twice to clear his throat. "Welcome, you and Faith have been… don't you think y'all been… sort of well-off in your situation here?" He watches her expression, notices when it grows wary around the eyes and mouth.

"I s'pose."

"You each has your own bed. And when it gets warm out, you have the sleeping porch all to yourself."

"So?"

"So, there's plenty of room in the farmhouse for Lucy. Don't you think she should come live with Mr. and Missus Randolph? It'd be like we was all together again, like before."

"No, I don't." Her tone is sharp. "Faith and I manage for Mary Alice. We don't need one more girl. Shoot, we don't really need Faith. I do near about everythin.'" He can feel her shootin' glances at him from beneath her lashes and strives to make his face look agreeable. "I s'pose she's a tiny bit helpful in the kitchen. Her biscuits are flakier than mine. But I'm getting better ev'ry day. Daddy says so."

"He ain't your pa."

"He is now. And he don't need one more girl in this house."

"Lucy's your sister."

"So what? She can find her own place. We have to look out for ourselves. Remember what Orbry said? Things can't go back to the way they was."

She's making him cross and he wants to scold her for not bein' nicer. He presses his lips together to keep from sayin' something he might regret. It used to be that he never had to swallow his words. Due to the harm he's brung his family, he now knows better. There's few that would show kindness to a boy who's killed his ma. If he's to bring Lucy to be with her kin where she belongs, he'll have to step carefully. Maybe Welcome needs to be reminded how fun things would be if Lucy was here.

He's thinkin' how to go about it when they come over a ridge to the top of the riverbank. Large pools of water are scattered as far as he can see.

"Whoa."

"Look at that. The creek overflowed. The water musta come all the way up to that line there," she says, pointing. "We've had so much weather lately; maybe the ground couldn't take no more."

Earl tips his head curiously as Welcome grabs a branch and pokes one of the puddles, making flicking movements.

"Whatcha doin'?" he asks, coming around where he can get a better look.

"There's fish stranded in some of these here pools," she says. "If we knock them onto the grass, it'll be easy to collect 'em for supper. We don't need poles or bait or nothin'." She makes a hooting noise that startles him. "We're fishing, after all!"

Earl searches along the riverbank until he finds himself a tall stick forked at one end. He trails beside Welcome as she makes her way through the patchwork of puddles left behind by the receding water. He copies her movements. Soon the two of them each have a half-dozen fish lying on the riverbank.

He leans over to study the puddles, large and small, that run along their side of the creek. They'll be gone by the afternoon; it's that hot. Then there'll be a bunch of dead fish on the ground. Buzzards will feast.

"I ain't never caught fish this easy," he says, shielding his face from the too-bright sun.

"It's like one of those plagues in the Bible," his sister says. "We learned about it at Sunday School. The plague of the fishes." She scrunches her face in thought. "I don't know… yeah, yeah. This is just like it. The plague of the fishes."

He jabs his stick into the ground and props one arm on it to take a rest. With his free hand, he pulls the handkerchief from his pocket. It's a sticky day, just like he knew it'd be. "Welcome, with this much water, the skeeters are bound to be fierce tonight. If that back porch screen has holes, I wouldn't sleep out there if I was you."

"Earl, listen to me." His sister's voice contains a tone that causes him to pause what he's doing. "You need to step away from your stick. Now."

"Why?" He sends her a puzzled glance then follows her finger with his eyes to where his branch stands upright in the mud. He freezes at the sight of a water snake slithering up the wood straight toward his hand.

"Run!" shouts Welcome.

Howling with terror, he lets go of the wood and races up the ridge. When he reaches the top, he bends to catch his breath and slow his galloping heart.

Welcome runs up beside him, huffing. Her eyes are wide as an owl's. "Was that a water moccasin?"

"I weren't hangin' around to find out."

"I never seen you run so fast," she says, smothering a giggle. "And you're always fast."

"It's good you saw that snake." He frowns down to where his stick remains standing. He jabbed that thing in the ground good. Now, the snake has coiled around the crook at the top and seems in no hurry to move. "I'm not leavin' my fish."

"What?"

"I'm not leavin' my fish." He searches the ground and pulls up a handful of stones. Pulling his arm back, he hurls one, smacking the creature in the middle of its body. It jerks and drops to the ground, slithering quickly toward the creek. They watch it go. As soon as it disappears into the water, they return to the riverbank and collect their fish, keeping a wary eye for unwanted intruders. Welcome uses the skirt of her dress like a net, gathering the edges together to hold their catch. With slow, careful steps, she follows Earl back to the farm.

As they come around the house, they spot the Model T parked by the front porch. Mr. Randolph rocks slowly, his eyes on them as they approach.

"What you got there, girlie?"

"How about a fish fry?" she says with a grin. "These here fish in my dress practic'ly threw theirselves out of the creek."

"Earl, do you know how to clean fish?"

"Yes sir."

"That can be your job."

He nods and walks over to fetch a bucket lying beside the porch.

"Where's Miss Mary Alice?" Welcome asks. "Is she still feeling poorly?"

"She's inside resting. Be quiet when you enter the house." He glances at Earl. "Son, I don't see that any progress has been made clearing the lower field."

He's bending over for the bucket, but now he stands, gazing at the man uncertainly. "No sir."

"Can you tell me why?"

He stares at his sister, his eyes accusing. Welcome stands awkwardly in the yard, her skirt still full of fish. She shoots him a quick glance, looks away.

Clamping his mouth in disgust at her deceitfulness, he tries to explain. "Mr. Randolph, sir, I thought it would be okay seeing as how wet the ground was and… and all." He hates to snitch on his sister. He gives her a meaningful look, waiting for her to speak up, to say her part in it, but she won't meet his eyes. She looks like ice wouldn't melt in her mouth, she's so cool. "Well, I thought it would be alright," he finishes lamely.

"I'm sure Welcome enticed you with the promise of a day off," the man says.

"What?!" His sister puffs up, acting offended at being mentioned in this conversation.

Mr. Randolph's pale gaze is stern. His mouth presses into a thin line. "You work for me, young man. Don't forget it. You take your instructions from no one else. Do you understand?"

"But…" Now that she's been implicated, his sister clearly wants to speak her piece.

"Girlie, I'll deal with you later." He gestures to the bucket. "Earl, go ahead and clean those fish. They'll make a good supper. Tomorrow, I expect you to move twice as many stones as you did yesterday. Do we understand one another?"

He nods sullenly. He doesn't know if he's madder at Mr. Randolph for taking a harsh tone or mad at his sister for not steppin' forward.

"Welcome, give the fish to Earl and come with me. We're going to get you bathed."

"I already had my bath this week."

"I don't care. You stink."

SIXTEEN

"Don't do it that way, Earl. I've told you before, you'll injure yourself, then you'll be useless to me. Do it like I showed you. Bend your knees. Squat to the stone. Grab it with both hands. Then straighten your legs to lift." Mr. Randolph demonstrates with one of the lighter stones in the field. He places it in the wheelbarrow. "Understand?"

"Yes sir."

"Repeat what I just said."

A spasm crosses Earl's face, then continues into a long shudder that rattles him to his toes. For a moment, it feels like he's falling. He grabs hold of the wheelbarrow handle, anchoring himself to the present.

"You okay, boy?"

"I'm fine." He takes a breath and concentrates on Mr. Randolph's instructions. "Bend my knees, sir. Squat down to pick up the stone. Straighten my legs to lift."

"You'll thank me later when you're not crippled with pain. We can't have you wrenching a muscle in your back."

"Yes sir. I mean, no sir."

The old man makes Earl uneasy. To have something to do while he's standing there, he uses his handkerchief to dab at the dampness along his upper lip. He's waitin' for the man to step away, to join Joseph and the mules, but he stays, his disturbing gaze causing Earl to sweat more than usual.

"Do you understand that any rocks you leave behind will cause the plow to pop right out of the furrow, dragging Frank with it? You wouldn't want that, would you?"

"No sir."

"Be thorough."

He frowns at the ground.

"Check to confirm you've removed everything, then check again. Two checks."

"I will."

Mr. Randolph cups both hands around his mouth and shouts toward the adjacent field. "Frank, how's it going?"

"All good, Professor."

The man turns back to Earl. His long arms hang loosely at his side, but his fingers curl and uncurl. Earl braces in case he's getting ready to be flicked. *Just like Orbry*, he thinks, resigning himself.

But a flick never comes.

"Sir? Was there more instruction you needed to tell me?" he asks.

The man jerks likes he's been lost inside his head. He brings his hands together and cracks his knuckles, then gives Earl a brief glance. "I'll leave you to it. I've got a contract I promised to look over for one of the deacons." He takes one more look at the other field where the team has reached the end of a furrow. "I expect you to put in a half-day before taking a break. When Frank leaves the field to water the mules, that's when you can eat lunch. One of the girls will bring you something to eat."

He knows all this but nods anyway like he's hearin' it for the first time. "Yes sir."

Mr. Randolph strides to a strip of land separating the two fields, his work boots picking up mud as he heads back toward the house. The missus won't like that, Earl thinks, watching him go. With a small exhalation, he stoops to pick up a stone. He stops. "Follow instructions," he whispers. Pulling his shoulders back, he starts over, bending his knees and doing it like he's been shown.

When he's got a full load of stones, he lifts the handles of the wheelbarrow and guides it toward the end of the field. The wheelbarrow wobbles back and forth, forcing him to wrestle it the whole way. A stone tumbles to the ground. He stops, parks the cart, and returns the stone to the top of the load. He lifts the handles again, pushing and wobbling until he reaches the drop-off. Mr. Randolph wants him to sort the rocks into three piles – small, medium, and large. The man talks on and on about his plans for a new pigsty, but Earl ain't ever seen one made of stone. *Pigs aren't like goats*, he thinks, *always trying to break through things*. Nothin' wrong with a wood fence.

His load sorted, he returns to the field with an empty cart. Soon, he has a rhythm going. He learns how high he can load the barrow without losing stones along the way. He's at the top corner of the field when he pauses to watch

Frank come around the turn with the team. The steel plow blade cuts through the soil and sends it curling over itself in crumbly waves.

"Stay haw… Stay haw…" Frank's voice is low and steady, guiding the mules to bear left as they near the end of the field. He guides them into the turn. "Gee now…"

Earl admires how well Dick and Dock behave. Frank makes it look easy. Maybe someday, if he pays attention, he can be a teamster, too.

He resumes his lifting but pauses when Frank hales him from midway up a furrow.

"Earl, come here. I need help."

He abandons the wheelbarrow and runs to the other field. "Somethin' wrong?"

"Dick threw a shoe," Frank says disgustedly, undoing one set of the plow lines. "It's this damn boggy field. Now, I'm going to have to replace the doubletree. Can you walk Dick back to the barn and bring me the other tack? It's hanging on the wall across from my bed."

"I can do that."

"Be careful walking him back. I've looked him over and he seems fine, but he needs to be in the stall until I can get a new shoe on."

"Don't worry 'bout a thing," he says, eager to be helpful. "I'll put him in his stall and return with the singletree. I can do that."

He accepts the plow lines from Frank, wrapping them around his arm and taking a firm hold near Dick's bridle. He makes his way carefully, scanning the ground for a hole or a stone that might cause the animal to stumble.

Arriving at the barn, he slides open the end doors with one push and leads the mule inside. As he enters, Mr. Randolph exits the tack room, followed by Faith.

"Hey, Faith!"

"Hi," she mumbles. Without glancing his way, she ducks out of the barn.

"Earl, is something wrong with the mule?" asks Mr. Randolph.

"Dick threw a shoe. The field's boggy from all the rain, I guess. Frank said I should put him up and he'll finish plowing with Dock. He'll put a new shoe on tonight."

"Let me see."

"That one there," Earl says, pointing to the unshod hoof.

Mr. Randolph lifts the leg.

"Frank checked," says Earl.

"I'm sure he did. Nothing wrong with me taking another look to confirm no nails are embedded."

Earl peers over the man's shoulder, watching as Mr. Randolph presses an area where a small piece of the hoof might have come off with the shoe. He glances at Dick to see how the mule reacts.

Gently setting the hoof back on the ground, the old man walks around the animal, rubbing his hand along each leg in turn. On one spot, he wipes off a smear of mud to peer more closely. "Earl, did you know cuts from a ragged nail can put an animal down if the injury isn't caught in time?"

"No sir."

"That's why you don't only check the hoof that threw the shoe. You examine the other legs, too."

"I'll remember."

"Good boy. I'll put Dick in his stall," says Mr. Randolph. "Was there anything else you needed?"

"Frank tole me to get the singletree."

"You know where it is?"

"Yes sir."

"Go ahead."

That night, Dick receives his new shoe and the boys continue their work without incident the remainder of the week. Saturday evening, after wiping down the two mules and putting them into their stalls, Frank approaches Earl's camp bed.

"I'm headed to town now. I won't be back till Sunday night. You're going to make sure the animals have their hay and water, right?"

"I won't forget."

"Turn Dick and Dock into the pasture to graze tomorrow morning. Not long. They'll get sick from too much of this new grass. A couple hours is fine, but no more."

"I know what to do," Earl says, forcing his voice to stay calm. He hides his hands beneath his legs so Frank won't see them shaking with excitement. Frank is leavin'. Earl gets the barn all to hisself for the weekend. He's in charge.

"Alright then. See ya later."

After he leaves, Earl walks around to check everything is exactly right. He sweeps up loose straw and puts out a pan of water for Puss. With these tasks completed, he's soon feeling lonesome. He considers searching for one of his sisters but knows better than to show up at the house. Maybe he better spend his evening right here in the barn.

Roberta's had her evening milking and is bedded down in the stall with a forkful of hay. Thinkin' about Roberta makes him wonder who took the calf. Since arriving at the Randolphs', the only meat he's eaten is pork and chicken. If there's veal, no one's shared any with him.

In the distance, a dog barks. A thousand crickets chirp. An owl hoots softly somewhere in the trees. These sounds are not unlike those of his home, the home he'd shared with his ma and Baby Mattie, with Orbry and Lucy. He wonders what Lucy is doing right that minute. He wonders if the Salvation Army found her a place to live and whether she knows where to write him. He wonders if Frank knows how to read. He might be willing to read Lucy's letter out loud. If Earl ever receives one.

With a tired grunt, he goes into the tack room. He stretches out on Frank's bed and tries to imagine he's back at the cropper cabin listening to Ma putter around the kitchen. She stacks clean dishes in the cupboard then moves to the rocker to take up her sewing. When she reaches a good stopping point, she'll come to his room and make sure he's tucked in for the night. While he waits for her to appear, he'll close his eyes…

He awakes with the sun. He hears the barn swallows first, returning from a dawn flight to deposit the bugs they've snagged into the gullets of their hatchlings, chirping now from rafter nests. He frowns when he opens his eyes to a wall covered in hooks and bridles, uncertain where he is, then realizes he fell asleep in Frank's bed. Smilin' 'cause he got away with somethin', he rises, stepping outside the barn to relieve hisself. Quietly, he puts a halter on each mule and leads them to pasture. It gives him pleasure to sit on the fence rail and watch them graze. From where he sits, he can hear Mr. Randolph bring slop for the squealing hogs, then enter the barn for Roberta's milking. He wonders if he should return to the barn and greet his boss. He stays where he is.

When he returns the mules to their stalls, he's pleased to find a covered basket on his bed. A greasy ham biscuit and two boiled eggs nest inside.

After devouring his meal, he returns the basket, hanging it on a hook by the kitchen door where one of his sisters will retrieve it. He knows Mr. Randolph and the missus will be gone all morning to attend church, staying late for a deacons' meeting and the ladies' auxiliary.

Feeling like he has nothing but time, he decides to return to the creek where he and Welcome had collected their fish. Making his way over the ridge, he's surprised to discover the creek looks entirely different today, no longer muddied by heavy rains. The water level is down. The ground is dry. He follows the water's meander until it passes through a clearing containing two large tree stumps.

Detecting a flash of unexpected white within the branches of a rhododendron bush, he pokes his head between the leaves for a closer look. He reaches one arm deep between the branches and feels soft fabric. Withdrawing his arm, he opens his hand to reveal a pair of knickers with a ruffle around each leg opening. He drops them to the ground like he's been stung. He glances around the wooded space. Is someone watching him? After a moment, he retrieves the undergarment and stuffs it back into the bush. Whatever this funny business is, he wants nothin' to do with it.

He misses Lucy. She may have been his younger sister, but she could make sense of things better than anyone. He stands in the middle of the clearing, his ears peeled for any sound that isn't from nature. He can feel his skin warm and then cool as the sun peeks from behind clouds, then tucks itself away again.

He closes his eyes and feels himself become invisible.

SEVENTEEN

Earl has a thing inside him, something that pecks. It's not there all the time, but when it is, he wants to yell and kick and break things. He figures this thing inside him comes from his pa. He tries to ignore it but it builds inside him, makes him jittery.

Feeling the pressure growing, he strikes out at the first thing that catches his eye, the toe of his boot connecting with a metal pail and sending it airborne. It lands with a crash against the pigpen rails, causing the hogs to squeal and scurry in distress.

Instantly, he feels bad for scarin' 'em, but a person can only take so much. Earl hasn't done one blasted chore but move rocks since he arrived. He's sick and tired of it. He no longer has to think about how to lift the rocks. The movement has become second nature. Already, his arms and legs are stronger than they were when he arrived. The chore presses on him, makes him not want to move from his camp bed in the morning. Surely he's good for somethin' besides moving rocks.

From where he stands, he watches as Frank turns the team toward the barn. Usually, he stays to help remove tack, but not today. Without a backward glance, he races to the creek to cool down. Stripping on the bank, he pauses to watch two yellow butterflies dance around each other in midair. It's a small thing but seeing the butterflies lifts his spirit. Dropping his clothes to the ground, he wades into the stream. The water clears away not only the grime from the day, but the heaviness inside him.

He misses his ma.

Quietly, he drifts on his back, moving with the current. His shoulder collides with a rock followed by a half-buried log and he realizes he's come to a river jam. He wipes his eyes and lifts his head. He sees the log with one jagged edge tipped out of the water. Resting on the edge are three turtles. There's so little wood for 'em to share that they've piled one on top of the other, fighting for the last sliver of sunshine. He can't help but laugh, which sends them diving into the water. For that, he feels sorry. Refreshed, he makes his way out of the creek and back to his sweaty clothes piled on the bank.

He returns to the barn, pleased to find a plate of pork and turnip greens covered with a tea towel. He shoos away the flies and gobbles the meal in a few bites. He's always hungry for more. Afterward, he finds himself a twig to pry loose the gristle in his teeth. When he hears the sound of running feet, he turns to find Welcome paused, breathless, in the doorway.

"Earl, come to the porch. Daddy has a letter."

His heart soars. Lucy found him! Somehow, she found a way to get a letter to the Randolphs. With a spring in his step, he follows Welcome to the front of the two-story farmhouse. As he comes around the porch, Miss Mary Alice places a frail hand on her husband's arm. Earl focuses on the old man, seated beside her in a matching rocker.

Welcome takes a spot on the edge of the porch and hugs the corner post, the hem of her skirt lifting lightly in the evening breeze. She sways to and fro, moving her gaze from one person to the next. Faith steps through the screen door and stops.

"Come around, Faith, where we can see you," says Mary Alice.

She moves to the top porch step and sits demurely, tucking her skirt beneath her legs.

Mr. Randolph removes his cheaters from a pocket and sets them on the tip of his nose. He seems uncomfortable and clears his throat a couple of times before speaking. "Girls, Earl, I'm afraid we've received sad news from your sister, Rose. She writes here that there's been an accident. Your sister, Frieda, has passed."

Earl swivels his head to find Faith, distressed to see her eyes filling with tears. Of all Lizzie Belle's children, she'd been closest to Frieda. Many times, he'd seen the two of 'em pouring over fashions in the Sears Roebuck catalog or giggling about a photograph in one of those glossy magazines from the five-and-dime.

A sudden, sharp memory pops into his head. It was from before Pa's trial, before Rose went to the sheriff. Frieda had a small pot of lip color. Earl couldn't remember where she'd gotten it. Maybe it was a gift from a beau. Maybe she lifted it from a store shelf. Faith was ten at the time. Earl knows this because it was before she and Welcome left home to live with the Randolphs. He'd been allowed in his sisters' room, a rare privilege. He sat cross-legged in the corner, promised to behave himself, and watched with fascination as Faith puckered while Frieda brushed red paint onto each lip.

Pa had come inside, seen his girls playing with the lip pot and flew into a rage. He hurled the jar against the wall, calling Frieda a 'hure'. Faith cried but Frieda simply stared at their pa with narrowed eyes. For a moment, Earl thought his pa was going to strike Frieda. He did not but he punched Kurt later and that seemed to make him feel better.

His sister's whisper pulls him back to the present. "What happened?" Faith asks, not bothering to wipe her face as tear after tear leaks down her cheeks. "What happened to Frieda?"

Mr. Randolph scans the letter then exchanges a look with his wife. "It appears there's not going to be a funeral. Rose writes that your sister is being buried in Fayetteville at a place, it says here, near Cross Creek." He glances up. "That sounds pleasant."

"What happened?" Faith repeats, her voice tight.

Earl studies his sister. There's a tension in her body that puts him on alert.

"It's not a story for young ears," Mary Alice says, leaning forward in her rocker. Watery blue eyes blink behind the round, wire frames. "We'll save the rest of this letter for when you're older."

Faith sends the old woman a look of pure steel. It surprises Earl. Perhaps the look surprises Mary Alice also.

"Frieda's my family," she says quietly. She looks hard at Welcome, then at Earl. "Do you want to hear how she died?"

Welcome nods. After a minute, so does Earl.

Faith returns her gaze to Mr. Randolph and to the letter in his hand.

"Very well," he says. His fingers tremble slightly on the notepaper. He glances up one more time to meet her eyes. "Your sister was in a dangerous profession, Faith. You understand what I mean by this?"

"I do."

Earl doesn't. He looks at Welcome. Does she understand? Why was Frieda in danger? Was it because she worked with the soldiers? Maybe the camp was under attack.

Deciding to keep quiet, he returns his attention to Mr. Randolph. The man lifts the letter and holds it where he can read it. "It says here she challenged her… the man she worked for. Evidently, other folks saw the exchange and speculate he may have been angered by her insolence. The local authorities in Fayetteville believe he felt the need to re-establish his authority with the… other girls. A witness came forward. This person told the police the man tied your sister to the train track. She was struck by the night train. She died instantly."

An inner trembling forces Earl to plant himself more firmly to the ground. He's afraid he will collapse and disgrace hisself. He presses his lips together, light-headed at the thought of his sister's final moments. Poor Frieda. She would have been scared. So scared and so helpless. She would have heard the train coming. There would have been a rumble on the tracks, a whistle piercing the night air. She would have screamed for someone to save her. She would have screamed for their ma.

Welcome glances at Faith. "And that's three. I knew tragedy weren't done with us. Her boss musta got the idea from that film we saw – remember, Faith? When Pa snuck us into the theater but the ushers made us leave before the main feature. *Barney Oldfield...* something... I don't remember the rest." She scrunches her nose. "It was an oldie even when we saw it. Course, the girl got saved in that one, didn't she? Poor Frieda. No one came to rescue her."

"Hush, Welcome. You... shut your ugly mouth!" Faith's voice breaks and she leaps from the steps. Her eyes dart feverishly to each face then she tosses her head back, howling a pain that rattles Earl so much, tears spring to his eyes. He's never heard such a mournful wail.

Welcome stamps her foot. "I don't see..."

Faith spins violently, pinning her sister with a glare and cutting off her words.

"What?" Welcome says, her chin jutting defensively.

"For once, try to think of someone other than yourself."

Faith bends like she's in physical pain, her breath coming hard and fast. Mary Alice reaches into her sleeve and removes a lace hanky. She extends it to the broken-hearted girl.

"Dear, I know this comes as a blow so soon after losing your mother. You can take comfort knowing Mr. Randolph and I are committed to putting you girls on a different path." The elderly woman sends her husband an uncertain smile that firms when he removes the hanky from her outstretched hand and gives her a reassuring pat. "It's terribly unfortunate, but I'm afraid your sister was the victim of her poor choices."

"You're wrong," Faith says flatly.

"I... what? I beg your pardon?" Mary Alice appears stunned by Faith's response.

Earl's sister lifts her head, eyes hot. "What 'choices' did she have? After Pa's trial there wasn't one boy in all of Sampson County whose family would let him court Frieda. She was damaged by association. She *had* no choices. She had no one to help her get a respectable job in town. And Pa never let us be educated. He didn't think women needed schooling. She was bright as anything, but she was the daughter of Reinhardt Hahn, a thief and a... a rapist."

Mary Alice gasps at the word.

Faith barrels on, heedless. "Frieda couldn't be anything but what he made her. My Pa used her, wrecked her, then tossed her aside when she got too old. Then he went after Rose."

She turns her heated gaze on Welcome, then Earl. "You don't know, but I know. Frieda talked about it after Ma's funeral. She didn't want to lift her skirt for the soldiers. She wanted a family..." Her voice cracks. Her body shakes like she's being battered by strong winds. "She wanted a home and a husband and children. Frieda was trying to change her life. She was keeping money aside for the future. Maybe that's why she got tied to the track. Maybe she was killed because she dared to hope she might be something more."

Earl holds his breath as he listens to Faith's outburst. She paces back and forth in front of the porch, twitching like a caged animal. She's filled with sorrow and anger, he realizes, but he senses there's more. He tries to pay attention so he won't miss it, whatever the more is.

She hurls a look of frustration toward Mary Alice, then turns her eyes on Mr. Randolph. Earl watches carefully, sensing there are words being exchanged, words she's not saying out loud and he wonders why. With a groan, she whirls and takes off running, tearing down the dirt path to the field. When she disappears into the trees, Earl frowns after her.

Thinking is hard work. It takes effort. He focuses on what Faith said, about Frieda being damaged by Pa. Was she damaged like Rose was damaged before the trial? Before Baby Mattie came?

If only he weren't so slow. Silently, he curses his pa and the two-by-four what struck him. He wants his wits, the wits he should have had. He can't pinpoint why, but he feels this new anguish in their family can be laid at the feet of their pa. He thinks maybe this was part of what Faith was trying to say. Reinhardt Hahn's own wife had called him a perversion. The judge said it, too. His pa arrived in this country with nothin' but hostility. He'd taken out his wrath upon the only people who might have been persuaded to his side. Was he the reason Frieda had died?

Troubled, Earl lifts his eyes to the old man seated on the front porch. Something scratches at him. He's only been at the Randolphs' farm a few weeks, but he's been listening since the day he arrived. Listening in the fields when the old man talks to Frank, using coarse language that makes Earl uncomfortable. He listens outside bedroom windows, cracked open to let in the spring breeze. Mr. Randolph is fond of pointing out that his family can be traced back in time to a hasty battle or a battle in some place called Hasty. Earl isn't sure. But Ralph Albert Randolph is a man of learning. A professor, deacon at the Baptist Church.

Earl is slow. But he's not incapable of forming connections, given time. He thinks about Welcome calling this man Daddy and climbing onto his lap to poke in trouser pockets for penny candy. He recalls Frieda, laughing with Henry Tate at Ma's viewing. There had been something in her eyes. Something he perceives now could have been a yearning, a secret craving for a respectful word from that young man. He considers Faith and her outburst, apprehends new jealousies between two sisters. He tips his head, pondering a pair of bloomers hidden in a bush and how his sister ducked her face when she'd sidled out of the tack room behind Mr. Randolph, hid herself like she was ashamed to look her brother in the eye. He frowns as another memory fights its way forward. Had the man's trousers been unfastened?

Earl is capable of making connections and he makes them now – between his father and the man slowly rocking on the front porch. He looks into Mr. Randolph's eyes and his pa looks back. And Earl knows he's seeing the true man. And Mr. Randolph knows that he's been seen.

"What?" asks Mary Alice, her voice quivering. She glances between Earl and her husband. Earl turns away, sick to his stomach. Poor Frieda. Poor Faith. Poor Rose and Ma and Welcome and Lucy. And poor Earl, too stupid to do anything about it. Shoulders slumped, he trudges back to the barn.

He's seated on the bed, his head in his hands, when Mr. Randolph approaches the stall door. "Collect your things," he says shortly. "We're taking a drive."

The bucket beside Earl's bed holds all his worldly possessions, hand-me-down shirts and trousers, and the small daguerreotype of his ma, taken when she was young. Lucy had kept it safe, passed it to him before he left home. He likes to look on it at the end of the day. The sweetness in her expression reminds him of the goodness he'd known from her every day of his life. Gently, he turns over the photo, so the face is hidden among the folds of his clothes.

He lifts the bucket and gazes calmly at the old man.

"Get in the Model T."

"Is it alright if I say goodbye to my sisters?"

"Faith hasn't returned. You can deliver your goodbyes to Welcome."

Earl follows Mr. Randolph to the motorcar parked in front of the house and climbs into the passenger seat, setting the bucket on the floorboard. He glances at the porch where Welcome still sways slowly, one arm wrapped around the tall post that holds up the roof. As the vehicle roars to life and turns toward the main road, she lifts her arm in a casual wave.

EIGHTEEN

Earl doesn't speak to the man beside him to ask where they're going. He stares out the window, his gaze desolate. It's a silent drive. Only when he recognizes Clinton's Main Street does he straighten and pay attention. The Model T pulls to a stop in front of a small frame house with a white fence. A corner streetlight provides a halo of illumination that encircles the vehicle. Tempted by something new, a moth flutters over to inspect the automobile's headlamp.

"Bring your things."

Lifting his bucket, Earl follows Mr. Randolph up the steps to a broad porch enclosed by wood rails. One tap on the screen door brings the Salvation Army lady, the one who gave him and Lucy the news about Ma.

The woman squints through the screen mesh. A thin coat has been pulled on top of her bathrobe. She holds the lapels closed with one hand.

"Mr. Randolph, is that you?"

"Miss Hazel, I'm sorry to disturb you so late in the evening. I've brought Earl Hahn with me. I'm afraid the Salvation Army will need to make other arrangements for his care."

"Has something happened?" She stares at Earl, hovering behind the tall man. "It seemed like a promising situation. You needed help around the farm. Earl needed a home. With you, he has proximity to sisters who can oversee his care as he matures."

"Yes ma'am." He rubs a hand over his chin. "The relocation appeared… fortuitous for both parties."

"Was he not a good worker?"

"It's my wife. She has concerns about the boy's… unpredictability. The incident with his mother, you see, it keeps her up at night."

"Hmm." She steals another glance at Earl, her eyes not as hard as they might have been. "I'm sorry to hear that."

"I apologize for depositing him without notice. The death of his sister, Frieda…"

"Yes, I'm aware. A tragedy, no question about it."

"It was unsettling news. It speaks to certain… character weaknesses, which we must guard against in the girls. To have to worry about the boy, too…"

She shows no expression as she examines the bearded man through the screen door. After a moment, she releases a puff of air.

"Leave him here," she says.

"Thank you. I hope you'll keep me informed of his new situation. His sisters will want to correspond."

"Of course."

With a curt nod, Mr. Randolph strides down the steps.

Earl watches the woman on the other side of the screen, not bothering to glance back when he hears the Model T start and drive away into the night.

"Young man, you look like you've just come from the fields."

"Yes ma'am."

"Did something happen?"

Her eyes are like a bird's, he thinks, peering at him without blinking.

"Today. Did something happen at the Randolphs'?"

He stays silent.

"Fine. If you don't want to tell me, that's up to you. Here's what you need to know before we go any further. My house is clean and you, at present, are not. You're going to have to wash off some of that country straightaway."

"I went in the creek today."

"Did you have soap?"

"No ma'am."

"Then it doesn't count. Meet me around back. Bring your bucket."

He makes his way down the front steps, peering along both sides of the street. He sees neat, tidy homes with square yards. Large trees stretch their branches over the road to touch leaves with trees on the other side. There's not a barn in sight. Lips pressed, he walks around the house to an unfenced grassy space that backs up to other homes. Miss Hazel stands beside a hand pump and a large washtub.

"Do you live here by yourself?" he asks.

She directs a hard look his way. "Earl Hahn, have you got mischief on your mind?"

His eyes widen. "No ma'am."

"Good. I won't tolerate it." She motions to the bucket in his hand. "You can set that down. I have two girls here with me at the moment. You're my third case. Your sister's here."

A slow grin spreads across his face. "Lucy's here?"

"Don't get worked up. I'm confident she'll be leaving soon, although…" the woman's brows pull together, "she's been harder to place than I anticipated. She's too old to be easily adoptable and too young to be much help in a domestic position. I had to teach the girl how to iron – can you imagine! What was your mother thinking?"

He feels a flash of temper at the insult to his ma. Coming on top of his sister's death and his abrupt departure from the Randolphs', it leaves him feeling off-balance. He lowers his eyes so this woman won't see he's on the verge of tears. He doesn't want to appear weak to her when she already has a poor opinion of his family. "I expect she thought she had time," he says, choosing his words carefully. "Lucy's young. And Ma had four older daughters to help with the women's work."

There's silence for a long moment, then the woman places a hand on his arm. "Earl, forgive me. You're right, of course. I was being careless. Your mother did the best she could in an intolerable situation. And I was sorry to learn of your sister's death. The truth is… Lucy's quick. I mean, yes, you're right. She's young. But she's got a bright mind. I showed her how to set a proper table and she performed everything correctly the first time."

He feels a glow of pride in his little sister.

She waits until he looks up to meet her gaze. "Why don't you get cleaned up and we can talk more in the morning? Lucy will be thrilled to see you." She hands him a bar of lye soap and a towel. "Use the hand pump to fill the washtub. Clean yourself head to toe with this bar of soap. Wash behind your ears. Wash the back of your neck and in-between your toes and all your…" she waves a hand vaguely, "all your private bits. Wash everything. I know boys take shortcuts. No shortcuts. Do you hear me?"

"Yes ma'am."

"There's a ladle here to use for rinsing. When you're dry, put on something you brought with you – whatever's cleanest. Put everything else into the washtub to soak. While you're doing that, I'll cover the sofa with a sheet. You can sleep in the parlor tonight."

"Yes ma'am. Thank you."

She starts up the back steps then stops. One hand on the rail, she turns slowly. "Your sisters, Welcome and Faith, are Mr. and Mrs. Randolph kind to them?"

He's uncertain how to answer. He doesn't want to lie to this woman. And he doesn't want to say something that might get the girls sent away like he'd been sent away. He feels loose-headed from all the thoughts trying to push their way forward. Earlier, he'd felt a certainty about something, but here, standing in this new place, he doubts himself.

"Thank you for finding them a place, Miss Hazel," he says finally. "And please pass my regards to… to your Salvation Army people. Y'all did a fine job. Real fine. My sisters have a roof over their heads. They have hot meals three times a day and a warm place to sleep come winter. I expect no one coulda done any better."

She doesn't move, her head cocked slightly as though listening for something left unsaid. After a moment, she gives him a small smile. "I'll leave the kerosene lamp burning in the kitchen and bread and jam on the table. Help yourself."

"Thank you, ma'am."

Alone in the dark, he gets to work. The water from the pump is lukewarm. He fills the tub halfway and stands in it to lather himself. He scrubs all over, wondering absently if Miss Hazel might be prevailed upon to give his hair a trim. He pumps briskly to release clean water so he can rinse, then towels dry. He decides his long johns are the cleanest thing he has to wear.

He removes the tiny portrait of his ma then lifts his bucket into the air, watching as everything he owns falls into the soapy water. He tosses the damp towel over the pump to dry and lets himself into the quiet house.

NINETEEN

Earl wakes as soon as he hears movement in the kitchen. He starts to walk out in his long johns, then he hears a voice he doesn't know. Worried it might not be proper, he grabs the sheet from the sofa and wraps it around hisself. Cautiously, he pokes his head into the sunlit room.

"Earl!"

He grins as his sister launches herself at him, giving him a tight squeeze. It warms every part of him to see her friendly face. He pats her on the arm.

"I sure am glad to see you, Lucy. I missed you something awful."

"How are Welcome and Faith?"

"Oh… they're fine, 'bout the same, I guess." He hooks the sheet around one hand and with the other, he gives a small wave to Miss Hazel where she stands at the stove. She gestures with her spatula toward a person he doesn't recognize.

"Earl, this is Clara."

He nods to a yellow-haired girl helping to set the table. "Mornin'."

"Clara is leaving today," says Miss Hazel. "She's going to be a kitchen maid up at the Biltmore House. Isn't that grand?"

He glances at Lucy, raising his brows in clear enquiry. She shrugs.

"That's real swell," he says, tryin' to be encouraging. "I hope you'll be happy there."

"Thank you," says Clara. "Do you take coffee in the morning?"

"Yes, please." He slips into an empty chair.

She walks all the way around the table to the other side of his seat then sets a cup down and pours the hot coffee into it. He sends his sister another look she understands right away.

"Miss Hazel is teaching me and Clara to serve food from the left and pour from the right." She slaps her knee, barking with laughter. "It's a bunch of hooey."

The woman at the stove releases a weary sigh as though she's heard all this before. "Lucy, you may think it's hooey now, but if you want to get any type of domestic position, you need to master proper serving etiquette."

"I don't want to cook and clean," his sister insists. She looks to Earl for support. "I'm gonna pick tabacca."

Clara's snicker is overshadowed by a gasp from Miss Hazel. "You'll do no such thing. That's not proper work for young ladies."

"Then send me to the cotton mill!" she exclaims loudly. "They're hiring girls younger'n me to clean looms."

She leans across the table and waves both hands in her brother's face. "On account of we got tiny fingers."

"And you'll lose one of those fingers if you start messing with those horrible machines." Miss Hazel smacks the spatula against a pan for emphasis. "Do you want to suffer in a hot factory twelve hours every day, inhaling cotton dust? Those girls get brown lung. They can barely breathe by the time they're twenty."

Lucy's brow furrows and her lips tighten while she struggles to come up with a suitable response.

Miss Hazel gives a small sniff. "That's what I thought."

"Well, I don't see why I can't get a job outdoors. There must be something I can do."

"No, there's not," the woman says shortly. "You need to learn useful skills so you can be placed in a respectable position. In time, if you're lucky, you'll find a nice husband and you can keep house for him."

"Horse feathers. I ain't gettin' married," she says. "I ain't never gettin' married."

"You say that now, but just you wait. It's not easy for a woman alone."

"You're alone."

"I wasn't always," Miss Hazel says firmly. "Until my Walter passed, he provided for me and I took care of him."

Lucy shoves herself back into her chair, arms crossed. "Fine," she says, through clenched teeth. "I won't get a farm job. And I won't get a mill job. I'll..." Her look turns triumphant. "I'll be a schoolteacher."

"Oh, sweetheart." Miss Hazel shifts the cast iron skillet to a back burner and turns off the gas. Wiping hands on her apron, she steps over to place a gentle hand on Lucy's shoulder. "Those jobs are for the girls who finish school and then some. Have you ever been to school?" she asks.

Lucy shakes her head, chin quivering. "I was goin' to attend the school in town. Mr. Edwards said I could. Come fall, the school car was gonna take me. Ma taught me my numbers and letters, so I'd be ready."

Miss Hazel looks at Earl. "What about you?"

"I went to school once, only I don't remember. I think Pa liked his children home."

"Without proper schooling, it's difficult to change your circumstances. Lucy, I'm doing my best to put you in a situation where you don't go hungry. I cannot guarantee you'll be able to attend school, too."

Lucy's face falls. She looks like she wants to cry. "It's not fair," she stammers, her words coming out in a whisper.

"No, sweetheart. It's not fair." The woman gazes at them both and her face doesn't look soft, but it looks honest. "See? You're already learning important lessons."

"Miss Hazel, what if Earl and I was to stay here with you? I could go to school in town and we'd work hard, whatever you wanted us to do." She meets Earl's eyes across the table. "Ain't that so?"

He nods vigorously, approving of this plan. "Yes ma'am. I'd do anything to stay here with you and Lucy. I could tend to the hens."

"I don't have hens."

He's never heard of such a thing. "Well, I can chop wood and look after a small garden. I'm real good at moving stones, prob'ly best in the whole world. I can fetch things and run errands, like if you needed somethin' from town I could fetch it for you."

Clara has paused in her task and watches the conversation swirling around the room, her own face difficult to read.

"I wish I could take you, Lucy. And Earl. And you too, Clara. I wish I had the means to give all of you an education and a safe place. Unfortunately, the bank is getting ready to take this house. You see, children, I cannot even earn my own living. I don't have the gumption your ma had. She did everything she could to keep things going, I know that. She cooked and cleaned for Mrs. Tate. She took in sewing and laundry. And she sold eggs to the grocer. I've tried to find a way to stay in my home. I offered piano lessons to the town's children. I embroidered pillowcases and agreed to share the income with Mr. Wilkins if he could sell them in his store. And I receive a small income, very small, by helping children like you find new situations. It's… it's really not fair at all…" She presses a hand to her mouth, eyelids clenching as though to hold back tears. After a minute, she releases a shaky breath. The others wait until her eyes reopen. She gives them a wan smile. "You see, children. Life never stops teaching us lessons, no matter how old we are."

"What will you do?" Lucy looks like she's forgotten her own worries. All her concern now is for the woman who's given them a helping hand. She hops out of her seat and runs to Miss Hazel, wrapping thin arms around her waist.

"Now, now. None of that. It's not the end of the world." She pats Lucy's shoulder. "Go take your seat. I have a little time to pay what's owed or vacate. Lucky for me, I have a sister in Spring Hope. Her family has agreed to take me in."

Earl glances at his sister, startled to see her eyes are damp. Miss Hazel sees it, too, and drops a kiss on top of Lucy's head.

"Don't fret on my account. Or on your own. I'm going to find you and your brother good situations. Wait and see. And, well, if we haven't found you something by the time I depart, Social Services will make sure you have a roof over your heads until you're placed." She claps her hands together. "Now. Let's eat our breakfast then I'll send an advertisement about Earl to all the best newspapers. The Salvation Army gives me a stipend to cover expenses related to your placement."

He tries to puzzle out how this will work. He's seen things advertised – shoes and tractors and bottles of tonic, but never people. "What'll it say, ma'am, this… advertisement?"

She reaches for a pencil and notepad and begins to write. "Healthy boy, age…?"

"Thirteen."

"…thirteen, available for hire. Farm work or manual labor. Room and board required." She sets her pencil down. "Does that sound acceptable?"

"You can put in there that I enjoy livestock, ma'am. Working with the livestock, like mules and such."

"The newspaper charges by the line, Earl."

"Oh. Okay." He considers and decides he'd better give her another bit of helpful information. "Then you might want to say that I'm an agreeable worker, ma'am. I work real hard."

She wipes a hand over her eyes then lifts her head with a smile. "Thank you, Earl. I'll see what I can do."

By the end of the week, he's settled into a new routine and feels blissfully happy. He's back with his little sister. She's every bit as much fun as he remembered. Once Earl's chores are done and Lucy has completed her lessons, they play all kinds of games together. They play hide-'n'-seek. And tag. They climb trees and enjoy picnics on the grass behind Miss Hazel's house. And with Clara gone, he receives a bed – a real bed, not a camp bed – to sleep in every night.

He wasn't foolin' when he told Miss Hazel he was a hard worker. He performs all his chores, eager to please. He climbs the ladder to clean her gutters and puts a new coat of whitewash on the picket fence so's anyone looking to buy a pretty house won't have to do the work later.

Miss Hazel spends most of her time with Lucy, teaching her skills she'll need to find a good place. She shows her how to use the Singer sewing machine. In no time at all, Lucy masters how to make a buttonhole and stitch a straight hem. She's bright, just like Miss Hazel said. Although sometimes she gets distracted. She and Earl are watching the yellow finches dart among dandelions when Lucy accidentally sews her finger to a pillowcase. Her screech brings Miss Hazel running to see what in the world happened. She raises the needle to free Lucy's hand.

"Keep your eyes on your task, Lucy. You must pay attention."

His sister's expression is vexed. She frowns, sucking a dot of blood from the tip of her finger. "I was paying attention!" she says, following with a whisper, "To the pretty birds."

In the evening, Miss Hazel shows Lucy how to prepare simple meals: roast chicken, or a pot of beans with ham hock. The best time of all comes at the end of each day. After the two children clean the kitchen, Miss Hazel plays the piano and sings hymns with them in the parlor. Their ma tried to give the children some church, so Earl knows the words to many of the songs. An enthusiastic participant, he joins at the top of his lungs. *"Bringing in the sheaves, bringing in the sheaves, we shall come rejoicing, bringing in the sheaves!"*

He sure does like living with Miss Hazel and Lucy. He wishes it would last forever.

TWENTY

"Miss Hazel, may I ask you a personal question?"

"Yes, Lucy. What's your question?"

She's silent for a moment, her fingers twitching restlessly. Earl peeks at her face to see if he can figure what she's thinkin'.

"Lucy?"

"I'm tryin' to decide if it's impolite to ask," his sister says, looking perplexed. "I have a curiosity 'bout somethin' and I don't know how to be satisfied unless I ask."

It's the Sabbath and the children have been given a reprieve from their chores. After morning Bible Study followed by a simple lunch, they gather in the parlor, each with a task. Miss Hazel knits. Earl's been given a wooden jigsaw puzzle to solve. Lucy works a cross-stitch pattern, but mostly she just looks cross.

Miss Hazel lays the ball of yarn and needles in her lap. "I'm listening."

"I'm curious to know what happened to your husband, Mr. Walter. Was he a soldier? Did you lose him in the war?"

Miss Hazel leans her head back against the sofa. A clock on the mantelpiece strikes the hour but her expression doesn't register the interruption. Earl stays silent, paying attention to the woman's immobility. She must be thinkin' deep thoughts. After a whispered 'Amen', she comes back to herself and gives each of them a gentle look.

"I suppose it's understandable to be curious about folks you're getting to know. I get curious about the two of you, too."

"You do?"

"It's only natural."

"But you know everything about us!" says Lucy.

"I'm quite sure I don't." There's a hint of laughter in her eyes that warms the children, makes them shift closer. "My Walter was in the war, but he wasn't a soldier. He was a mechanic."

"He fixed motorcars?" Earl asks.

"Walter could fix anything he put his hands on. But he went overseas to work as a mechanic on planes flown by the French and American pilots. He stayed in France the entire time America was in the war. After the armistice was signed, I expected him to ship home. But he wrote and told me he was needed a little longer."

"Why was he needed if the war was over?"

"It was because of the bodies, Lucy. There were simply thousands of dead, young men lying in temporary graves all over Europe. People were needed to help identify them and bury them in proper, marked graves." She presses both hands against her cheeks, her eyes filled with remembering.

"Oh, children, it's been such a long time since I talked about any of this. And two years since I received my last letter from him." She drops both hands into her lap. "I'll never forget the way he described it. You see, in trench warfare, the fighting would move back and forth over the same piece of ground. One side would hold a position, then the other side would get it back. After a deadly battle, each side would dig large battlefield graves and try to make notes about who was in them. Often there'd be bad weather and mud, and the graves were trampled and hit by bombs or overrun by tanks. Walter was very affected by his work on the burial detail. They'd have to dig up and rebury all the soldiers who died in battle. Sometimes, the bodies were so damaged…" She stops. "Well, I've probably said more than I need to about that. I don't want to give you nightmares."

Earl shudders at the images her words put into his mind and looks to his sister. She hangs on every detail, her eyes full of dark emotion. After a minute, she stands and walks to the sofa, slipping next to Miss Hazel. She pats the woman's hand.

"Thank you, dear." The woman reaches into the pocket of her apron with her other hand and removes an ivory handkerchief, dabs at damp eyes. "Walter was being paid for the work, but that's not why he did it. He wanted every soldier who had served his country to be buried in a grave with his proper name on it. He wanted the families of those men to know where they could be found so they could one day pay their respects and thank them for their service."

"He sounds like a real nice man."

"Oh, he was, Lucy. He was."

"Somethin' terrible happened, didn't it?"

"We all thought the influenza epidemic was over," Miss Hazel whispers. "The first wave of flu cases wasn't too bad, but the second wave took so many people. Millions died. Walter escaped both waves. He was a hearty fellow. But I've always suspected that working on the burial detail wore him down. The third wave caught him, and he died of the flu in a camp hospital in France. They buried him there."

Two tears slip from the cradle of her eyes and make their way down each cheek. Earl's surprised to see that Lucy's crying, too. And she didn't even know Miss Hazel's husband.

"I'm sorry I made you remember such a sad story," Lucy says, brokenly.

Miss Hazel pulls her close for a hug. "The end of the story is sad. But I had many wonderful years with Walter. I miss him every day, but I hold onto my happy memories more than the sad ones. Someday, I pray you'll find someone to love, and feel loved as much as I did."

Lucy looks doubtful but she doesn't say anything.

Wiping her cheeks, the woman gives the children a wet smile. "I don't know about you, but I could use some fresh air. Why don't you two play outside? I'm going to dig in my old war garden. I always feel better when I've got my hands in the soil."

"What did you plant?" Earl asks.

"Let's see. I've pulled radishes and taken a cutting of collard greens. This week, I'll bring in the asparagus. Lucy, I have a wonderful recipe you can prepare with the asparagus.

Green beans will be ready to pick soon. Whatever we don't eat, I'll take to my sister's." She stands. "Now, off you go."

After putting away their things, Earl and Lucy sit on the front steps and discuss what to do.

"How far is it to Ma's house?" she asks.

"Too far," says Earl. He's run the distance many times but doubts Lucy could make it there and back.

"I want to get Ma's spoons out of the wall."

"What spoons?"

"After Pa left and Farmer Tate said we could move back to the cropper cabin, Ma got four spoons and sealed them inside the kitchen wall. I saw her do it."

"What'd she do that for?"

"She said it was to keep hunger from our family."

"Golly, Lucy. I remember bein' hungry all the time."

"But you didn't starve, did you?"

"No."

"I forgot about the spoons till after we left but I want to hide one in the wall wherever I'm goin' next."

"I want to hide a spoon."

"That's why we gotta go back to the house."

"Maybe someone new is living there. Maybe Farmer Tate brought in a new family."

"If we go to Ma's house, we can walk over to Farmer Tate's and visit Mattie. Would Missus Tate mind, do you think?"

"Mattie might not know us no more, on account of she's just a baby," he says, feeling a wave of sadness. He puffs out a breath and stares down the quiet street, pondering Lucy's words. "Even if Farmer Tate did let someone new move into our house, they's prob'ly scared all the time. I bet that house is full of haints."

She frowns. "Why would you say that?"

"Well, where do you think Ma is?"

"Heaven."

He's not convinced. "I don't think Ma's goin' to Heaven without her children. I expect she's got Frieda with her and she's waitin' for the rest of us to catch up."

"At the rate Hahns are droppin', it won't take long."

"Now you sound like Welcome."

She's silent for a long time.

"Earl?"

"What?"

"I'm scared."

Surprised, he stares at his sister. Lucy's as fearless as anyone he knows. "'Bout what, Lucy? Do you think Miss Hazel won't find you a place?"

"No," she whispers. "I'm afraid she will, but I don't want to go. I want to stay here with Miss Hazel and you. I want to be near Mattie and Ma's ghost."

He scoots down a step and presses against her side, giving her a gentle headbutt like Dock used to do when the mule wanted attention. "Maybe she'll find us a place together, Lucy. Even better than stayin' here with Miss Hazel. You'll go to school. I'll drive a mule team. We'll be safe. We'll be together. And we'll get cold Co'Cola every day. Won't that be fine?"

She snorts with laughter. "You are too much."

He grins, relieved to see her smiling.

"Want to walk into town?" she asks.

Town meant boys and taunts. Besides, they didn't have one penny for lemon drops.

"What if we was to go visit Rose?"

Lucy shakes her head. "I went to see her one day and she didn't have any time for me. I think she wants to forget all about her kin."

"That can't be true."

"She does. I'm sure of it."

He tries to wrap his head around this but gives up. "I know. What if we was to visit the auction barn?"

"They're closed Sundays."

"Yeah, but they always got rabbits in cages. I like the rabbits."

She purses her lips like she's hopin' a better idea will come to her but nothing does. "I s'pose."

When they get to the county auction, the arena and seats are empty. However, there's livestock in pens and farmers stroll the grounds, looking to see what will be offered for sale in the coming week. Sampson County is big into hogs, but a few pens hold steers and one wall is stacked with poultry cages.

As soon as he enters the main barn, Earl calms right down. There's somethin' about a barn that's like a tonic to him. He'd been to the auction with his pa and his brothers, looking for good layers mostly. Sometimes Ma got her chicks and feed mail-order. She preferred Plymouth Rock hens and Rhode Island Reds. She didn't buy Leghorns 'cause she said their eggs was puny.

Thinking about hens makes him feel queasy so he hurries past the squawking birds to a dark corner of the barn stacked with hutches. Each holds a large rabbit. There's every color imaginable. There are ten-pound rabbits and twenty-pound rabbits and every size in-between of brown and black and gray fur.

"That one looks like a good breeder," says a man in overalls, pointing to a brown buck.

"I got one looks just like that." The farmer next to him carries a thick chaw in his cheek. He spits his tobacco juice near Earl's feet. "I breed him seven times a week. Sometimes, twice in a day."

"Damn."

"Remember when you could do that?"

The man sniggers. "Mebbe when I was twenty."

Chuckling, the men wander off to another area of the barn. Earl's been waiting for his opportunity and sidles up to the cages. One of the does is sound asleep. Its foot twitches. "Look, Lucy. She's dreamin' about running through fields." He sticks a finger through the bands of wire and rubs the smooth hair. "Isn't it softer than anything you ever felt?"

"I like this one," she says, peering into a nearby hutch. "Look how her ears and nose are fringed in black, like she poked her head in the chimney."

"That's a good-looking rabbit, alright."

"I guess it don't matter what they look like," she says. "It only matters how they taste."

He frowns, considering her words. He likes the rabbits. Then again, he likes rabbit stew. "As long as they're good breeders, they won't get eaten, right?" he asks.

She shrugs. "For a little while, I guess. But their babies will."

He ponders this while Lucy tugs him over to the hog pens. There's a big mama sleeping on her side. Lucy sticks a hand through the fence to feel her bristly skin, only the stock boy sees and yells at them to get lost. They're racing through the outdoor pens when they hear an unwelcome voice. The nasal twang destroys Earl's good spirits.

"Lookee here. If it ain't Clinton's own village idiot." James Purvis climbs down from the rail where he's been regarding a large bull. "Ain't they locked you away yet?"

Earl tries to hustle past the Purvis boy without makin' eye contact. That's why he doesn't see the shove when it comes, knocking him into his sister and her hard to the ground.

"Hey!" he grumbles. "That's mean." He helps Lucy back on her feet.

"Ooh, that's mean," the boy mimics in mincing tones. "Why don't you grow a pair?"

Earl feels a movement at his side and turns to see what it is. He watches with confusion, then horror, as Lucy grabs a shovel from a nearby wheelbarrow and swings it toward the other boy. The shovel's ev'ry bit as big as she is, but she manages to knock James Purvis to the ground. Immediately, she drops the shovel and begins pounding him. She doesn't speak a word but hits him over and over again with her fists.

When he hears the boy groan and sees blood spurt from his nose, Earl wraps his arms around Lucy, lifting her into the air. He can hear her gasping for breath as she struggles in his arms. After squirming for a long moment, she eventually relaxes, becoming dead weight. Watching her carefully to make sure she's not still riled, he sets her on her feet.

"Ma says it's not right to kick a man when he's down," he scolds.

"Today I'm Pa's child and I've had enough of this boy. I bet James here knows all about kickin' a man when he's down, don't you?" She pulls her leg back and boots him in the ribs for good measure. He whimpers, wrapping one arm around his head and covering his private parts with the other.

She crouches so she's right in his face. "From now on, you leave us alone, James Purvis. Or I'm gonna sneak up on you when you least expect it. I will find you and whup your ass every day including Sunday. You hear me?"

His only response is a low moan. Earl wipes a hand over his mouth and stares at the boy who's tormented him for so long. He's got a busted nose, for sure, and prob'ly bruised ribs. But he's breathing.

"Come on, Earl." With a sharp motion, Lucy gestures for him to follow her. She marches toward Miss Hazel's house.

He casts one last look at the whipped boy, then catches up with his sister. "Don't you think you were awfully hard on him, Lucy?"

She stops and spins to face him. "Don't you say that to me!" she shouts, tears pooling in her eyes. "I was standin' up for you 'cause you don't never stand up for yourself. I swear, when Pa hit you with that board, he didn't just knock the sense out of you. He knocked out ev'ry bit of gumption. Orbry was right. You need to grow up."

Whirling back around, she stomps off. He follows, careful to keep space between them. His feelings are hurt but he doesn't know what to say to make things better. As they approach the front of the house, he can see Miss Hazel seated in her porch swing. When she spies the two of them, she waves excitedly. She holds a piece of paper in each hand.

"I've been so busy, children, I forgot to check my mail. Come to find out, I've received responses to both my advertisements. Isn't that good news!"

TWENTY-ONE

"Earl Hahn, you let go of that porch rail right now."

"No."

"Get in the Ford."

"No."

Miss Hazel casts an exasperated glance toward Lucy, who sits on the top step watching the drama. "Can't you be helpful?"

She looks to where her brother has wrapped himself around a rail and refuses to depart for his new place. "Earl…"

"No."

She looks at Miss Hazel and shrugs.

Earl watches the woman's jaw tighten, then release. With a slight shake of her head, she climbs the front steps and takes a seat. She reaches out to clasp Lucy's smaller hand in hers.

He regards the two females warily, suspecting them of tricks.

Miss Hazel leans back and appears to be taking in her whole property, the large dogwood shading one corner of the yard, the bright geraniums growing from window boxes and the feeder where tiny birds feast on sunflower seeds. Her face softens.

"Earl," she says thoughtfully. "I'm going to tell you something my Walter once told me. He said an unoccupied man cannot be happy. Any man – or woman, for that matter – who has nothing to do or no purpose in life will certainly become a pest to society." She sends him a somber look. "Do you want to be a pest?"

"I'm not a pest."

"I believe you," she says simply. There's a moment of silence. "You might like this place, you know."

"Not without Lucy."

"Lucy has her own place, Earl. It's the best I could do. Now, I need you to meet me halfway."

"I don't understand."

"I need you to be on your best behavior. I need you to try… just try to make this work. Show me you can make something of yourself."

He presses his forehead against the wood, his eyes aggrieved. Nothing is going his way.

She reaches up to the porch and strokes the leather traveling bag she's packed for him. "Do you like your new bag?"

He does like the bag. It's way better than a bucket. It feels smooth beneath his fingers and possesses a shiny clasp that fastens on one side. It's big enough to hold everything he owns. It even has a small pocket inside where Miss Hazel tucked his picture of Ma. She told him the bag had belonged to Mr. Walter, a dead man. She said she'd be pleased for him to have it.

"I like the bag," he says finally. "I expect it's the nicest bag anyone could ever have. I'll take real good care of it."

"I know you will." After a short pause, she seems to make up her mind about something. "Earl, if you truly don't want to leave with me today, I'll turn you over to one of the other Salvation Army case workers to find you a place. I know Sampson County has been your home for a long time. Your sister Rose is here. But you need to understand that Lucy and I are leaving regardless. You can give yourself a fresh start with a good family, folks who have a lot to offer. Or you can stay and wait… and maybe never have another opportunity this promising."

He tugs the collar of his new shirt and refuses to meet her gaze. The shirt had also belonged to Mr. Walter. It's stiff and starched and makes him feel like a stranger to hisself.

"I need your decision, Earl. Are you going to open yourself to new people and new skills so you can be productive in this world? Or are you going to remain in this town that has given you nothing but heartache?"

He scratches his cheek and tries to think. It makes his brain hurt. Finally, moving in slow motion, Earl pulls himself to a standing position. He brushes his hands down each sleeve and brushes his trousers. With a heavy heart, he holds out his hand. Miss Hazel passes him the traveling bag.

Lucy lifts her own bag, smaller and covered in quilted tulips, then follows her brother to the automobile. Silently, they climb into the back seat of Mr. Walter's Model T.

It's a long drive. The two children hold hands, their eyes on the passing scenery. Familiar landscapes move into view then are gone. Soon, both realize they've traveled further than they've ever been. Flat, dusty fields of corn and cotton give way to gentle hills and densely packed pines.

Earl's half asleep when Miss Hazel turns the car up a long, paved driveway. He startles, his heart thumping at the sight of an imposing, brick structure facing a wide, green lawn. "What's this place?" he asks, wary he's been tricked. What if she's brought him to the mental asylum?

She parks the motorcar and twists to face the back seat. "This is the Phipps Estate, Earl. This is where you're going to stay from now on."

This is a new word for him. Estate. His lips move silently as he tries it out.

"How many families live here?" he asks.

"You're far from home now," murmurs Lucy.

Miss Hazel looks at them like she's tryin' hard to be cheerful. Earl thinks she might be sad on account of she's moving to her sister's. During the drive, Lucy whispered another idea. She thinks Miss Hazel might be sad on account of having to say goodbye to the two of them.

"How do we make her unsad?" he'd whispered back.

"We let her put us in new homes."

He frowned at her then, unwilling to give in so easily.

"I'm going to take Earl around the back," the woman says, her eyes on Lucy. "The gardener said he'd meet us. Can I trust you to stay here by yourself for a few minutes?"

He feels like he's going to throw up. He can't stay at this place, no matter how many families they have. It's not the place for him. Miss Hazel is going to make him say goodbye to Lucy and it's happening now. He has too many feelings. He can't decide where to put his gaze. He can't speak because he's liable to cry. It's too much. When his sister clears her throat, he turns with desperate eyes, praying she has a new idea.

"I want to come," Lucy says, her face set in stubborn lines. "I want to see where Earl's going to live." She shifts closer to him and lifts her chin as though challenging the woman to stop her.

Something flickers in Miss Hazel's gaze. "Come on. I guess it's better for you to see than to wonder."

As they slip out the passenger door, Earl grabs hold of Lucy and bends close to her ear. "When you get to your new place, you send for me."

"I'll try," she says.

"You're the only family I got left, Lucy. You can't leave me here."

"I don't know 'bout this place I'm going," she says. Her voice sounds tight to his ears. "I don't know how they'll feel about you joining me. You heard what Miss Hazel said. Mr. and Mrs. Ingold already got five boys. What they want is a girl. Jus' a girl."

"You'll change their minds. I know you can do it. Get yourself settled. Then promise you'll come back and get me."

Lucy's silent, her face grave. She shoots Miss Hazel a quick look. The woman frowns at them from the front of the automobile. "I promise," she says.

"And write me letters."

"You don't know how to read."

"I'll find folks that do."

"Come on, you two. No more lollygagging." With a crook of her finger, Miss Hazel beckons them to get a move on. Earl peers around. There doesn't seem to be anyone to welcome them. No curtains stir in windows. No sound can be heard from inside or out. Holding hands, the two follow Miss Hazel to the back of the house. There, they find a wrought-iron gate set within a tall, black fence.

"Hello?" Miss Hazel squints through gaps in the fence, her eyes searching the dense foliage. "Hello, Mr. Johnson, are you here?"

After a minute, an older man shuffles up and unlatches the gate. "You'd be Miss Hazel?"

"Yes, and this is Earl." She pulls him forward, has to poke him to hold out his hand. He places his hands behind his back and stares at the man. This man doesn't look like anyone he knows. He's a slender, dark man with silver in his hair. He looks nothing like the burly, red-necked men who'd worked the fields with his pa. What kind of farmer is this? Maybe these Salvation Army folks are puttin' something over on him.

Miss Hazel wraps an arm around his shoulders. "Mr. Johnson, allow me to apologize on behalf of my young charge. I assure you he's a good boy. Since his accident, he's lived a very… insular life."

The man is quiet, nodding at what she says, but keeping his eyes on Earl. "Son, do you like dogs?"

He thinks for a moment, then nods. The truth is, he's partial to dogs, but not cats. Mr. Randolph's barn cat scratched him when Earl was only trying to be friendly.

"And if a yellow dog walked up to you right now, what would you do?"

He ponders this question. "Pet it," he says.

"Of course, you would, a kind boy like you. You'd pet it." The man nods thoughtfully. "And if a brown dog followed the yellow dog in, came over sniffing and rubbing up against you like dogs will, what would you do?"

"Pet it."

"Yes sir, that's what I thought. Now, the way I see it, you is the yellow dog and I is the brown dog. We jus' be two dogs in two different colors, but I expect there's all colors of dogs in this world, don't you?"

He thinks about this. Pastor Jack has a copper-colored hound dog that's just about the best pointer he's ever seen. And Farmer Tate has a black-and-white dog that's smart as a whip. Those are two fine dogs. He nods at the man.

Mr. Johnson holds out his hand. "Now, son, give me your grip."

Earl extends his hand and the man shakes it firmly then gives him a pat on the shoulder. "Good boy. Now, let's get down to it. Do you know much about gardening, Earl?"

He scratches his ear and ponders how to answer.

"Speak up," says Miss Hazel.

"One time, I helped my pa and Farmer Tate plant tabacca. And I can pick field peas and shuck corn."

"I'm talking about a different type of gardening. Don't worry if you don't understand now. I'll teach you. You'll help me with all the outside chores, everything from planting flowers to pulling weeds to fence repairs. I'm going to need you to go up ladders. Are you afraid of heights?"

It's Earl's opinion that he's the best climber in Sampson County. He's climbed into the rafters of Farmer Tate's barn many times to watch the workers hang tabacca leaves. He's climbed trees and railroad trestles and water towers. He shakes his head at the man, then registers the look Miss Hazel gives him. "No sir. I ain't scared of heights."

The man motions for them to follow him down a path of small paving stones.

"Will Mr. and Mrs. Phipps be coming out to meet Earl?" Miss Hazel asks. "I believe Mrs. Phipps is acquainted with one of my associates in the Salvation Army. I was looking forward to meeting her."

"No ma'am. They send their apologies. One of Mr. Phipps' factories is in Durham and the two of them drove over to take care of some business. They promised to come meet the boy when they return."

"I understand. And where do you live, Mr. Johnson?" she asks.

"My son took me in last year. He lives downtown. I take the streetcar as far as it goes and walk the rest of the way."

"I see."

Earl tunes out the grown-up conversation. He's busy gazing in silent amazement at everything around him. In the summertime, his ma had kept a garden of cabbage, corn, okra, peas and bright red tomatoes. She canned everything she could to tide them through the winter months. She even kept a small bed of petunias next to the hand pump. She'd pinch off the dead flowers all through spring so new blossoms could form. The sudden memory of his ma makes him stop in his tracks. It's been months since her funeral, but grief still has the ability to take the wind right outta him. Lucy's behind him and gives him a shove. Unstuck, he moves forward automatically.

He's been told he's goin' to work in a garden. He's yet to spy one single bean plant or tomato vine. However, each side of the path overflows with flowering plants of every color imaginable. And all shape of blossoms, too. There's droopy ones and ones shaped like bells and purple, spiky flowers on tall stalks. In one bed he sees giant puffballs with more petals than a person can count. And there are square shrubs. He pauses for his sister to catch up and points. "How ya think they get 'em to grow square like that?"

"Maybe they grow 'em in boxes."

He steps over to a stone fountain and trails his fingers through the water, watching as a bee darts among the flowers. The air smells green and piney and sweet.

The man stops at the back of the property and unlocks a small outbuilding constructed of concrete blocks. Evergreens grow beside each wall. Stooping slightly, he steps through the doorway and waves them inside.

A shaft of sunlight from the open door delivers partial illumination. Peering into the shadows, Earl can see it's a large toolshed, even bigger than the bedroom he'd shared with Orbry. He's never seen so many gardening tools: shovels and rakes, ladders of all sizes, watering cans and three wheelbarrows! Smaller tools hang on the wall. Some he's never seen before, but others he recognizes, like trowels and hacksaws. He inhales, smelling iron and earth and grass clippings. Beside the opposite wall, there's a metal bed. What looks like a horsehair blanket covers the thin mattress. A potbelly stove faces the center of the room. The flue goes straight up and out the roof.

"I'll make sure the boy has plenty of firewood come winter," Mr. Johnson says. "He won't be cold. I've slept here, and it gets toasty with the stove going. Cook will provide him with three meals a day, simple fare. All he has to do is tap on the kitchen door and she'll have a bowl of beans or a ham biscuit made up for him. Mr. and Mrs. Phipps are good people. He'll get on fine."

Miss Hazel gives him a smile, a blend of relief and gratitude. "That sounds agreeable, Mr. Johnson. I'd say he's most fortunate." She touches the young man beside her. "Earl, you can say goodbye to your sister now."

He places an arm awkwardly around Lucy's shoulder and gives it a pat. What he wants to do is grab her arm and keep her there beside him so he won't be alone. Feeling eyes aimed in his direction, he makes himself let go. "Don't forget," he says hoarsely. Then he steps back, keeping his head down. Miss Hazel is going to leave now. She explained it. She'll take his sister to her new home and he'll be alone. He places one hand against his chest and presses on the pain that blooms there.

"Earl, you pay attention to Mr. Johnson. Do what he says, do you understand?" Miss Hazel waits until he meets her eyes.

"I understand," he whispers.

"Mr. Johnson, you know how to reach me."

"I'm not worried. The boy is young, and he looks strong. I'm no longer either one. He'll be a great help."

She places a hand on Earl's shoulder, squeezes, then steers Lucy back the way they'd come. His sister-bossy and beloved-takes a quick peek behind her. He stands stiffly in the shed doorway looking after them, knowing he should remember this, always remember when the last of his people left him.

PART III:

AMERICAN HOLLY

ILEX OPACA: An evergreen tree native to the southeastern United States. The tree forms a strong canopy which offers small creatures protection from predators. Slow to mature, many varieties of songbird are nourished by the bitter berries of this plant.

TWENTY-TWO

Late Summer–Early Fall 1922

As Miss Hazel leaves the garden with Lucy at her side, Earl feels he has finally become what others call him - trash. Something to be discarded.

The man named Johnson offers to introduce him to the plants within the garden. Earl observes mutely, not saying anything now that Miss Hazel isn't there to prod him. Recent events have taught him caution. He's never sure when he'll be met with meanness.

"Everyone here calls me Mr. Joe. Think you can remember that?"

Earl tries not to roll his eyes. He might be slow, but he's not stupid.

The old man starts to talk. And talk. Only, this man doesn't talk the way some folks do, going on about theirselves or maybe about a neighbor they don't like. This man talks about different kinds of dirt and how some plants like the sun and some plants hate it. He talks about weeds and weather and how to water different plants – as if there was a right way and a wrong way. Who ever heard such a thing?

Gradually, Earl finds himself paying attention, intrigued in spite of himself. He keeps his mouth shut but follows along as best he can. Mr. Joe doesn't appear to mind that Earl's not adding to the flow of conversation. He walks and talks from one side of the garden to the other, warming to his topic. He shows off prize-winning rose bushes and azaleas with blooms gone but described in great detail. He points out special grasses and shrubs. Everything has a name. Variegated this or ornamental that. Earl's never heard such big words.

"Mr. Joe, will there be a test on this?" It surprises Earl to learn that tending to plants might be considerably harder than tending to a mule. "It's an awful lot to remember, and there's a thickness in my brain."

"No, Earl. There's no test. Whenever we're working with a plant in the garden, I'll give you a bit of information – just a little at a time. Before you know it, you'll be able to tell me what's what."

He gives Mr. Joe a slight nod, but his heart isn't in it. He'll never know as much about one plant as this old man knows about all of them.

"Today, I'm going to give you a simple task. Are you ready?"

Earl rubs a hand over his mouth, his eyes taking in the unfamiliar landscape. It's a big place. Well-marked paths meander every which way. Flowering bushes so high he can't see over them dot the property. Whatever the task is, he knows it will end with a slap to his head or an ugly word. Still, if he doesn't give it a try, where can he go from here? He puffs out a breath. "Yes sir, I am ready to begin."

"See this?" The man leads him to a nearby spot and points at a green, leafy plant growing close to the ground. "This is common chickweed. I want you to make your way around the garden, checking the ground and all the flowerbeds. Every time you see one of these plants, you gently pull it from the roots, like this." Mr. Joe demonstrates. "I'm going to give you a trowel. Dig out any loose stem fragments so they're not left behind in the soil. Can you do that?"

"Can I take that one with me?" Earl points to the plant in the man's hand. "To match up so I don't make a mistake?"

"I don't see why not." Mr. Joe shakes the dirt from the roots and hands the plant to Earl. "If you see something that doesn't match this plant, you don't pull it. We'll tackle other kinds of weeds another day."

Earl spends the afternoon working his way through the garden on his hands and knees. He pulls a straw basket alongside him. Every place he sees chickweed, he digs at the roots and removes the plant from the ground. The sun is low in the sky when he takes the full basket and shows it to his boss.

"You did well," the man says.

Earl's lips lift briefly.

"In a minute, we're going to walk that basket over to the back door and deliver it to Cook."

"I thought maybe you was goin' to burn it."

"The chickweed? No sir. Why, Cook will put every bit of it to good use. First, she'll make a salad out of the leaves. Then she'll chop the rest and infuse it with oil to make a salve for sore muscles. Now, let's get you washed up at the hand pump. I'll introduce you and Cook can give you your supper."

"Will I meet the mister and missus?" He's nervous about meeting the folks that live in the big house. He recalls how simply passing near Miss Mary Alice would cause her to reach for her husband.

"I haven't seen their automobile come up the driveway. But don't worry. They'll be pleased to have you here."

He has his doubts but decides to submit no further questions. Accepting the bar of soap he's offered, he scrubs his face and hands to remove every bit of soil. Once he's presentable, Mr. Joe walks with him to the back door. There's a pretty patio and tables and chairs and flowers in pots. He can imagine folks sitting here to enjoy their cup of coffee in the morning.

Mr. Joe knocks on the wood frame and a large woman comes out, wiping floury hands on a dish towel. She has ruddy cheeks and kind eyes. After greeting Earl and thanking him for the chickweed, she brings him a plate with ham, cornbread and collard greens.

"There's a table yonder on the patio, hon, where you can have your supper," she says. "When you're finished, simply tap on the door and I'll take your plate."

"Yes ma'am. Thank you."

Mr. Joe walks with him to a small seating area situated beneath tall pines. "Earl, what are you going to do after I leave?"

He places the plate on the table and keeps his eyes cast down. Is Mr. Joe afraid he might get into trouble? "I don't rightly know," he admits.

"Do you read? Would you like me to bring you some magazines tomorrow?"

He relaxes his shoulders and considers the offer. It might be nice to look at magazines if they have pictures of mule teams in 'em. After a moment, he shakes his head. "I don't read so good," he says softly. "I like to listen to the night noises."

"Listen to the night noises?" The man stands, hands on hips, watching him curiously.

Earl squirms under his gaze.

"I tell you what," Mr. Joe says softly. "When I get home, I'll see what my grandson has that might interest you. Do you play jacks? Do you know how to whittle?"

"I'm not too good with jacks, sir. My pa tried to teach me to whittle once."

"Okay, Earl. We can discuss this more tomorrow. Tonight, make sure to pull the door shut to the shed before you fall asleep. You don't want varmints gettin' inside."

"Yes sir."

"There's a kerosene lamp on a crate behind the bed and matches on the shelf. Don't knock the lamp over in your sleep." Mr. Joe places a hand on his shoulders, giving him a light squeeze. "When you're done with your supper, return everything to Cook."

"Yes sir."

With a last look around the garden, Mr. Joe gives the boy a nod and departs. Earl watches him leave, then digs into his supper. The ham and collards taste good. He pockets the piece of cornbread to eat later. Taking the plate and fork to the hand pump, he rinses them. Then he taps on the kitchen door and returns everything to Cook.

"That supper was real tasty. Thank you."

"What a helpful boy you are. You didn't have to rinse everything. It's my job to clean the dishes after you're done with them."

"Yes ma'am. I wasn't sure."

"That's fine." She looks him over head-to-toe. "You're a skinny thing with heartbreak wrote all over your face." She purses her lips, her expression thoughtful. "Did you get enough to eat? Do you need anything else before you turn in for the night?"

"No ma'am."

"There's a tin cup on a hook in the shed. You can get water from the hand pump whenever you need it. Did Mr. Joe show you where the privy is?"

"He did."

"Okay. You get yourself a good rest. In the morning, come tap on the door and I'll give you your breakfast."

"Yes ma'am. G'night."

Earl follows the garden path back to the shed. The sky is streaked with fading light behind gray clouds. It's too early to turn in, so he sits on the ground and crosses his legs. Slowly, he takes in everything his vision can reach. It's a pleasant place to sit. This morning, he felt jangled knowing he was in for another change. But as he relaxes with the soft hum of the garden around him, he can feel himself becoming calm. Soon, if Mr. Joe can be believed, he will know the names of things. Some of 'em, anyway. Won't that be something? Lucy would be proud of him.

Thinking of his sister elicits a whimper. Clamping his lips together, he wraps both arms around his legs in an effort to hold himself together. If Lucy was here, she'd give him a fun game to do. On his own, he can't think of nothin'. So he sits. He sits for an hour, watching caterpillars inch along a twig. He listens to soft voices wafting through the open windows of the big house, a man and a woman he can hear but not see. A baby bunny comes near and sniffs his knee. Earl holds his breath, not moving even an inch, until the bunny hops away to explore something else. Swallows swoop in the dusky sky, snatching insects in mid-air.

When it becomes too dark to see, he stands, brushing off his britches, and enters the shed. He latches the door from the inside. Fully dressed, he stretches his body on top of the mattress. He doesn't light the kerosene lamp. He's afraid he might start a fire. It seems safer to simply lay still and wait for sunrise. He doesn't want to think. He doesn't want to feel. More lonesome than he's ever been in his life, he waits for Mr. Joe to come in the morning and give him another chore to do.

TWENTY-THREE

Earl learns something new every day. He learns how the greenhouse helps plants grow even in wintertime. He learns how to start flowers from seeds in tiny trays of soil. As the seeds grow, they're moved to small pots, then bigger pots until the roots are strong enough to move into the garden. He learns about plants that can grow brand new from a piece of stem or leaf. Mr. Joe likes to say that Mother Nature works in mysterious ways. Earl believes it.

His newest skill is working the push reel mower. This machine possesses a blade that revolves to keep the Phippses' lawn trim and tidy like a picture in a magazine. Earl decides mowing is almost as good as driving a mule team. He can turn a corner and see immediately the clean, straight row behind him. This accomplishment gives him all kinds of satisfaction, which is why he decides to mow again two days later.

This prompts an entirely new learning for Earl. Never mow at daybreak. Dew grass really gums up the works.

Other tasks aren't near as fun as mowing but he knows they're important. He's still figurin' out how to identify which plants belong in the garden and which plants do not. But when he accidentally pulls the wrong plant from a flowerbed, Mr. Joe doesn't punish him. The first time it happens, Earl lowers his head, bracing for a slap that never comes. Instead, Mr. Joe shows him why he got confused and helps him understand how to do better the next time.

He's sad to see each day come to an end. Mr. Joe leaves. The sky grows dark and he grows so awful lonely – wandering the garden in the moonlight, missing his ma, missing Lucy – until the morning sun reappears alongside his boss, slipping through the pines with a friendly, "Hey, Earl."

Now, after finally startin' to settle into his new routine, he's received a disturbin' piece of news.

"I don't understand. You're not coming to the garden tomorrow?"

"Mr. and Mrs. Phipps like Sunday to be a day of rest. I'll stay in town with my boy and you'll stay here. You can have the entire day to relax."

"But what will I do?"

There's no sister to keep him company. The estate has no animals to tend. He's trapped, surrounded by black, wrought-iron fence that forms the border of his entire world.

"Use the pocketknife I gave you. Whittle yourself a whistle out of one of the willow branches. Or you can ramble over to the creek and do a little fishing. If you look in the greenhouse, behind the potting table, you'll find fishing poles stacked in a corner."

"I can leave the garden?"

"Of course, Earl. Go through the gate at the back and enter the woods. You'll hear the creek. Just don't go onto other people's property. As long as you keep to the woods, you'll be fine."

He gives the man a dark look. It's bad enough he has to be alone every blessed night with no one near. No abiding presence to provide assurance that whatever might come in the darkness, there's someone to face it with him. Now he's going to be alone all day, too. He doesn't like it. He doesn't like it one bit.

"It's only one day, Earl. I'll be back bright and early Monday morning. We'll start construction on the new side porch."

He considers this information. "I'm pretty good with a hammer." He gives Mr. Joe a sideways glance, wonderin' if he'll be caught in the lie. Neither Pa nor Orbry ever let him wield a hammer when they was workin'.

"I'm pleased to know it. In that case, we'll split the work evenly. I can hammer on one side while you hammer the other. Does that sound good to you?"

"That side porch is lookin' a bit rickety."

"You're absolutely right. That porch isn't safe. That's why you and I are going to build a new one. A strong, sturdy one. Now, go see what Cook's made for supper. I'll see you on Monday."

When the next morning dawns, Earl taps on the back door like always. Cook hands him a bowl of hot grits with a runny egg on top. She wears a bright blue dress with tiny white flowers. A blue hat is perched on her head. "Hon, today you can rinse the bowl at the hand pump when you're done eating. Leave everything by the back door, and I'll see to it later."

"Where're you going?"

"I'm off to church, then I'll be over at my sister's house." She hands him a pail. "Inside, you'll find a ham biscuit and some cukes. Put this in the shed and save it for your lunch, do you hear? Wait till the sun's directly overhead. Don't eat now, or you'll be starving later. I'll be back this evening in time to give you your supper. Do you understand?"

"Yes ma'am. Don't eat it now. I'm to wait till the sun's overhead and then eat."

From the gate at the front of the garden, he watches as the Phipps family climbs into their motorcar to go to church. On his second day, Mr. Joe introduced him to the folks that live in the big house so they'd know who he was and not worry about seeing him in the garden. Now, from a safe distance, he admires the fine clothes they wear and the polish of their fancy automobile. There are two people with 'em he knows to be their grown son and his child. The boy, the Phipps grandson, glances at the gate, making eye contact with Earl before entering the motorcar.

On his own now, Earl strolls the garden. He cuts a thin willow branch and tries to use the pocketknife Mr. Joe brung him. Trying to whittle a whistle is harder than it looks, like so many things. He closes the knife and sticks it in his pocket.

He's kneeling near one of the moist flowerbeds when he discovers the tiny black roly-poly bugs. They delight him, the way they tighten into little balls when touched.

He constructs a tiny fort out of sticks, with the bugs gathered inside.

He creates a wall they can't crawl around, then uses a stick to line the dirt, drawing thin roads for them to go places. There's no tellin' how much time passes, he's so focused on his project. That's prob'ly why the sudden mouth-clearing catches him off guard. There's a noise like a giant ball of phlegm being coughed up from deep inside a chest. When Earl looks up to see what it is, a giant gob of green snot hits him smack dab in the middle of the forehead.

Stunned by the action of the boy standing in front of him, Earl takes his sleeve and wipes it across his forehead. He gazes in disgust at the smear on his shirt.

"Golly." He frowns at the Phipps grandson. "What'd you do that for?"

"My father says you're a killer." The boy narrows his eyes, steps closer. "Are you?"

In his heart, Earl wants to say no. He doesn't feel like a killer. But he can't tell a lie when this boy already knows the truth. Reluctantly, he nods. "I guess I am." He rises from the ground, brushing the dirt from his hands. The younger boy takes a step backward.

"Are you going to hit me?"

Earl rubs the back of his neck with one hand. After a moment, he shakes his head. "I ain't gonna hit you."

"You're sure?"

"I'm sure."

The boy watches Earl for another moment then glances at the ground. "What are you doing?"

"Buildin' a home for the roly-poly bugs."

"Let me see." The boy squats, taking in the construction project of dirt and twigs. "I'm Harold."

"Pleased to meet you, Harold." He hesitates, unsure if that's true. "Does anyone call you Harry?"

"Not unless they want another gob of snot in the face."

Earl presses his lips together and prepares to make a run for it.

"How old are you anyway?"

"Thirteen," he answers warily. "How old are you?"

"Ten. But I'm advanced for my age." The boy stands, giving Earl a bold stare. Dark hair flops over a forehead sprinkled with light freckles. He's on the pudgy side, which reassures Earl. This boy can be outrun.

"I don't miss much," the boy says. "I'm going to be watching you. If you know what's good for you, you'll stay out of trouble." Squinting intently, he points a finger at Earl's chest. He holds it there so long, Earl looks down at hisself to make sure there ain't something there worth seeing.

He's relieved when the boy turns and re-enters the house. After a moment of quiet watchfulness, he crouches to check on his bugs. Left alone, they've scurried every which way, not even followin' the roads he built.

A low rumble in his stomach prompts him to narrow his eyes at the sky. Lunchtime.

Because his hands are covered with soil, he washes at the pump before retrieving his pail and plopping down on a grassy patch to eat. Long spears of cucumber taste like summer in his mouth. The country ham is chewy and salty and reminds him of breakfasts when Wilhelm and Kurt were still at home. Every year, his brothers raised a hog then butchered it in the fall to tide them through the cold winter months. There weren't nothing in the world like one of Ma's homemade biscuits filled with salt pork.

Feeling tears spring to his eyes, he swallows and looks around for an idea about what to do next. The salty meat makes him thirsty, so he grabs his tin cup and washes his lunch down with cool water from the hand pump. Scrunching his face in concentration, he tries to think what he'd do if Lucy was here. If they was together, they'd prob'ly want to climb a tree.

He spots a tree that looks promising. The lowest branch is within reach. Nimbly, he swings himself up. He's several branches into his climb when he stops. From here, he can see the entire property. Below him is the garden with pretty paths and every shape of flowerbed. The landscape grows wilder outside the fence where plants go untended. The wood line stretches as far as he can see. Staring toward the horizon, he can make out the tip of a stone tower piercing the trees – another estate. Faintly, he hears the distant clang of the trolley car.

"What are you doing?"

Earl swivels to find the Phippses' grandson leaning from a second-story window. Now, with a bit of distance between them, he pays closer attention to the boy's well-fed cheeks, the starched collar of his white, button-down shirt. He doesn't have the weasel face of James Purvis but that don't mean they couldn't both be varmints.

"Hello," he says cautiously. He wonders if the boy's spitting ability extends as far as the branch he's holding.

"Are you spying? What are you getting up to in that tree?"

Frowning at the boy because it seems obvious to him, he looks around, gauging his height. "About midway, I'd say." He glances skyward, where sunlight brushes the highest branches. "It's a tall tree."

Harold stares at him blankly for a moment then shakes his head. "You think you're clever. I'm gonna keep a close eye on you."

Earl gives the boy a hesitant smile. "In that case, do ya wanna do somethin'?"

"Like what?"

"There's fishin' poles in the greenhouse. Mr. Joe said there's a creek."

"There's a creek but I don't feel like fishing." The boy taps his lips with one finger, appearing to size up Earl. "What if we went to the woods and played soldier?"

"You'll have to show me what to do."

The boy gestures impatiently. "Climb down."

Earl makes his way down the tree, dropping to the ground just as Harold comes around the side of the house.

"Follow me," the boy says.

With Earl close on his heels, Harold opens the wrought-iron gate separating the garden from the woods. Finding a path that leads through the trees, they follow it for a short distance. Pine needles muffle the sound of their footsteps. Exposed tree roots twist out of the ground next to a deep ravine that appears menacing in the afternoon shadows.

"That's my trench," Harold says, pointing. "Those knotty logs are my barb wire fortifications."

Earl understands the trees are not really wire. They're imaginary. Lucy had been fond of pretend play.

"Over there is where you fight," Harold continues. "That's the German line."

"I'm German."

"That's what I said."

"My pa came from Germany, before the war."

"Oh." The boy's eyes widen. "I'm fighting a real Hun. Swell." He begins searching for something. "Find yourself a long stick to be your rifle."

Earl climbs over the knotty log that's really the barb wire and kicks at the ground. On his second kick, he strikes something solid. With both hands, he digs beneath layers of old leaves and pulls out a skinny branch. If he tries hard, he can see where it has the general shape of a rifle. He pulls the knife from his pocket and opens it. Carefully, with strokes that move away from his body, he shaves off small pieces from the branch.

"You've got a knife!" Harold's tone is admiring. "Here, do mine, too."

He hands over his own slender branch and Earl smooths it for him before closing the knife and returning it to his pocket.

"Now you go over there," says Harold, pointing. "Hide behind that barricade. I'm going to try and shoot you. You try and shoot me."

Earl feels uneasy about the game Harold's selected. On the other hand, he's pleased to have someone to do things with. The Phippses' grandson hasn't spit on him again, so that's good.

He takes his place behind a fallen tree and places his stick rifle across the rough bark. He waits to see what Harold will do. He sees the boy's head pop up from the ravine with his stick extended. "Pow," the boy shouts. "Pow-pow!"

Earl doesn't think that sounds much like a rifle, but he doesn't like to say so. He hunkers down behind his barricade. He's startled when a large chunk of mud flies over his head and lands a few feet away.

"What was that?"

"Grenade," shouts the boy. "You better run."

Earl rises halfway from his hiding spot and hurries in another direction. He hears Harold's muffled 'kapow' and assumes that's the sound made by the object he's thrown.

"You've got to shoot back, Earl. It's your turn to fire now." Harold's voice holds a hint of exasperation.

Earl lifts his eyes and aims his stick rifle toward the top of the other boy's head, just visible below the edge of a gully. "Pow," he says.

"Louder!"

"Pow-pow!" he shouts.

"Better."

They fire at each other in this way, back and forth, and then Earl watches with surprise as Harold sneaks out of the gully and dives behind a tree. He continues shooting at the boy, who pretends to fire back, now from the cover of a giant sycamore.

Earl's startled when Harold suddenly runs from cover, rushing forward with his stick held out. At first, Earl's reluctant to continue firing. It doesn't seem sportin' to shoot at someone who's got no cover. But an angry look from Harold makes him lift his pretend rifle and take aim. "Pow!" he shouts loudly.

Harold spins where he stands. Dropping his stick, he

clutches at his stomach with both hands. Earl's stunned to see a dark stain spread across the boy's white button-down shirt, right before he collapses with a cry.

Earl grabs his own stomach, gives a violent heave, and deposits his midday meal all over the ground. Feeling shaky, he tries to focus where the boy has fallen, startled to see Harold racing over. He straightens, his eyes traveling over the boy who now appears alive and well.

"Eww, that's disgusting," Harold says, glancing at the mess Earl upchucked onto the ground. "If you felt unwell, you should have said something."

Earl points at the boy's shirt. "What's that?" he asks hoarsely.

Harold glances at the dark stain spread across his white button-down. "Neat, huh? There's wild blackberries growing next to the ravine."

He shakes his head back and forth. "I don't want to play this game," he whispers.

At that moment, a man's voice reverberates through the wood, a shout coming from the direction of the house. "Harold!"

"That's my father," the boy says. "He's going to have a fit when he sees what I've done to this shirt." He starts to trot off but pauses, turning back to Earl. "That was a good battle. If you want, we can do something else next week."

"You'll be back next week?"

"We come on Sundays."

Earl watches as the boy races off through the woods. He gives a trembly sigh and kicks the stick he dropped. He has one week to come up with something different for them to do.

TWENTY-FOUR

Earl flicks a beetle, then turns to Mr. Joe. "Did you see that? I knocked it right out of the air."

"Don't harm the beetles, Earl."

"Why not? I thought they ate the plants. They get into my hair. I don't like it. I like the roly-poly bugs. They're bugs and they're balls at the same time."

"Every creature has a job to do, even the beetles."

"Like what?"

Mr. Joe pauses in his task, removing a red handkerchief from his trouser pocket and wiping his face. Earl watches then casually removes the blue cloth he carries with him always. He mirrors his boss's actions, pressing the worn handkerchief against damp skin.

The older man gives a half-smile and points toward a group of trees. "See those magnolias by the side of the house? Those trees wouldn't exist without beetles."

"No kiddin'?" Earl frowns at the trees, trying to

figure out how something so tall could be dependent on something so small.

"Beetles are attracted to the white magnolia flowers. They're drawn by the chemicals the flowers produce. They feed on the nectar inside the flower and gather the pollen there and spread it, you see, to the other plants."

"What's 'pollen'?"

"Well, it's… it's food, I guess, for the creatures that like it. But it wouldn't taste good to you, Earl. For the beetles, it's tasty and nutritious – exactly what they like to eat most in the world."

"Oh."

"The beetles take the pollen, these little golden grains, from the center of the flower. As they fly about, they carry the pollen to other flowers on other trees. When pollen is transferred between flowers of the same species, the plants can reproduce."

"What's that?"

"Well… every living thing, including plants, wants to reproduce. This means they want to create offspring so the species can survive for another generation."

"Offspring?"

"Babies."

"Plants have babies?"

"They do. They have tiny seedlings that grow into saplings that grow into tall trees. Just like folks. Today, you're a sapling. One day, you'll be a tall tree."

"What's a species?"

"Groups of things that are alike. All folks are one species. And dogs are a species, called canines. And there's thousands of different tree species."

"Does the tree get fat?"

"I beg your pardon?"

"Before Rose was going to have her baby, she got fat."

"No, Earl. The tree doesn't get fat. Instead, for the magnolia, a cone-shaped fruit with red seeds will appear, decorating the tree over the winter. Remind me to show you when it happens. When the cones fall, the seeds bury themselves inside the ground then grow when conditions are right. It's because of all the beetles that North Carolina has so many beautiful magnolia trees."

"Do they have names?"

"The trees?"

"The beetles."

"Oh, sure. There's sap beetles and tumbling flower beetles and leaf beetles."

"Golly." It was astonishing that every kind of beetle had a name. "I named the roly-poly bugs," he whispers to himself. He wonders if there's another name they have. Then he wonders if they have lots of names. Who gets to decide?

Mr. Joe finishes tying slender branches to a trellis. "There. That's the last one."

Earl picks up the gardening tools and heads to the shed. Every tool has a place and he's learning how to put things away to Mr. Joe's satisfaction. When everything is tidy, his boss claps him on the shoulder. "What have you got planned for Sunday?"

"If Harold's able to come out, I thought we could take the poles down to the creek and fish."

"If you boys catch anything, be sure and keep your fish in a pail with some of the creek water. When you're done, take the fish to Cook. She'll know what to do."

"I can clean fish. If I tell Cook, maybe she'll let me help."

"I'm sure she'd appreciate it."

When Harold arrives in the garden Sunday afternoon, he doesn't seem thrilled with the idea of fishing. He suggests playing Chicago gangster. Then he suggests cowboys and Indians. Earl will not be swayed. "No shooting games," he insists.

"You're no fun," the boy responds.

"Let's climb trees and see who can go the highest."

"Nah."

"If you got glass marbles, we could shoot marbles."

"Grandmother won't let me play marbles on Sunday."

"Maybe you could ask Mr. Joe to put in a horseshoe pitch."

Harold snorts. "Seriously?"

"I guess it's fishing then." With a pleased smile, Earl gathers the poles, a pail and a box of fishing tackle. He opens the gate and leads them out of the garden.

Every evening of the past week, after Mr. Joe left to catch the streetcar, Earl raced through his supper then headed to the woods to explore. He found the perfect place for fishing. He also discovered a small farm on the other side of the wood. The fields aren't as big as Mr. Tate's farm, but the owner has a herd of dairy cows. After Lucy comes back to get him, he figures they might get themselves a cow and chickens. Every morning, he can milk the cow and collect the eggs. He would be a big help to his sister on a farm. And when it's time to plow, he'll hook up the mules, like Dick and Dock, but he'll give them new names. If they get girl mules, they'll be jennies. But he won't name

’em Jenny ’cause he don’t know anyone by that name. He’ll name one after Frieda. And maybe Lucy would like a mule named after her, too, on account of she can be stubborn and hard-headed.

He’ll drive the mules down the furrows exactly like Frank did it. He smiles, thinking about Dick and Dock. Those had been two friendly mules. Frank was only sometimes friendly. He wonders about them and how they’re gettin’ on. He thinks about Welcome and Faith, too, but that’s harder. It hurts his head.

“Come on, slowpoke!”

Harold’s got ahead of him and waves impatiently. Earl steps up the pace, thinkin’ about all the fish they’re gonna catch and how Cook will be so pleased. Maybe she’ll give him two pieces of fried fish for dinner.

“This is the place.” He points toward a grassy bank surrounded by trees. “It’s the best place I seen for fishin’, on account of the shade will hide our shadows from scaring the fish.”

“Fish are stupid. I don’t think they get scared because of a shadow. How is it different from a tree’s shadow? They swim through shade all the time, don’t they?”

“I guess so,” Earl says, realizing this is true. “But maybe people shadows move differently than tree shadows. My pa tole me to fish on a cloudy day or t’ always face the sun. That way, I’m more likely to catch somethin’.”

“Was your father a smart man?”

“I don’t know.” He frowns, thinkin’ about the trial and where his pa is now. “I expect he ain’t so smart.”

“Then why take his advice? Besides,” Harold takes a seat on the grass, “I want to be in the sunshine.”

"Suit yourself."

Grabbing a trowel from the tackle box, Earl stabs it into the moist earth and removes a mound of soil crawlin' with earthworms. He delivers one wiggler to Harold, who receives it with a look of mild distaste.

Next, he baits his hook and moves to a tree root sticking out of the bank. He casts his line then watches as Harold drops his own hook into the water. Now, they wait. He fills his lungs with creek air, noting the smell of water and pine. He catches a flicker of movement and spies a turtle peeking above the water, but it disappears before he can point it out to Harold. He eyes tiny eddies on the water in case somethin' swims his way, but his bobbin never sinks beneath the surface.

When the shade shifts and his line still hasn't moved, he reels in the hook. The worm is still there, drowned. He needs a worm with life. He digs another hole, pleased to uncover a fat, squirmy one. He rebaits his hook and returns it to the water. He fishes for an hour this way, changing worms repeatedly. He doesn't get a single bite. Earl can tell Harold is gettin' restless.

"Harold?"

"Hmm?"

"Your pa brings you to visit Mr. and Mrs. Phipps every Sunday?"

"We have church and Sunday dinner with Grandmother and Grandfather every weekend. We've been coming since I was a baby."

"Where's your ma?"

Harold's silent for a long moment, his expression difficult to read. "She doesn't come with us anymore." He stares intently into the water.

"Why not?"

"Mother's not well. She… likes how the house is dark and quiet when my father and I leave. She stays home all the time now."

"Oh." He sucks the inside of his cheek, watching a leaf swirl downstream. When Harold speaks again, Earl cocks his head, detecting a new tone in the boy's voice.

"My father says she's in despair and angry with God."

"Angry with God?" Earl whispers the words, not wanting God to overhear.

"My baby brother died a few months ago. I overheard Father talking with the minister. He believes my mother is…" He stumbles over the words. "Trapped inside her grief."

That sounded terrible. Anything trapped must be sufferin', for sure.

"I miss her." Harold casts a sideways glance at Earl. "I miss who she used to be."

"Who was she?"

The boy gives him a twisted smile. "Just my mother… my mother without her heart broken."

He nods gravely, understanding this. "Some hurts are so big, they take a lifetime to feel better. That's what I think. I miss my ma every single day. I expect I might never stop missin' her."

"You weren't angry with your ma when you shot her?"

"Golly, Harold." Earl pushes away the disturbin' image conjured by these words. "I wasn't angry. It was an accident."

"Then that's sad." Harold's eyes grow solemn, an expression Earl hasn't seen before on his new friend. "I'm sorry I hurled that goober at you. It wasn't right. I didn't know you then, but it doesn't matter. I shouldn't have done it."

Earl sighs, gazing around the creek. It don't seem like they're going to catch anything today. "If you don't want to fish no more, we can do something else. We could explore."

"I've explored all these woods. There's nothing to see. Although..." Harold's eyes light with a sudden memory. "My father and I walked beside this creek one time and we found an arrowhead. That means American Indians used to hunt here, maybe right where we're sitting. Shakori, I bet, hunting bear or wild turkey."

Earl peers into the darkness between trees. He recalls the photo he seen on Mr. Wilkins' wall at the five-and-dime. That feels like ages ago. The grocer said it was a fearsome chief who lived out west. If there was people like that in these woods, he better keep a look out.

"Do they still come to this place, you think? The ones that left the arrowheads?" He cups a hand around his mouth and speaks sideways to Harold. He doesn't want to be overheard by anyone lurking in the shadows.

The other boy pulls his fishing pole out of the water. He removes the drowned worm and tosses it into the creek, then reels in the loose line. "I've got an idea."

Earl copies Harold, pulling in his pole and tying everything neatly. "What's your idea?"

"We should hunt for buried treasure."

"There's buried treasure?"

"Have you ever heard of the book *Treasure Island*?"

Earl shakes his head. His ma kept the Sears Roebuck catalog and the Farmer's Almanac. They made good privy paper. The only book that didn't become privy paper was Ma's Bible.

"There are these pirates, see, and they bury treasure on an island in the middle of the ocean."

"What kind of treasure?"

"It's a chest full of gold coins and jewels. Later, they have to come back and try and find it."

"Why?"

"So they can spend it, of course."

"Oh."

"I bet Indians buried treasure, too."

"Like arrowheads?"

"No, the Indians would have had wampum."

"What's that?"

"Well, it's like a special belt made from small seashells strung together. Except if it's been buried in the ground then it might be kind of, I don't know, rotted away and stuff, but it would have historical value. I bet we could sell pieces to the history museum or to the university. We could split the money. Not fifty-fifty, of course. This land belongs to Grandfather, so I should get the bigger share. Maybe sixty-forty."

"Okay."

"Or seventy-thirty."

"Okay." Hunting for treasure seems like a fine plan to Earl. He likes that it doesn't appear to involve shooting. "Where should we look?"

"Let's take these poles back to the house and get a shovel. We'll need it for digging." Harold wipes damp hands down his trousers and gathers his pole. "I better get paper and a pencil, too. I'll need to draw a treasure map once we find the wampum."

"What for?"

"So we can find it again, of course."

"I thought we were going to sell it." Earl struggles to keep up with Harold's thinking.

"Sure. But we'll want to keep it hidden until we've negotiated a fair price. The map will make sure we don't forget where the treasure's buried."

He nods admiringly. "That's a real good thought, Harold. You have a sharp mind."

"Yeah, someday I figure I'll go into business."

As they walk back to the greenhouse to exchange fishing poles for shovels, Earl tries to imagine what he'd do with his share of a treasure. For sure, he could join his sister. He and Lucy could prob'ly live on treasure their whole lives.

TWENTY-FIVE

"Dig there." Harold points to a fallen tree. "That looks like a good place hunters might have built a campfire."

Earl puts the tip of the shovel into the ground and presses with one foot. The ground gives way easily. He tosses a few shovelfuls of dirt to the side, then realizes Harold hasn't moved. "Why aren't you digging?"

"I'm thinking."

"Oh." Earl waits, uncertain what to do next.

"Local tribes wouldn't hide their treasure here."

"They wouldn't?" He gazes around the open area. It seems like a good spot, filled with light and no shadows.

"They'd want to hide their treasure beside a particular tree or a big rock – a landmark that meant something to them. This area isn't special enough." Harold snaps his fingers. "I know just the spot. Follow me."

Earl takes the two shovels and hurries to keep up. They go farther than he's explored on his own, past the property line and into an area thick with trees and ferns. Harold stops and points. Peering through the trees, he can see massive boulders and rock formations in the distance.

"Father says those boulders have been here for thousands of years. The area around them might have changed, but those rocks would have been here even before American Indian tribes arrived. Let's dig there."

The boys make their way carefully over fallen logs and across soft ground thick with decayed leaves. When they reach the boulders, Earl gazes upward in fascination. "I expect God dropped these stones here like they was marbles."

"Look around. Maybe we'll find a clue."

Earl props the shovels against a tree. When they get around to the other side, they discover a place between two large boulders where natural footholds provide a place they can climb. He clambers up after Harold, blinking when they come out of the darkness of the woods into sunlight. He clenches his eyes, grabbing hold of the rock to keep his balance.

Harold turns at the sound of loose stones slipping off the ledge to ping on rocks below. "You alright?"

"I'm sun-stunned," Earl says, panting lightly. "I can't see."

"Your eyes need time to adjust to the light, that's all. Give it a minute."

Carefully, he inches one eye open. Then he unclenches the other. He stares around the wood from his new height. "Look at that tree, there."

Harold follows his gaze to a tall sycamore. Bare limbs reach to the sky like dry bones.

"Would that make a good place to bury treasure, do you think?"

"You might be right. That tree looks like it's been here for a long time. Anyone on these rocks would see how it stands apart from the other trees."

The boys make their way back to the shovels, carrying them to where they believe the sycamore to be. Things look different from the ground. Every few moments, they look up to get their bearings. At last, they identify the correct tree not far from a smaller pile of tumbled stones.

"Look, Earl. Footprints!" Harold drops to the ground, staring intently at impressions left behind in the moist dirt.

"Indians?"

"They're not moccasin prints. But someone has been in these woods."

Earl pulls back when a darkness on his left appears to bend in the light. It looks like the outline of a man. A closer look reveals it to be nothing more than a shadow, shifting as the sun's rays find their way through tree branches. He notices something sparkly on the ground. Expecting it to be a piece of glass or tin foil, he kneels to examine the spot. He pushes dirt and leaves out of the way, exposing what looks like a ring.

"I found treasure," he whispers.

"Did you say something?"

He looks to where Harold is drawing on his pad. "I found treasure," he says, louder.

"Don't shout it, Earl. We don't want the whole world to know."

Harold's tone sounds exasperated, but when the other boy looks to where Earl is pointing, his face takes on an expression of curiosity. Dropping his pad to the ground, he picks up the ring and brushes off caked dirt. He spits on it, rubbing the metal vigorously to make it shine.

Earl looks over his shoulder, admiring the jewelry. "That was a good idea you had, Harold. The treasure was right where you said it would be."

"It's missing the main stone."

"What?"

"These prongs here are supposed to hold a small stone. I bet it was a diamond. You can see there's two tiny diamonds on each side, next to where the center stone was." Harold drops to the ground and begins digging with his fingers. "Help me, Earl. See if you can find a stone that would fit this ring. It would be something cut so it sparkles."

Earl joins the other boy, using his fingers to dig into the dirt. He pushes aside leaves and twigs then runs to get one of the shovels, turning over ground so Harold can run the soil through his fingers. He clears a space all around the spot where the ring was found.

Finally, Harold sits back on his heels. "I give up. I don't think there's a diamond anywhere around here."

"What do you s'pose happened?"

"Maybe there was a woman wearing the ring and she didn't realize it slipped off her finger."

"Why's the stone missing?" Earl has a sudden inspiration. "Ooh… I know. Maybe the ring dropped on the ground and knocked the stone loose. A bird thought it was a shiny bug and swallowed it!"

"I think a bird can tell a bug from a diamond. Maybe the stone fell out of the ring somewhere in the woods.

When the owner couldn't find the diamond, she threw the ring down in an angry fit. That's what I think."

Earl nods, accepting this explanation. If someone was having an angry fit, they was likely to throw things. His pa threw things all the time when he was in an angry fit.

"I think the ring is pretty, even without the stone," he says. "Don't you? Maybe you can sell it to somebody that has a stone to put in it."

Harold stares at the ring, turning it in the sunlight. He points to the band. "See this? It's called filagree. Mother has this on one of her rings, although this is different than anything I've seen. The design is some kind of plant – ivy, I think."

"I bet there's not another ring like it."

"You know, a jeweler could cut a new diamond to fit this setting. He might even help us sell it."

Harold hands the ring to Earl. "Keep this safe until I can do some research. There's too many help poking around at my house. One of the maids might take it. I'm going to see if there's a pawnbroker in Raleigh who'd give money for something like this. Next Sunday, I'll have a better idea what to do."

"What's a pond breaker?"

"Pawnbroker, Earl, pawnbroker – it's a kind of a shop. You take stuff to them, and they give you money for it. But if you don't buy back your things, they can sell your stuff to other folks."

"Oh." He gazes around the darkening woods. "Do you think we should search for more treasure?"

Harold glances at the sky. "It's getting late. Father will wonder where I am."

He retrieves his pad and Earl gathers the shovels. As they walk back to the estate, Harold taps Earl's pocket where he tucked the ring. "I'm counting on you to keep that safe. Don't show it to anybody, not even Mr. Joe."

"I won't. It'll be our secret." He's quiet for a moment, thinking. "It's a real pretty ring. You could give it to your ma, you know, to lift her spirits. I wouldn't mind."

Harold stops, then turns to look at Earl. "I didn't think of that. If it had a new diamond and got a bit of polish, it'd make a swell present." He nods thoughtfully. "That's a fine idea. I'll think about it."

The hint of a smile appears on Earl's lips. Surely any sad woman would be cheered if her son gave her a pretty ring.

TWENTY-SIX

The Carolina sun was too much. It hurt Earl to open his eyes. Some bright days, he begged Mr. Joe to only work in the shade, the pain was that bad. One morning, his boss brung him a battered straw hat to wear. Earl thought it was fine. He wore it every day, even when it was cloudy. When work was done, he hung the hat on a hook inside the shed. Then he filled a bucket from the hand pump and poured the water over his head, a ritual cooling off that gave him something to look forward to at the end of the day. Well, that and Cook's supper.

"You know, Mr. Joe, when it was this hot back home, me and my sister would sneak beneath the house. It'd be dark under there and the dirt was soft and sifty, like baking powder. It was my favorite place to get cool."

"It's been hot, that's for sure. It got so scorchin' yesterday, I saw two trees fighting over a dog." The man chuckles.

Earl stares at him blankly.

"Get it? 'Cause dogs pee on trees?"

"Yes sir, they do. Dogs'll pee on just about anything."

"Never mind." Mr. Joe hangs up the hedge trimmers. When he's done, he puts his hand into his pocket and withdraws a small coin. He hands it to Earl.

"What's this?"

"I worked you pretty hard this week. I thought you could use a treat. Tonight after supper, why don't you walk to the trolley stop? The grocer keeps an ice chest inside the store. You can get yourself a Co'Cola."

"Golly, thank you, Mr. Joe." He brings the coin close to his eyes, turning it from front to back. It's different from the coin Mr. Purvis had given him. "What's it got on it?"

"A buffalo."

"What's that?"

"It's a furry cow that lives out west." Mr. Joe removes his handkerchief and moistens it at the hand pump. He releases a soft sigh as he presses the damp cloth against his face and neck. "Have you ever had a sody pop, Earl?"

"Back home, after a day barnin' tabacca, Farmer Tate feeds all the workers. His boy Henry cooks a pig in a pit and Missus Tate serves it with pinto beans and warm pop. And one time, after my pa was on trial, Mr. Purvis gave me and my sister a coin for a cold pop. But his son was a bad egg and he poured that soda on the ground. I was upset about that."

"Well, now you can have a cold pop all to yourself. It's just the thing on a hot day."

"Thank you, Mr. Joe. I sure appreciate it."

It's too hot for hot supper, so Cook gives him a cold pork sandwich with chilled lettuce and salted tomatoes for his evening meal. After he returns the plate, he holds the door for a moment wanting to say somethin'. Speakin' to Mr. Joe earlier made him remember.

"You got something on your mind, Earl?"

"Yes ma'am. I wanted to say that if I get any mail, you'll let me know, won't you?"

"Of course. Are you expecting mail?"

"Yes ma'am. From my sister, Lucy. She's livin' with a new family 'cause they got all boys and they wanted a girl. I expect she might send me a letter any day now. I wanted you to know in case it came and all."

"I'll keep an eye out for it, Earl. I sure will."

"Okay then." He hovers for a moment, then steps back. "Thank you."

He gives Cook a wave as she closes the door then lets himself out the garden gate. He whistles as he walks, cheered by the thought of his sister sending him a letter and telling him about her new place. Then he feels sad 'cause she's not here to share his special treat. Ever since James Purvis dumped their cold soda on the ground, he's wanted to make it up to Lucy.

He knows his way to the trolley stop but he's never ridden the trolley car. Mostly because he doesn't have coin for a ticket. But also because it's full of people, and Earl doesn't know if they're nice or not.

He's been inside the grocery, though. Several times, Cook has sent him to the store with a shopping list and a small wagon. Earl hands the list to the grocer and the grocer's boy fills the wagon with supplies. The grocer seems nice. Nicer than Mr. Wilkins back home. Sometimes it's good to know folks who aren't only Mr. Joe and Harold.

It's a short walk, but Earl's already gathered a sweat when he pulls open the door with the tinkling bell. This shop is smaller than Mr. Wilkins' store, but it carries many of the same things. Shelves filled with canned goods reach all the way to the ceiling. Along one wall, round bushel baskets overflow with cantaloupe and cucumbers, summer squash and sweetcorn. There's always something fresh from nearby farms.

Being in the store with the smell of ripe vegetables tickling his nose reminds him of an unpleasantness. Before he went on trial, Pa took him and Welcome to town to run errands. Once they was inside the store, Pa told his sister to distract the grocer. As though she hadn't a care in the world, Welcome stood by the cash register and kept up a steady chatter. That girl liked to hear herself talk. Earl had stood mute, frozen by the knowledge they was doing something his ma wouldn't like. When Pa gestured sharply to Earl, he made his way to the back of the store, unable to keep his eyes from the hard salami his pa was stuffin' down his trousers. "Pay attention, boy." He grabbed Earl's shoulder and forced ten cents in change into his hand. "Bring die münzen to the kashier. Und dis." He passed a bag of cornmeal into his son's other hand.

Earl shakes off the memory. He sure wished Lucy was here. He didn't need a soda pop all to hisself. Catching a look from the grocer, Earl doesn't dawdle but walks directly to the ice chest. He lifts the lid and leans over the edge, grinning as the cold air flows across his skin. There are a bunch of flavors to choose from. His sister, Frieda, had been partial to cherry Cheerwine. He wonders how the red pop tastes but finally reaches for what's familiar.

Closing his fingers around the blue-and-green contoured bottle, he shuts the lid and hands over his coin.

"Thank you, son." The grocer presses a key on the cash register. The drawer pops out with a ping and the man drops the coin into the tray.

"Where can I open the bottle?"

The grocer takes the bottle and flips off the top using a steel opener nailed to the counter. He returns the pop as a thin swirl of white condensation rises from the chilled glass.

Earl takes a swig before any more coldness can escape. He smacks his lips.

"Good?" the man asks.

He takes a second sip. Then a third. "Delicious every time."

A thin woman enters the store with a straw basket. She wears a white apron over her dress. A lace cap is perched on top of her head. She spies Earl and comes closer. "You're the boy works in Mrs. Phipps' garden."

"Yes ma'am." He recalls seeing her with Cook. They'd been seated at the kitchen table snapping the ends off green beans.

"I'm Miz. Fowler. I keep house for the Brooks family, down the way."

"The house that looks like a castle?"

She turns to the grocer. "It's the stone tower that does it," she says matter-of-factly. "I don't know where they got it into their heads to have such a thing. No one ever uses that room either. Pretty sunroom stays empty the whole year round."

Earl's not sure if he's s'posed to be listenin'. He takes another sip of his drink and wonders if it would be impolite to slip out the door.

"What's that you got?"

He glances where the woman's finger is pointing, his eyes widening. Ever since Harold tasked him with protecting the ring, he's been wearing it looped around his neck with a boot lace and tucked inside his shirt. When he leaned over the ice chest, it must have slipped out. He wraps his hand around the end of the cord, not wanting to share the treasure with strangers.

"It's nothin'," he mumbles. He moves to tuck it back into his shirt.

"That's not nothing." She swats his hand and lifts the makeshift necklace for a better look. "I know this ring. It's Mizzus Brooks' ring what she had stolen last month."

"I found it," Earl says. He steps back, his hand returning to protect the ring. "I found it. I didn't steal nothin'."

She narrows her eyes. "When Cook told me Mrs. Phipps had taken in a homeless boy, I figured you'd be trouble. Anyone ain't got no people is bound to be trouble. I told her as much, but she pooh-poohed me. Are you a boy who steals things? I bet you're a boy who steals things. You need to give that over. That ring belongs to Mizzus Brooks."

Earl's face tightens. Distressed, he turns to the grocer. "I didn't steal nothin'. I found this ring. I found it in the woods with my friend, Harold."

The woman gives a sniff. "Your friend."

"Untie the cord, son. Let me take a look."

He sets the bottle of soda on the counter and lifts shaking fingers to untie the lace. He passes his treasure to the man.

"That ring is pure platinum." The woman moves closer, her eyes sharp on the small object held between the grocer's finger and thumb. "Yep, I knew it. See that design on the side? That's from Mizzus Brooks' family crest. She was an Ivey before she married Mister Brooks. He had that ring made special for her in New York."

"The center stone is missing," says the grocer.

The housekeeper pins Earl with a glance. "What'd you do with it?"

"I found it like that, jus' like that. There weren't no other stone in it. Harold and me, we looked, honest."

"Miz. Brooks has been heartsick over losing that ring. The men what broke into the house took her silver tea set and her cameo, but it was losin' that ring had her in tears. They oughta lock you away, that's what they oughta do. There's no telling what a person will do, one that don't have no family."

"Why are you sayin' that? That ain't true." Earl's face crumples, his eyes darting between the stern housekeeper and the grocer. He didn't steal nothin'. He shouldn't be locked up if he ain't done nothin' wrong.

"Madam, there's no call accusing this young man when we don't know the full story." The grocer turns to Earl. "Son, do you know anything about a silver tea set or a cameo?"

"No sir. I don't know about those things." He doesn't tell the man he's unsure what a cameo is, but he's pretty sure he hasn't seen it. Or anything silver like a tea set.

"Did Mrs. Brooks file a report?" the grocer asks, returning his attention to the woman.

"She sure did. The sheriff said they wasn't the first house the robber hit." She gives Earl the evil eye and he ducks his head, shaking it sorrowfully.

"In that case, this situation should be easy to resolve. I'll hold onto the ring, and the sheriff can send someone over to inspect it, confirm it matches the description of the one that's missing."

"I can do better'n that. I'll go tell Miz. Brooks to come over here, and she'll confirm it herself."

At mention of the sheriff, Earl feels dizzy. He remembers the sheriff, the metal cuffs on his wrists and the taunts of the officers. Maybe the police will take him to the jailhouse for findin' a ring and not turning it in. If they lock him away a second time, he'll be all alone with no Pastor Jack to rescue him. His eyes darken with another frightening thought. Maybe this time, they'll take him to the prison and lock him in a cell with his pa. Too late to stop it, he feels a warm liquid make its way down his leg, dampening his pants and leaving a pool of piss on the floor.

"Lord, have mercy!" The housekeeper gazes at him with horror.

"No. No. No." His whisper is barely audible. His head hurts and he doesn't know what to do. His heart skitters with agitation. He rakes a trembling hand through his hair. He prob'ly shouldn't take chances. "I'm not waiting for no sheriff," he says, striving to keep the panic out of his voice. "I di'nt do nothin' wrong."

With a last desperate glance toward the grocer, he pushes past the woman and barrels out the door, the bell tinkling behind him.

As soon as he hits the road, he takes off running. He's in trouble. And just like the last time he'd been in trouble, he hadn't seen it coming. One minute, life is good. There's sweetness and the hope of pleasant things. In the blink of an eye, it goes to pieces.

TWENTY-SEVEN

Earl races toward the Phipps Estate at a flat dash. He's halfway there when he realizes the garden will be the first place the sheriff comes looking for him. Before he can blink, he pivots, pausing to catch his breath only when he's reached the dark shadows of the wood.

He stumbles toward a knotty log that had been a barricade in Harold's wartime battle, then a seat for traveling Indians cooking around a campfire. Now, it's a spot for him to slow his heart and think what he should do.

Mr. Joe is gonna be upset with him. Mr. and Mrs. Phipps might be upset, too. When they learn the police are searching for him, they're likely to regret takin' him in. When they learn he found someone's special ring and didn't tell 'em, well, it makes his heart hurt to picture their disappointment. Earl fists one hand and bangs it against his forehead. "Think. Think." He peers watchfully around the woods.

He better not stay in this place. If someone comes lookin' for him, they'll look here, too. Feeling shaky, he reaches into a pocket for his handkerchief but it's not there. He remembers. He left it crumpled on top of his mattress. With a sigh, he lifts his tattered shirt hem to wipe the sweat from his face. He tries to think what to do, then remembers the dairy farm on the other side of the trees. Maybe he can hide there tonight.

He hurries through the dark wood, frightening to him now, full of strange shadows looming everywhere he turns. Several times, he glances backward, certain he's bein' followed. It's hard to see where he's goin'. He trips over a tree root that leaps out at him in the darkness. Then he trips again over his own feet, somersaulting down a small ridge before bouncing upright. "Whoa," he gasps. He better watch where he's going or he'll break his neck.

When he reaches the far side of the wood, the ground changes, becoming a long row of tended fields – crops for the family or feed for the herd. He stays low to the ground, making his way toward a large barn. As he nears the building, he sees the glow of a dimly lit lantern and hears a voice speaking softly. It's the farmer soothing the cows as he performs the end-of-day milking. The barn doors nearest to Earl are closed. He crouches there, hidden from view. He can make out a small hayrick on the other side of the building, a wood cart and a pen where pigs doze.

He waits until the farmer finishes his chore. The man exits the barn, heading toward the two-story farmhouse. Quietly, Earl slips inside. A few cows have lingered after the milking, snuffling in loose hay. Tall milk cans line one wall. He peers out the door. Not seeing or hearing anything, he grabs one of the cows and pulls her into a milking bay. She doesn't resist, but watches him curiously with large, dark eyes. He pitches a forkful of hay onto the floor and waits until she's dipped her head to munch the dry grass. Glancing around cautiously, he cocks an ear. The night is still. Parched from his dash through the woods, he slides beneath the udder and squeezes each teat, drinking the last dregs of warm milk the farmer left untapped. He avoids the cow's switching tail and restless hooves. Clearly, she's tired and wants to be done with manhandling.

He rises from the floor and wipes a sleeve across his mouth. He pauses again to listen then leads the cow to the door so she can make her way outside. Moving to the back of the barn, he finds a row of unused stalls. He crawls into the farthest one, covering himself with loose straw. He feels hidden but takes no chances when he hears the farmer return to the barn. Keeping as still as he can, he breathes shallowly to avoid making any noise. Fear of discovery causes his heart to pound inside his chest. He's relieved when the farmer begins removing the milk cans, the clang of metal masking his small breaths.

Finally, the last can is withdrawn, the lantern is extinguished and the door bolted. Earl releases a slow breath and closes his eyes. Immediately, an image of the ring appears to him. He gave it to the grocer. How can he explain to Harold why he handed over their treasure? He remembers the woman with the hard eyes. She had no call to be mean. Why did she say he has no family?

His thoughts turn to Mr. Joe. Tomorrow, the gardener will arrive at the estate to perform the day's chores and Earl won't be there to greet him. His boss will wonder at it. He'll check the shed and find it empty. He'll call Earl's name and receive no answer. And if the sheriff, contacted by the grocer, should search for Earl, will he make it as far as the dairy barn?

His nose twitches. The straw's tickly, but he doesn't mind. Bein' in a barn is better than bein' alone in the woods. Bears and bobcats can't sneak up on him in a barn. *There's always work needed on a farm,* he thinks sleepily. If he has to leave the Phipps Estate, he's going to need a plan. He doesn't want to come to a bad end. He becomes aware of the dampness lingering on his trousers and feels ashamed. It's a good thing James Purvis hadn't been around to see that. Earl struggles to hold back tears, wishing Lucy was there to help him. He tries to figure what he should do next, but the day gets the best of him. Every single part of him weary, he sleeps.

When he awakes, it's to the sound of footsteps outside the barn wall, inches from his head. The farmer's heading to the pigpen. As quietly as he can, Earl slides out of the stall. He peers around the dim space. It's daybreak and the farm is starting to stir.

Tiptoeing, his steps soft as shadows, he moves to the back of the building. He presses one eye to a thin gap between the double doors and watches as the farmer lifts two large buckets over the pig trough. The pigs press excitedly toward the contents as they pour out. Earl's stomach rumbles.

As soon as the farmer returns to the house, Earl darts to the trough. He squints through the plank fence, finding it hard to tell what's in the slop. If the pigs can eat it, maybe he can too. Keeping his fingers as far as possible from the hungry snouts, he sticks a hand in the trough, grabs at whatever's there and pulls it through the fence rails. In the pale morning light, he can make out an apple core, a broken corn cob and what looks like potato peels. Picking out a green chunk of something, he puts one corner in his mouth to taste. Cucumber. He shoves the rest into his mouth.

He pockets the apple core and the potato peels and tosses the corn cob back into the trough. Checking to make sure the farmer isn't in sight, he sprints toward the woods. He'll find a place to hide near the boulders, someplace with a view. He needs to know whether the police are huntin' for him. He wonders if they'll have dogs. Dogs could root him out, even from the boulders or a tall tree. Then he has a thought. If he walks back and forth all over the woods and climbs up and down trees, dogs might get confused. They won't know which scent trail is the path to where he's hiding.

He wonders how he knows to be wary of the dogs. It's because of Pa, he realizes. Pa was always talkin' about coverin' his tracks so no one would find his still hidden in the woods.

When Earl reaches the tree line, he turns his gaze back to the farm. All is quiet. The pastures are tinged with soft purple where the rising sun meets morning dew. He finds a secluded spot behind a tree and sits cross-legged on the ground. Concealed from prying eyes, he reaches into his pocket and retrieves his breakfast. He bites the apple core in half, chomping it, seeds and all. Next, he makes quick work of the potato scraps. It's not nearly as satisfying as what Cook prepares. He'll get a drink from the creek later and forage along the bank.

With the edge off his hunger, he heads for the place where he and Harold discovered the ring. He goes slowly, taking his time, careful to make sure no one else is around. As he advances toward the ancient boulders, he feels himself becoming more calm, soothed by the scent of fresh pine, the skittering of small squirrels and warblings from the trees.

For an hour, he walks one way, finding a small creek that branches off the bigger creek behind the Phippses' house. He crisscrosses it several times then heads in another direction. He climbs up trees, dangles from branches and leaps to adjacent trees, chuckling low in his chest. Finally, he loops around to a spot near the old sycamore. He scans the ground carefully. He doesn't think Harold missed anything the last time they was here. He's too sharp. Still, for his own peace of mind, he wants to confirm there's no gleaming stone hiding beneath the moss and leaves, waiting for a sliver of light to strike it just so and make it found. If he found the missing diamond and returned it to the grocer, maybe all would be forgiven.

He explores for over an hour. Finding nothing that connects to the treasure, he returns to the boulders and climbs to the top to see what he can see. Over the trees, he identifies the tops of two chimneys belonging to the Phipps Estate. The only sounds are nature sounds – hoots and clicks and chirrups. He stays a while to see if anyone shows up in the wood. Eventually, he gets bored. He climbs down to forage along the creek, finding late summer berries next to the ravine where he and Harold had played soldier.

Wandering along the creek, he recognizes a cluster of dark mushrooms growing from the trunk of a fallen oak tree. These growths are different colors but they remind him of the turkey tail his ma collected last winter. Maybe they'll taste like it, too. The whole clump gives the impression of a dark waterfall growing out of the tree bark. He takes his pocketknife and slices several scallops from the tree. They're dry and bitter, but he makes himself eat them. If only he had a skillet and some lard, maybe a little salt, he could fix these mushrooms right up.

He's on his way back to the stones when he hears his name being called. He picks up speed, staying low in the dim light of the wood. He climbs to a spot in the rocks where he's hidden from view. He knows it's Mr. Joe. The back of his throat tickles from wanting so badly to call out, to run down and make himself known. He clamps a hand over his mouth to stay quiet. If he calls out now, he'll cause trouble for Mr. Joe, a man who's only been kind to him.

"Earl! Earl, where are you?"

The snap of a nearby branch makes him think the older man must be walking along the creek bank. From there, Mr. Joe can see the large stones. Will he come closer?

"Boy, wherever you are, come talk to me."

He does not come close. The sound of Mr. Joe's voice grows fainter as he continues to follow the creek north. Earl drops his head onto his knees, desperate with worry. If only he was smarter, he would know what to do.

TWENTY-EIGHT

Voices wake him. He hadn't meant to fall asleep. At first, the voices are part of a dream, something jarring that makes him feel anxious inside. Then he's listening to the voices, making out words, and dimly aware he's no longer sleeping. One voice is gravelly, the other high and tight. He lifts his chin, focuses his attention. Two men stand at the base of the boulders. Their words carry upward to the place where he hides, curled within a crevice.

"What'd you get?"

"Candlesticks, some kind of silver tongs like claws."

A metallic clinking sets Earl's teeth on edge.

"What's these for anyways?" says the gravelly voice.

"Sugar cubes, mebbe." There's a sound of shuffling. "Hot damn. Look at this. Do ya think this here picture frame is silver?"

"Let me see."

"Whadaya want me to do with the photo?"

"I don't care. Toss it in the crik."

"Right."

"Any jewelry?"

"Rings an' things was shut up in a cab'net. I di'nt have time to pick the lock."

Earl winces at the cuss words that spew forth at this news. He's afraid to move from his spot, afraid to make any sound that might give him away.

"Boss, why haven't we hit the red-brick house?"

"There's always someone home."

"Not on Sunday mornings. I been watching. Family goes to church Sundays. The housekeeper don't come on weekends. Their cook leaves right after the family does."

Earl holds his breath, waiting for what might come next.

"What about the gardener?"

"I ain't never seen him Sundays. I seen a kid a couple o' times in the back."

Earl's head races with more thoughts than he knows what to do with, even as the two men fall silent. Perhaps they're pondering this new information. He wonders how long he can keep still when the conversation continues.

"As long as we entered through the front, no one'd know we was even there. We could be in and out in ten minutes."

"Whadaya thinking, Boss? What if we pretended we was painters?"

"That's one idea. We could get buckets and ladders."

"Buckets could hold a lot of stuff."

"Let me think on it. Right now, I gotta git back. Can you carry this haul to the truck?"

"Sure, Boss."

Earl sits quietly within the hidden space, listening to the sounds of the men packing and clearing the area. A thin bar of light flickers, rising higher on the stone as the sun goes down. He watches the sun streaks and thinks about all the homes he's passed on his evening explorations. Thinking about the fine houses reminds him of a story his ma used to tell. None of the houses he saw was built from straw. That would be silly. A smile flits across his lips and is gone. However, there are houses of stick… built from wide boards with striped awnings over porches. Two houses are built of gray stone. And, not surprisingly, there are houses of brick. There's yellow brick and white brick and brown brick. He only knows one house built from red brick. Maybe the men he overheard want to rob the Phipps Estate.

He presses both hands against his eyes. He pictures Mr. and Mrs. Phipps. He ponders them taking in a boy they don't know, someone who done somethin' terrible. He pictures Mr. Joe placing a hand on his shoulder and explaining to him about the plants in the garden, how special they are, how useful. He considers his new friend, Harold, trusting him to guard a treasure while he goes home to a sad ma in a dark house.

In his heart, Earl knows what he has to do. He failed to protect his own family. He doesn't want to be responsible for failing to protect Harold's. But what can one boy with a slowpoke brain do against two bad men?

Feeling a rumble in his belly, he sucks on the inside of his cheek, trying to figure what to do for his supper. He considers the pig trough and wrinkles his nose. He doesn't want slop for supper. He doesn't want dry mushrooms sliced from an old tree or berries gathered from a ravine. He doesn't want to spend the night tucked inside hard rocks or hidin' beneath a pile of straw on a stall floor.

His ma always told him to look for a bright side. Earl tries it now. First, he thinks about the worst thing that can happen. If he came out of hidin' and got sent to jail for stealin' a ring, the police would have to feed him, right? There's ladies at that nice Salvation Army, like Miss Hazel, who won't let him starve. At least, he doesn't think so. And if he's in the jailhouse and another house gets broke into, the sheriff will know then that Earl's not a robber.

Still, he worries. He worries he might get kept in jail. He might get kept for things he has done – like telling a lie or keepin' a secret that shouldn't o' been kept. For helpin' his pa steal from Mr. Wilkins' store or poison Mr. Stan's well. Or, scariest of all, he might be kept in a cage forever and ever for shootin Pa's gun when he wasn't s'posed to touch it, and what that had meant for him and all his family – and for Ma who looked after him with tenderness.

He's feelin' pretty low when his thoughts turn to Mr. Joe. What would Mr. Joe want him to do? When he asks himself this question, the answer comes easy. He'd want Earl to look after Harold's grandma and grandpa.

Feeling his way carefully, he climbs down from the boulders. He walks to the creek and scoops a handful of water to splash his face, keeping an eye out for snakes. He sinks his arms into the water and scrubs his skin, even under his fingernails. He stares at his reflection in the water and pulls loose bits of straw from his hair and lets the stalks flutter to the ground.

From the creek bank, he sees a piece of paper snagged against a tree root. Earl remembers what the man said about throwing somethin' in the creek. He lifts the torn image with his fingertips and presses the wet paper against his trousers. Holding the photo up to the light, he can make out a woman. She has a kind smile. Seeing it, he feels homesickness spread into ev'ry part of him. Standing on one side of her is a person who's been torn partway, a young boy maybe. And on her other side is a girl with dark curls who makes him think of Lucy. Is his sister happy? He hopes so. More than anything, he hopes they'll be a family again someday. Like the family in the photo, but together, not torn. Carefully, he tucks the picture into his pants pocket.

A short while later, he lifts the latch on the back gate and lets himself into the garden. The door to the toolshed is shut, but it opens easily. Mr. Joe left it unlocked for him when he departed for the day. This small action reassures Earl he might still have a place here.

He approaches the house and knocks softly on the back door. When there's no answer, he knocks harder.

"Well, I'll be." Cook appears behind the screen. "You sure gave us a fright, Earl. Where you been?"

"Hidin'," he says, ducking his head slightly.

"Hiding where?" She waves a hand like she's wiping away the question. "Never mind that. Come inside and sit at the table. You must be starving." Pushing open the screen door, she steps forward to grab Earl's arm, tugging him into the kitchen.

"Are Mr. and Mrs. Phipps home?" He rubs nervous hands down his trousers. "I need to talk to 'em. It's important."

"Don't you think you should eat first?"

"No ma'am. I think I better speak to 'em." He's not entirely sure they'll want to feed him once he speaks his piece. His eyes dart to meet Cook's. "Do I look presentable?" He glances down at his shirt, stained from the barn and the woods and him having used it as a rag to wipe his face. "I should have changed into a different shirt."

"Don't you worry. You look fine. I'll fetch Mrs. Phipps. She'll be glad to see you're safe."

After she leaves the room, Earl rocks slowly back and forth. In minutes, he hears Cook coming down the hallway to the kitchen. From the footsteps, he can tell there's two folks with her and they're chattin' softly.

"Earl, honey, we're glad to see you've returned to us." Mrs. Phipps approaches and stands beside him. She has silver hair and tiny lines on her face. Her blue eyes look tired, but also clear and kind.

He takes a breath and reaches for his courage. "Thank you, ma'am. I should prob'ly explain why I didn't work today. The grocer was goin' to call the sheriff, on account of a ring me and Harold found in the woods. It scared me 'cause I didn't want to go back to the jailhouse. I didn't know the ring was stolen, ma'am, honest, I didn't, but that's no excuse. I should have let Mr. Joe know I found it. And I shouldn't have run away. I'm sorry. I'm ready to take my punishment."

She pats his arm. "Earl, you can come to us with anything that's troubling you. I hope you know that."

He watches the woman, tryin' to make sure she's not puttin' something over on him. He's spent very little time with Mr. and Mrs. Phipps. It begins to dawn on him that running away may have been unnecessary. The kindness in her eyes makes him think it might be okay to ask a question.

"Was the ring we found… was it the same ring that was stole from Miz. Brooks?"

"I believe so." Mrs. Phipps exchanges a glance with the man standing by her side. Mr. Phipps has remained quiet, letting his wife do the talking. Now he speaks up.

"It appears there have been several burglaries in this area over the summer. The police did stop by the house yesterday evening, Earl. They wanted to speak with you in order to find out where the ring had been found. We visited with Harold this morning and he explained you boys were out in the woods digging for treasure. There was no way you could have known the ring you discovered had been stolen."

Earl nods, accepting this explanation. "Thank you for telling me, sir. That's good to know. I expect the men who stole that ring are going to rob your house next."

There's a moment of stunned silence. "I beg your pardon. Did you say the robbers are coming here?"

Mrs. Phipps' brow crinkles and she reaches out to touch his arm. "What do you know, Earl?"

"I was hidin' in the large stones and I fell asleep. I didn't mean to, but I did. When I woke up, there was two men talkin'. They had stuff with them. I didn't see what they had, but I heard 'em talking about it. There was some silver, I think, candlesticks." He removes the torn photo from his pocket and hands it to the woman. "This one feller, he threw this in the creek. I'm pretty sure it came from a picture frame they stole. They never did say which house they robbed."

"But you heard them say something about our house?"

"The men said they could pretend to be painters and break into the red-brick house. I don't know but one red-brick house, ma'am. And that's this one, in case you was wonderin'. They said they would do it on a Sunday morning 'cause that's when folks is gone, I guess on account of it's the day of rest." He takes a deep breath and releases it. "I guess they been watchin' the house."

"I see." Mrs. Phipps turns to Cook, who's hovering in the background. "Cook, why don't you fix a plate for Earl?"

"Yes ma'am. Right away."

"Earl, you've been very responsible to come and tell us this." Mr. Phipps' expression is grave. "If we invited the sheriff here to speak with you tomorrow, do you think you could tell him everything you've told us?"

"The sheriff?" Earl hears the tremor in his voice. He's sure gonna get it now.

"You have nothing to worry about." Mr. Phipps takes the photo his wife hands him and stares at it, his mouth set in grim lines. "We'll be right here with you the whole time. The sheriff is going to listen to your story, and he may ask you questions." He makes eye contact with Earl and holds his gaze, his expression serious. "Any details you can remember will be important. We want to help the authorities catch these men and bring them to justice. Would you be willing to assist the police in this investigation?"

"Golly." He looks from Mr. Phipps to Mrs. Phipps. When they put it like that, it seems like it's his duty. He doesn't know what to do. On the one hand, he definitely does not want to talk to the sheriff. That man is not his friend. On the other hand, these folks have treated him real good and they don't seem like they want to punish him. He swallows past somethin' stuck in his throat. Finally, he nods.

"Thank you, Earl."

Cook sets a plate on the table along with a tall glass of milk. She motions for him to come and sit.

Mrs. Phipps gives him a gentle smile. "We're going to let you eat your supper now. I imagine you're starving." She places a light hand on his shoulder. "Thank you for coming to us with this information. Mr. Phipps and I are fortunate to have you looking out for us."

With a final nod from Mr. Phipps, the couple leave the room. Earl glances at Cook. "Golly."

"Sit and eat. You're going to need your wits when you speak with the sheriff."

TWENTY-NINE

He rubs his belly with satisfaction, pleased to be in his own bed surrounded by familiar smells. He breathes in the scent of potting soil, grass clippings and rusted iron. "It's a fine thing," he says aloud, enjoying the use of his voice after a day of being silent. To some, his bed may seem like a thin mattress in a cinder block toolshed, something to sneer at. For Earl, it's become something to treasure, so much better than hard rocks or a barn floor. He's asleep before the crickets make their first strum of the evening.

When morning sunlight pierces a crack around the door frame, he leaps from bed, bouncing at the prospect of facing Mr. Joe. He wants to say he's sorry, for running away first of all. Also, for not comin' back when he heard Mr. Joe callin' his name. It's going to be a hard thing, but Earl knows he has to do it.

He swallows a biscuit filled with fried egg and bacon, barely taking the time to chew. He thanks Cook for the meal, overwhelmed with gratitude. A biscuit with egg in it is better than pig slop. After washing his breakfast down with cold water from the pump, he stands at the gate, gazing down the driveway.

Eager to set the day in motion, he shifts from one foot to the other. A sudden thought has him racing to the shed to throw open the door. He double-checks that everything inside is neat and organized. He dashes back to the gate. He watches the road, keeping an eye out for strange fellers loitering about who might be robbers. All is quiet. When he doesn't think he can take one more minute of waiting, he sees Mr. Joe turn off the road and head toward the house.

He opens the latch and waves his arm as high as he can, pleased to see Mr. Joe wave in return. He might be in trouble, but he can't help the grin spreading across his face. Every time he tries to rein it back, it breaks out again. He trots down the driveway, unable to hide his happiness.

"G'morning, Mr. Joe!"

"Good morning, Earl." Mr. Joe clasps his arm. "You sure did have me worried. Where you been? I looked everywhere."

"I know you did, Mr. Joe. I sure am sorry I made you worry. I got scared on account of the woman at the grocer said my ring was stolen from Miz. Brooks and she was goin' to call the sheriff. And I didn't steal the ring but, all the same, I was afraid the sheriff would make me go to the jailhouse, and I didn't want to go."

"You should have come to me. I would try to help you; I hope you know that."

He nods his head vigorously. "Yes sir, I should have done that."

"Did you speak to Mr. and Mrs. Phipps?"

"Last night. Cook gave me my supper, and I told Mr. and Mrs. Phipps big news. I told 'em the robbers might go after their house next."

Mr. Joe stops in his tracks. "Boy, what did you say?"

Earl explains everything, about how he'd been hiding so he didn't have to go back to the jailhouse and about falling asleep in the stones and then overhearing the robbers' plan to break into the Phippses' house come Sunday morning.

"Whooee! That's something, Earl. That sure is something."

"Yes sir. Mr. and Mrs. Phipps think so, too. After morning chores, Cook is going to call me to speak to the sheriff. Mr. Phipps said the sheriff absolutely will not take me to the jailhouse and I can have his word on it. The sheriff is going to come this afternoon and I'm s'posed to tell him everythin' I heard."

"Well, that's good. I sure am glad you stepped up. That's a fine thing."

A warm glow passes through him.

"Tell me, are you feeling up to some work today? If you're not a hundred percent, I can start on my own. You could join me after your interview with the sheriff."

"I ate breakfast and I am ready to go to work. I am definitely ready for some work." Earl's about to bust open with the energy gallopin' through his body.

"That's what I like to hear." Mr. Joe claps him on the back then leads the way to the greenhouse. "I've got seeds we can start for the fall flower beds. Mrs. Phipps likes to have lots of color around the house when the leaves change. She puts on this autumn gala every year with pumpkins and candlelight and Cook prepares apple fritters and hot cider. Wait till you see. We'll have every color of chrysanthemum, like a rainbow, Earl, and black-eyed Susans for the bees and butterflies. We'll mix those in with red celosia and giant clusters of marigolds."

"Golly. I don't know any of those plants."

"You will soon. Autumn is my favorite season in the garden. It's hard work, I won't lie. But it'll be worth it once we've transplanted the flowers into their beds and you can see for yourself how fine everything looks."

"Can I put the plants into the ground?"

"Absolutely. And I'm going to need your help tending to the sprouts till the plants are hardy enough to survive outdoors."

"Yes sir." Excited by Mr. Joe's vision of transformation, Earl stretches to his tiptoes then bounces once more for good measure. "I'm ready."

For the next few hours, he assists Mr. Joe at the long worktable. Bags of seeds clutter the surface. A parked wheelbarrow holds mounds of rich soil. Buckets of compost mixed with strips of newspaper and crushed eggshells provide a starter mix. As they put seeds into small pots, Mr. Joe keeps up a running chatter about what they're doing.

"See this hard coat on the outside of the seed, Earl?"

"Yes sir."

"This is the seed's protection. It's a barrier against damage or injury. This outside coating protects the seed even if a wild bird eats it, allowing it to survive the bird's stomach juices so it can sprout wherever the bird's droppings land."

"That must be a strong seed to survive bird poop."

"Exactly. Which is why I put these seeds in water to soak before I left last night. It softens the outer shell."

"Mr. Joe, how does this little seed make a flower? It don't seem possible."

"That's the beauty of nature, son. Inside this tiny seed is an embryo – sort of like a baby chick inside an egg. This baby plant needs nutrition to survive, so there's tissue around it and everything a plant needs to make roots and shoots and leaves."

"That's a lot of stuff in one little seed."

"Indeed." He takes one of the pots into his hand and fills it with soil and compost. Rays of light streaming through the glass illuminate each motion. "Germination occurs when you get just the right blend of elements needed by each type of flower."

Earl frowns, his mind scrambling to process new words.

Mr. Joe appears to understand his confusion. "Earl, you understand what temperature is, right? And sunlight? And you understand that your body takes nourishment from the things you eat in order to be healthy?"

"Like Ma's kraut juice can fix a sore throat?"

"Sort of like that, yes." A smile breaks across his face. "Each plant needs its own type of kraut juice in order to thrive. There's a perfect blend of temperature and sunlight, water and nutrients, that's just right for each kind of plant. And when the seed receives the right mix of these elements, well, it swells. And when it can't swell anymore, it bursts wide open."

"It's broken?"

"Becoming broken is an important step – understand? – to allow the new life to come through. After the rupture, the plant begins to grow. One part grows downward into a root that anchors it to the ground, while the top grows upward into a green shoot that unfurls through the soil where it can catch the sunlight. With sufficient time and proper care, it will transform into something glorious."

Earl feels dazed by this vision of dark magic. "I seen things grow on Farmer Tate's farm. I had no idea so much stuff was goin' on a person can't see."

"What type of plants did he grow?"

"Every spring, Farmer Tate made a hotbed to start tabacca seeds. I guess they didn't need much light right then, 'cause he'd cover 'em so's they was in darkness, but he give 'em lots of water. Then one day, he'd uncover the bed and there'd be green sprouts everywhere. When they was ready, each sprout was moved into one of the field rows. I helped one time and I thought my back would never straighten out."

"Planting is hard work, Earl. Whether it's in furrows or flower beds. Your back and knees take the brunt of it."

"Yes sir. But those tabacca were pretty plants. They'd grow real bushy and the leaves were long and green and they smelled like…" He stumbles, unsure how to continue. The plants had smelled like earth, like home, like everything he loved in the world. He falls quiet.

After a moment, Mr. Joe casts a sideways glance.

"Earl, you explained what happened at the grocer's the other day, about why you run off."

"I got mixed up."

"I understand. Anyone can get mixed up. It's a good idea to have someone to talk to about things, Earl. That's my advice. The next time you feel sad or scared or confused, you talk to somebody. Talk to me or Cook or even to Mrs. Phipps. It's helpful to hear another point of view."

"That's a smart thing you're sayin'. I know that now." Earl imitates Mr. Joe's movements, adding more soil to a pot. "You know, I sure am sorry about another thing – besides runnin' off, I mean."

"What's that?"

"I bolted out of the grocer's so fast, I never got to finish my Co'Cola. And it was good, jus' like I remembered." He feels sweat pooling on his lower back and imagines what it would be like to have a nice cold drink that very minute.

"I tell you what. Once these robbers are caught, how about if you and I take a walk down to the grocer together? You can apologize to him for running like you did. Running off that way might have made him think you were guilty, Earl, even though you weren't. He doesn't know you like I do, so how would he know what you said was true? But once the robbers are caught, then he'll know it and you can look him in the eye. And we'll each get ourselves a nice, cold drink. How about that?"

He nods, taking Mr. Joe's words as a solemn promise. "That's a swell idea."

At lunchtime, Cook hands each of them a plate of sliced tomatoes and cucumbers covered in salt and pepper, along with a wedge of butter cheese and a biscuit. After he's finished eating, Earl washes at the hand pump. He changes into a clean pair of trousers and the shirt that used to belong to Mr. Walter. He's nervous about meeting the sheriff and holds tight onto his arms, trying to keep from shakin' apart.

"It's going to be okay, Earl." Mr. Joe places both hands on the boy's shoulders, anchoring him in place. "Take a deep breath and blow it out. All you got to do is tell this man what you told me."

"How do I look?" Earl lifts a hand to his hair and presses it down in the back. "Sometimes I get a cowlick. If you want to take the shears to my hair, you can. Miss Hazel, she's the lady from the Salvation Army, she cut it one time but she didn't know about my cowlick and it stuck up somethin' awful."

"We'll take care of that another day. You look fine."

They both glance up when Cook comes to the back door and motions for Earl to come inside.

Mr. Joe gives his arm a reassuring squeeze. "I'll be here when you're done. If you have any nervousness, you look to Mrs. Phipps. She'll help you out."

"I'll do that. Yes sir."

Earl follows Cook into the house. For the first time since arriving at the Phipps Estate, he leaves the familiarity of the garden for parts unknown, staying close behind Cook as she navigates the house, turning down one hallway, then another. He bumps into her when she halts outside the entrance to a small sitting room.

"Mrs. Phipps, Mr. Phipps, Earl is here to speak with the sheriff."

He bites his lip as Cook turns to look at him. She gives him an encouraging wink, then makes her way back toward the kitchen. He takes a hesitant step, poking his head into the brightly lit room.

"Come inside, Earl. You can have a seat next to me, here on the sofa." Mrs. Phipps rests her hand on the seat cushion.

He notices Mr. Phipps standing near a small hearth and gives him a head bob. A man he doesn't know is seated in an armchair covered with large, yellow flowers. He's glad he changed into clean clothes. This is the nicest room he's ever seen in his life – full of pretty colors and brass bowls that gleam from frequent polishing.

The seated man rises and approaches with his hand extended. "Earl, my name is Sheriff Warren. It's nice to meet you."

He shakes the man's hand, filled with wonder and relief. "Why, you're not the sheriff I know at all."

"No, Earl. I don't believe we've met. Why don't you take a seat?"

He sits on the sofa next to Mrs. Phipps and listens attentively as she explains what's going to happen. "The sheriff is going to ask you a few questions. Take your time answering. All you have to do is share as much as you can remember from the woods yesterday – the words you heard, what the men's voices sounded like; any details you're able to recall will be important. Can you do that?"

"Yes ma'am, I'll do my best."

The sheriff resumes his seat and withdraws a notebook. "That's good, Earl. Let's begin."

THIRTY

The following Sunday before daybreak, Earl stands at the back fence with Mr. Phipps as he opens the gate for two police officers entering the property. The officers approach through the woods, finding their way in the dark with a small lantern to guide them.

Surprisingly calm given the circumstances, Mrs. Phipps waits at the kitchen door and invites the men into the house. She gives Earl a pat as he brings up the rear of their small party. Cook hands each man a ham biscuit and a cup of hot coffee. "'Watch y'all don't break anything, hear?" Her voice is low, meant only for the officers. "I don't want any of Mrs. Phipps' pretty things getting damaged whilst you're trying to catch them thieves red-handed. I packed away a few things but the missus wanted the place to look normal."

The men accept the breakfast, their expressions growing appreciative as they take their first bite. "We'll do our best, ma'am."

Earlier in the week, the men had discussed their plans with Mr. and Mrs. Phipps. Now they go over the details one more time to ensure everyone is clear. Earl stands in the corner and watches the officers quietly.

After concluding their meeting and the meal, the policemen wipe their hands on napkins. Earl nods his approval, knowing how a greasy hand can leave a mark on a polished surface. They thank Cook for the nourishment, real polite, and make their way to assigned areas of the house to wait and watch.

One man takes a position behind pale blue draperies in the front parlor. On their previous examination of the house, the police determined there were valuable items on display in the parlor likely to be of interest to the robbers. Earl makes several passes by the room until the officer shoos him away with a sharp motion.

The second man hides near the dining room. Earl believes this is on account of the robbers like silver and Mrs. Phipps has plenty of that. He watches the man settling in, finding a spot with a view of the front entry. The officer wears a black belt with a baton attached, plus a leather holster snapped around his revolver. This is joined by a thin chain and a length of rope, but it's the metal cuffs clipped to his belt that make Earl uneasy.

Observing the locations of the men, he remembers the ring he and Harold found in the woods, the one that was stole from Miz. Brooks. He recollects his ma's slender gold band, discovered by Frieda in the nightstand. Jewelry is something folks like to keep close. "Shouldn't someone be on the second floor?" he asks the officer.

"If an intruder takes the stairs, I'll see him. I can pursue and apprehend him, while Officer Davis neutralizes the downstairs man."

"Oh."

"Don't worry. We're trained in arrest tactics. We know what to do."

Earl decides these men are alright and exits the house without complaint when Mrs. Phipps tells him it's time. As soon as Harold arrives with his father, the family departs for church as usual. Cook pins the blue hat to her head and leaves to visit her sister. Earl understands that anyone watching the house will see an ordinary Sunday morning.

After the house is empty – except for the two hidden officers – he locks the toolshed and lets himself out the front gate. He whistles slightly as he heads toward the trolley stop. The whistling was Mr. Joe's idea. He thought it would add a special touch, like Earl didn't have a care in the world.

In his pants pocket, he possesses two shiny nickels. Mrs. Phipps gave him careful instruction. He's to take the trolley to town and explore on his own till all the churches let out. After the church bells peal the noon hour, then he can return to the garden. By then, Mr. and Mrs. Phipps will be home and the police will be gone.

Earl feels uneasy but tries to pretend everything is fine. He's out of the garden, on his own, and with money in his pocket. He slips a hand into his trousers to make sure the coins are still there. Arriving at the trolley station in good time, he decides to sit a spell. The platform is empty and the single bench unoccupied. Loitering near the edge, he rubs both nickels through the fabric of his trousers. It's enough money to buy a day-trip ticket, plus a soda pop in town. It takes him a few minutes to realize somethin' else. If he doesn't go to town, he can keep his two nickels. Then he can afford a bottle of soda pop *and* a Moon Pie. Or he can wait till Harold's able to join him and they can both have a treat. The abundance of options makes him light-headed.

Hearing the trolley bell in the distance, he presses his lips together, gazing absently down the track. He can't buy a soda pop now cause it's Sunday morning and the store's closed. The trolley will arrive in a few minutes and he's s'posed to get on. Only, he's unsure how to go about it the right way. What if he gets off at the wrong stop? What if the trolley takes him somewhere far and he can't get back? He wonders if he should have mentioned to Mrs. Phipps he's never ridden the trolley before.

Then he wonders what's taking place back at the Phipps Estate.

From his spot on the bench, he becomes aware of a hum beneath his skin, a sense of something he can't put a word to. It occurs to him he should be at the house, to keep an eye out. Mrs. Phipps prob'ly hadn't thought about that, about how helpful he could be. She might not know how good he is at bein' invisible.

He rises from the bench. Instead of heading back the way he'd come, he takes the long way round to the other side of the woods. The last time he was at the boulders, one of the robbers mentioned having a truck parked close. He'd sounded like a big fella. Earl worries he might be a mean fella, too.

He sneaks around the edge of the woods, trying to find where the robbers might have hidden a truck for their getaway. He smacks his forehead when a new thought comes to him. The robbers said they might pretend to be house painters. If they do that, they'll pull their truck into the driveway like they's s'posed to be there. The more he thinks about it, the more it makes sense to him.

Turning toward the Phippses' place, he cuts through the woods. He moves like Harold did when they was playing soldier. He ducks behind one tree, peeks around, then darts to the next tree. Soon, he's crouching in the shadow of three thick magnolias surrounded by shrubs. From here, he's got a clear view of the Phippses' front porch.

He doesn't have to wait long. He catches his breath when a beat-up, black truck turns into the driveway. The vehicle makes its way up the long drive and brakes to a stop. Three men climb out and walk around to the back of the truck. They act like they're in no hurry, like they have ev'ry right to be there. Earl's nearly convinced hisself, they're so natural in their movements. Maybe they aren't robbers, he considers briefly, maybe they's house painters. All along, the plan was to have the house painted while Mr. and Mrs. Phipps was attendin' church. Then he has another thought. Maybe they aren't robbers or house painters. Maybe this is the police pretendin' to be house painters. Then he dismisses that idea too. The police are inside the house right this minute, waitin' to spring out and catch the robbers. He pictures them inside. Waiting.

Two of the men remove cans and tarps from the truck while the third carries an extension ladder to the house and props it against the brick.

"Golly," he whispers. The robbers are outside the house in broad daylight, right where anyone could see them.

He glances toward the road. It's quiet on a Sunday morning. Even if someone was out for a drive and noticed something unusual, they might not think to investigate.

One of the men climbs the ladder toward the upstairs window. He wears a tool belt buckled around his waist. Removing a crowbar, he pries open the window. The man pauses to stare in all directions. Earl presses himself to the ground behind the tangle of shrubs. He peers through a gap in the bushes. The man lifts his leg over the sill and enters the house.

He shifts his attention to the front porch where the other two men stand with large paint buckets. One of the men wears white coveralls. Earl can see the pails swinging lightly in their hands and realizes they're empty. He remembers the sunny sitting room he visited, how everything gleamed. It hurts his heart to think of them bein' in that pretty room and spoilin' it.

Returning his gaze to the top floor, he tries to detect movement and fails. All three robbers are now inside the house. The police said they was expecting two robbers and there's two police. Only now there's three robbers and two police. He chews his finger, waiting and watching. Should he move closer? Time passes. He's too far away to hear anything. His eyes move from one window to the next, anxious for any sign of activity. Have the police caught the bad guys? Are the bad men inside already bein' handcuffed?

He blinks when the second-story robber climbs out the upstairs window. A bulging pillowcase bangs his hip as he makes his way awkwardly down the ladder.

Where are the police? Earl wonders, feeling his agitation build. *Why aren't they coming out to catch this man?*

Panicked at the idea one of these phony painters might get away, he leaves the shadow of the trees and dashes toward the house. As soon as the man reaches the ground, Earl launches himself. The robber swivels to evade him, but he grabs the man's leg. The man stumbles then rights himself, with Earl hanging on for dear life. The man takes a few steps forward, grunting with the effort. It doesn't feel good to scrape along the ground, but Earl clenches his teeth and holds on harder. Heavy items inside the pillowcase clatter together as the robber trudges forward, dragging Earl's dead weight behind him. Suddenly, the man swings the pillowcase, striking him in the head.

"Ow!"

"Get offa me, boy, or I'll whack you agin!"

"You better drop that pillowcase. Those are Mrs. Phipps' things. They don't belong to you."

The man swears, swings the case a second time and misses.

Using his fingers, Earl inches himself up the man's leg. He feels the man's trousers slip.

"You better stop movin'. You're gonna be nekkid any second. You know you can't run if your trousers are down."

"Get the hell away from me!"

He has a sudden memory of his pa teaching him and Orbry to wrestle. He hadn't cared for the lessons on account of Orbry got all the praise and Earl got all the slaps, but he never forgot 'em. Maneuvering to get a better grip on the man, he pivots, thrusting his hip, and sends the man to the ground with a thud. Earl's legs strain to keep him still. With one hand, the robber maintains his hold on the pillowcase. With the other, he slams a fist into Earl's head.

Earl looks at the man with astonishment as lights explode behind his eyes. His head's filled with images racing one after the other so fast he can barely keep up: his pa's twisted face lifting a board, eyes black with fury. He sees his ma – Ma! – with a split lip and puffy eyes, sweeping him up with an expression of terror on her face. He sees his brother, Kurt, grab his pa and wrench him sideways. A sharp pain sears through Earl's head and he bellows like a wounded animal.

With renewed energy, he grabs the arms of the robber, pins him to the ground.

"Be still," he huffs. "Be still right now."

At that moment, the front door busts open and two men stumble through, locked in a scuffle. One of the police officers pulls his arm back and jabs the robber's jaw with a move that snaps the man's head. Without pausing for breath, the officer lifts his captive and slams him on the grass, then flips and cuffs him. The second officer steps outside, shoving the remaining robber before him, cuffed and quiet. The officer stares at the front lawn where Earl struggles to contain the third robber.

"Hold him," the man shouts. "Don't let go." He steers his prisoner to the edge of the porch. "Lie down." The man lays on his belly. Pulling a length of rope from his duty belt, the officer tethers the robber's legs by looping the rope around his thighs just above the knee and pulling tight. He uses the other end of the rope to secure the hobbled man to the porch column.

As a police patrol wagon turns into the driveway, the officer motions to Earl. "Can you stand him up without losing him? I have to get another pair of cuffs."

The robber twists on the ground, fear of capture giving him renewed energy. Earl clenches his legs tight, tighter, until the man expels a whoosh of air, giving in. Once he's subdued, a worn-out Earl helps the man to stand, keeping a firm grip on his arms. Defeated, the robber drops the pillowcase as the officer retrieves a pair of metal cuffs from the newly arrived vehicle and secures each wrist. Recalling somethin' Cook said, Earl scrutinizes the robber's hands. There ain't a speck of red on 'em.

With the prisoner secure, Earl steps back, feeling woozy. Gingerly, he lifts the pillowcase and cradles it to his chest.

"Do you need this?" he asks.

"Those items need to be catalogued so they can be used as evidence against these men. Once the court case is concluded, everything will be returned."

"Is it alright if I hold the bag till Mrs. Phipps comes home? I won't touch nothin'." He figures she'll want to see for herself what the robbers took.

The officer puffs out a breath, struggling to keep his prisoner in line. "If I leave it with you, I got to put your name on the chain of custody form."

Earl looks at him.

The cuffed man tries to trip the officer, who scowls and slaps his head. "Watch yourself." He glances back at Earl. "Don't touch anything in the bag. Sit on the front porch where I can see you. I'll be there in a minute to take a statement."

"From me?"

"You disabled one of the robbers. Good work, by the way. Give me a sec. I have to put this fella in the wagon, then I'll come back for the pillowcase. Don't touch anything."

Concentrating on each step, Earl makes his way to the now-empty front porch. Reaching out a hand to make sure he doesn't miss the bench and hit the ground instead, he sits. He raises trembling fingers to the spot above his ear where he was struck and flinches from the pain.

"I'm gonna be awful mad if I get dumber 'cause of this," he mumbles.

He closes his eyes to be calm and tries to concentrate when the police officer returns and starts asking questions. Spying the Phippses' automobile turn into the driveway, he heaves a sigh of relief. "Missus Phipps is here now. I need to show her this stuff."

"We'll bring her over. Don't worry. You sit tight."

"Do you have more questions?"

"I've got what I need. I'll return with Mrs. Phipps and collect the pillowcase."

Earl waves to Harold as the boy exits the car. He runs over, his eyes jumping with curiosity.

"Did the police catch the burglars?"

"They caught three," he says, rubbing his eyes tiredly. "I thought there'd be two but there was three. I guess two robbers was stealin' stuff downstairs, and one robber was stealin' stuff upstairs. All the stuff in this here pillowcase was taken by a man on the second floor. The police say they have to take this stuff because it's..." He pauses, hesitates over the word. "Eva..."

"Evidence."

"Yeah." He opens the pillowcase so Harold can peek inside.

"They took Grandmother's music box. She won't be happy about that."

"The police promise they'll give everythin' back when they's done," he says.

"I thought you were going to town."

He wipes his mouth and looks out toward his hiding place near the driveway. "I started to, then I had another thought. I thought I might stay nearby and be a watchout."

The officer returns, escorting Mrs. Phipps. "I've made a list of items taken from the second floor. Here it is. You can match it against what's in the pillowcase. The stolen goods need to go to the station to be checked into evidence."

"Of course, Officer." She glances at Earl. "Young man, I thought you were going to take the streetcar into town."

"Yes ma'am, I was." He scratches his nose. "Then I didn't."

"Your yard boy tackled one of the robbers as he came out the second-story window," the officer explains. "My partner and I had our hands full with the ones who entered through the front door. Your boy here made sure the third perpetrator didn't escape."

"Nerts!"

"Harold." Mrs. Phipps places a hand on her grandson. "No slang, please." She turns to Earl. "Young man, I'm indebted to you for your bravery."

He gazes at Mrs. Phipps with wide eyes. Is she talking to him? He glances around, then back to her face. Feeling reassured, he allows himself a small smile.

"Why is the side of your face all red?"

He touches the injury and a shudder runs through him. "The robber hit me," he says, wishing he could lie down.

"Harold, go into the house and bring Earl an ice pack."

"Yes, Grandmother."

She makes a *tut-tut* sound. "You were not to put yourself into harm's way, Earl. That pillowcase is filled with trinkets, nothing more. There's not one stick of anything in that house worth you getting harmed. Do you understand me?" She places a hand on his cheek. "I need you to promise you won't be so reckless in the future."

He meets her gaze, feeling uncertain. He's unsure what 'reckless' means but he thinks she's telling him not to get hisself hurt. He hadn't been trying to get hurt, and he hadn't expected it. It had come as a surprise to him, too. "I'll try to do better, ma'am," he says finally.

"That's all any of us can do."

Harold returns to the porch, breathless, carrying a tea towel full of chipped ice.

Mrs. Phipps takes the cold towel and shifts next to Earl. "Here. Press this where you were struck. Be gentle. It will help reduce swelling."

He hands the pillowcase to the officer and takes the chilled towel from Mrs. Phipps. He holds it for a moment, looking at the older woman, wanting her to press her hand to his cheek again.

"Like this." She applies the ice pack lightly to the side of his head. "Hold it here until I tell you to take it away. Do you understand?"

"Yes ma'am."

With a final, brisk glance to make sure he's following her instructions, she walks with the officer over to the patrol wagon.

Harold sits beside Earl. "Don't mind Grandmother. She tut-tuts like that whenever I get hurt."

The young boy stretches his arm along Earl's shoulders. Side by side, they watch the activities taking place in the yard. One officer keeps an eye on the patrol wagon, crowded now with three handcuffed robbers. Harold's father and grandfather move to Mrs. Phipps' side, forming a protective barrier while she reviews events with the officer in charge.

"Earl, did you really throw yourself on that burglar? That's pretty jake."

"He was tryin' to steal your grandma's pretty things. I was afraid he might get away."

"But you stopped him."

"Yes." He shifts the cold towel to a new position. "I did."

THIRTY-ONE

The side of Earl's head is black and blue for a week then tinged an unsightly yellow for days after that, a reminder of his bravery, or his foolishness, depending upon who you ask. Cook makes a fuss over him until Mr. Joe politely asks her to stop. It's time for Earl to focus on his chores, he tells her.

Which is fine with Earl. He prefers a routine he can count on – sunrise breakfast accompanied by birdsong, the scent of pine and freshly mowed grass; his tin cup hanging on a hook where he can reach it any time he wants. Still, it's a treat when Cook sneaks him a cookie after dinner or gives him an unexpected pat on the cheek. It makes him feel safe in a way he's never felt before. Not even when he lived with Ma after his pa had gone to prison.

He begins to understand he'll never go hungry living behind the big house. There's food enough in the Phippses' pantry to reassure even his demanding belly. One of Mr.

Phipps' workers from the factory delivers two cords of firewood and stacks them behind the shed. Earl realizes he can light the cast iron stove through the coming winter and never run out of heat. For the first time in his life, he doesn't fear that a punch or taunt or sudden tragedy is crouched in wait, something awful he won't see coming. And because this feeling is so pleasant, and so unfamiliar, he frets about it.

Some nights, he opens the tin containing the piece of paper with Pa's release date and considers the day he'll have to face the anger of the man who made him. It puts a lingering dread in his heart that weighs heavy when he's alone at night in the garden.

It's not the only thing that gnaws at him. He's yet to receive a letter from his sister. Is Lucy okay? Is she safe? Is she happy? He knows she can write because he watched her work on her letters with Ma. She knows whole words and could surely write him a page about the place she's at. He misses her all the time now and feels sure she must miss him. He asks Cook to check and double-check the postal delivery. Each time, she reports back there is no letter addressed to Earl Hahn.

He cannot understand it.

It's good that Mr. Joe has a never-ending supply of chores for him to do. Even Harold comes up with a project, something Earl can look forward to as he goes about his day. It's agreed the two boys may build themselves a clubhouse, a place in the trees just for them. Mr. Joe provides spare pieces of wood left from the construction of Mrs. Phipps' side porch. Earl and Harold promise to put the boards to good use, practicing safety at all times.

Each boy receives a small bag of nails and a hammer. They spend most of a Sunday afternoon fetching and climbing, sawing and hammering. It's a big job.

Now, stepping back from the tree, Earl studies the uneven boards making their way up the trunk, stair steps to larger planks that lay crossways over the more even branches. It isn't a high treehouse, and the walls aren't built yet, but it's shaping up fine.

"It's like a watchtower," says Harold. "We can use it to scout enemy troops."

"It's a place to nap with a cool breeze on your face," Earl responds. "Or a safe place to hide."

The other boy hands him a nail. "Can I ask you something?"

With single-minded attention, Earl lays a new board, making subtle shifts until it nestles into the perfect spot. He accepts the nail and positions it above the board. "What?"

"Do you know how to swim?"

"Sure." He hammers the nail, accepts another.

"You do?"

"Pa taught all us boys. We had to swim and row and box and wrestle. He liked when we did athletic stuff." With easy grace, Earl returns the hammer to the loop of his trousers and climbs back along the tree limb to assess his work. "He said when he was a boy growin' up in Germany, all the boys had to know how to swim in the summertime."

"Do you want to come swimming with me next weekend?"

He cocks his head, bracing one hand against the rough bark. "Where?"

"Father wants to take Mother to the lake. He says it will be healthy for her to be outside and enjoy the fresh air. I don't mind going if it makes her happy. It'd be more fun if I could bring someone."

"Golly, Harold. I don't know." The invitation catches him off-guard. It feels like a risk, to leave the safety of the garden. "I guess I'd have to talk to Mr. Joe."

"He's not your pa, you know."

"But he's my boss, ain't he? I don't want him thinkin' I've run off again."

"We'll go Sunday afternoon. That's your day off."

"What about the treehouse? We still got lots to do. Mr. Joe said we could take one of those old tarps from the greenhouse and nail it to the roof for waterproofing."

"We'll work on the treehouse the week after. You don't want to work on it without me anyway, do you? Come with us."

"What'll your ma think? Maybe she won't want me coming to the lake with y'all. Maybe this is s'posed to be a family day, only family."

"Nah. I'll sort it out. You'll see."

He can no longer think of an argument not to join his friend. "Alright." He points to an assortment of tools scattered on the ground. "Pass me that clamp, will ya?"

The proposed day trip already forgotten, Earl secures the next board and prepares to nail it into place.

"Earl?"

"Huh?"

"What do you call someone who refuses to fart in public?"

His face goes blank. He thinks about this a long time

but can't make out how he's supposed to answer. "Golly, I don't know."

"A private tutor." Harold sniggers into his hand.

"What's a tooter?"

"Ah, gee, Earl."

A shaft of light through the trees strikes his eye. He squints, shielding his face with one hand as he stares into the distance. "Sun's goin' down."

"We should clean up and head back."

Earl takes the pocketknife from his trousers and bends over the board he's hammered into place. His tongue pushes through his teeth as he etches letters into the wood. E-R-L. "Earl," he whispers. His ma never worked with him on his schoolin' like she did Lucy, but he'd eavesdropped on enough lessons that he figured he could sign his name.

"Did you put your name on the board?"

"Now everyone will know this place belongs to somebody." He closes the knife with a snap and holds it out to Harold. "Your turn."

The boy climbs beside Earl and accepts the knife. With less concentration but more finesse, he scratches his name into the plank. "There."

Between them, they carry the remaining boards and tools back to the potting shed to store until they can return in two weeks. When everything is put away, Harold runs inside the house. Earl walks to a picnic table, crosses his arms and rests his chin on his hands. Sometimes, if it's not yet time to leave, Harold's allowed to come outside and keep Earl company a while longer.

His hearing perks at the sound of voices coming

through an open window. He realizes Harold and his father are talking about him.

"Why don't you invite one of your school chums?"

"We're going to the lake on Sunday. I spend Sundays with Earl."

"I'm afraid it might set the wrong expectation, Harold, to bring Earl with us."

"Why?"

"Your friends from school, they're… they're age-appropriate. They're maturing at the same rate you are. I understand Earl is your friend now, but you're going to surpass him. If you're honest with yourself, you know you already have. I don't mind if you boys spend time together when you're visiting your grandmother. I know you get bored with no young people around. I just think you're better off inviting one of your friends."

"Earl's my friend. If I go to the lake without him, he'll be here alone all day."

"It's only one day."

"Father, I don't know if any of my friends will be my friends next year. I don't know if I'll go to the lake next year. Earl's my friend today. You'll be busy with mother. And I want to show him the lake."

"Does he even know how to swim?"

"His pa taught him."

"What did you say?"

There's a silence Earl's unable to interpret.

"I beg your pardon," Harold says, his voice stiff. "Earl's father expected his children to have athletic skills. He knows how to swim."

From his seat at the table, Earl hears a sigh and

recognizes it for what it is: the sound of giving in.

"He's going to need swimming attire."

"Yes, sir. I'll inform Grandmother."

Moments later, Harold comes running out the back door. "We're going to the lake, Earl! You and me."

He gestures toward the window. "I could hear your pa. He didn't sound very happy."

"Don't worry. It'll be fun. I promise." Harold climbs onto the picnic table. "When was the last time you went swimming?"

Cautiously, Earl probes his history and locates the memory he's seeking. "It was last summer. Me and my brother swum in the river that runs by Farmer Tate's lower tabacca field. Orbry's a better swimmer than me. He beat me every time."

"Where's your brother now?"

"Oh, he's prob'ly in the Army. He was mean. I don't miss him a lick. I miss my sister, Lucy. When she gets settled, she's goin' to come fetch me."

"I didn't know that."

"Oh, sure."

"Why hasn't she come visit?"

Earl's brows knit together. Sometimes, he can't help wonderin' if Lucy might not want her slow brother around anymore. Then he thinks about how much fun they used to have runnin' around the farm and feels sure she'll come for him.

"I expect she's got to get everythin' ready for me," he says, feeling subdued. He swings a leg over the bench and stands, stretching his arms as far as they'll reach. A gust of air catches his sleeve just right and blows in one side of him and out the other. He shivers. "Are you stiff from all that climbin'? It's different from plantin' flowers or workin' in the garden."

"I feel fine."

"You wait. Tomorrow mornin', ev'ry part of your body's gonna ache like the devil. How many times did you go up and down that tree?"

"I bet you money I'm not sore tomorrow. I bet you a dollar."

He turns wide eyes to his friend. "Golly, Harold, can we wager somethin' else?"

"Ah, never mind." The boy waves away his comment. "I just know I won't be sore."

Earl shakes his head knowingly. "You'll see."

THIRTY-TWO

"Oof." Earl grunts, his first movements of the morning not going well. Most days, he springs from bed, eager to greet the day. He considers springing, and groans. Using gentle fingers, he massages the top of his legs till he decides they're awake enough to support him without buckling.

Weighing each motion, he stands, keeping one hand stretched in case he should fall. He ponders long and hard about takin' a step. He steps, and stops, releasing a shuddering breath. As his limbs loosen, he makes his way to the privy, then to the hand pump. Like a child learnin' to walk, he arrives finally, awkwardly, at the back door. He taps on the wood frame. A distracted Cook hands him a bowl of milky oatmeal.

When Mr. Joe arrives, he notices right away something is amiss. "Earl, are you ailing?"

Earl finishes tying down a young sapling and unbends his body. He braces a hand against his hip. "I can explain.

Me and Harold was up and down this oak in the woods yesterday, sir, buildin' our treehouse. You should see it, Mr. Joe. It's fine. Only, I can see now I might have done too much climbing for one afternoon."

Mr. Joe's lips twitch and it takes him a moment to find his words. "It's obvious you're in discomfort. Go ask Cook for some of her chickweed salve. Once you rub that into your muscles, you'll feel better."

With stiffness in every step, Earl approaches the back door. At his knock, Cook calls for him to come inside. When he steps through the doorway, he's surprised to see the housekeeper from up the road, the same one who accused him of stealing.

He freezes halfway through the doorway.

"Don't stand there letting in flies," Cook says.

He comes all the way inside and lets the door swing shut, slapping him in the behind. He squeezes his hands together, keeping his eyes on the other woman. She's seated at the table with a cup of hot coffee. Cook bustles around the room. A pot of collard greens simmer on the stove, filling the kitchen with steam and an unpleasant odor. He wrinkles his nose, watching as she tosses a pinch of sugar and a splash of white vinegar into the pot. With one eye on the stove and the other on Earl, she motions toward the table.

"I'm not sure you've been properly introduced to my friend, Maevis Fowler. She does housekeeping for the Brooks family."

He bobs his head. "Mornin.'"

Cook turns down the heat and spins to face him. "Was there something you needed?"

"Mr. Joe sent me to fetch some of that chickweed salve you made."

"Is he feeling poorly?"

"It's for me, ma'am, on account of my legs are sore from the tree-climbin' me and Harold done yesterday."

She steps over to the pantry and opens the door. Reaching to a high shelf, she grabs a small tin and hands it to Earl. "Here you go." She closes the door and stares at her friend. "Mae, wasn't there something you wanted to say to Earl?"

The woman frowns at Cook. After a moment, she inclines her head and looks him in the eye.

"Young man, I owe you an apology. I accused you of something you didn't do. I shouldn't have rushed to judgment. I'm sorry I caused you distress."

He watches her uncertainly for a moment then glances at Cook. She nods her head reassuringly.

"Did Missus Brooks get her ring back?" he asks.

"She did. You might be interested to know a police officer came by after the robbers broke in here. I guess the police visited a boarding house where one of the robbers was staying. An officer found stolen items in a trunk, Miz. Brooks' family silver and a bag of jewelry. Everything is going to be returned. She has you to thank for that."

"What about the stone?"

"What's that?"

"The diamond what was missing from the ring. Did they find it?"

"Mizzus Brooks is to go down to the station house tomorrow and examine some loose stones. I guess one of the robbers liked to break apart the jewelry he stole.

Maybe he thought the jewels would be easier to sell that way. Hopefully, one of the stones will be hers."

A weight he hadn't known he had lifts from his shoulders. "Thank you, ma'am. I sure am glad to hear that."

Cook pats his arm. "Okay, Earl. You've got your salve. Go on before Mr. Joe comes looking for you."

Back at the shed, he removes his trousers and rubs the salve into his legs, placing the ointment everywhere it hurts. He's surprised to discover his legs feel better right away. Capping the salve for later, he joins Mr. Joe in the garden. The two work all morning, trimming back the summer growth on the hedges and marking branches for fall pruning.

A couple days later, the tin of salve sits empty, but Earl's pleased to discover he no longer needs it. He feels good as new. Well, except for bein' overheated. The week is ending warm and sticky. Every flower in the garden droops. Most days, he droops too.

"After lunch, let's walk to the trolley stop," says Mr. Joe. "Now that you've settled things with Missus Fowler, it's probably a good idea to clear the air with the grocer."

Earl hasn't been back to the store since the day he run off. After his return to the garden, Cook told him she'd enjoy a walk to the trolley stop with the supply wagon, a welcome break from her routine. He wondered at it but felt grateful not to have to return to the scene of his embarrassment. Every time he remembers how he wet hisself, he wants to disappear. He dreads facing the grocer, but understands Mr. Joe is looking after him to make sure he's a straight fella.

"Mr. Joe?"

"What, Earl?"

"I still got those nickels Mrs. Phipps gave me to take the trolley. Would it be alright if I buy you a treat? On account of how good you been to me."

"Thank you, Earl. Go get those nickels and we'll see what the grocer's got in the store today."

When they step through the tinkling door of the small market, he looks to Mr. Joe in case he wants to say somethin', only he just stands there, lookin' at Earl.

Earl walks to the counter and faces the grocer.

"Sir, I want to say how sorry I am for running away that day, on account of the ring I had. I know it wasn't the right way to behave. Everythin' is okay now cause the robbers what stole it have been caught red-handed, except not really 'cause there was no red on their hands. But maybe there was and I didn't see it. And I spoke with Miz Fowler and her, ah, her Missus Brooks has her ring back from the police, and maybe the stone, too, that was missing from inside it." He pauses to take in air.

The grocer glances at Mr. Joe. "I heard talk the robbers struck the Phippses' place. Is everyone okay?"

"Oh, yessir," says Earl. "The robbers tried to take Mrs. Phipps' pretty things, but the police caught 'em. Well, I helped. But mostly, it was the police."

The grocer holds out his hand. Surprised, Earl reaches to clasp it.

"I appreciate you coming here to let me know how things turned out. I think you deserve a reward, something that will take the edge off this weather we're having." The grocer steps over to the ice chest and removes a cold

Co'Cola. He flips the top and hands it to Earl. "Here you go. On the house."

Earl looks to Mr. Joe, concerned. His boss gives him a wide smile. "He means it's a gift for you."

He looks at the grocer. "Thank you, sir. I'm much obliged." He retrieves the two coins from his pocket and sets them on the counter then sends a hesitant smile toward his boss. "And this is for Mr. Joe so he can get anythin' he wants."

Mr. Joe places a hand on his shoulder. "You go ahead and take your pop out to the bench, Earl. I'll join you in a moment."

Feeling a new lightness in his heart, Earl makes himself comfortable, watching as folks climb on and off the trolley car. As he sips his Co'Cola, he files away a new piece of information: how 'on the house' means he don't have to pay a nickel. The soda slides down his throat like liquid winter, cooling him from the inside. Eventually, Mr. Joe joins him on the bench and unwraps a honey bun. Earl leans back, pleased with the day.

Once his snack is consumed, Mr. Joe sighs with contentment and tosses the wrapper into a trash bin. "That was tasty. Thank you, Earl." He rises from the bench. "Ready to head back?"

The two take their time, in no hurry to resume work on such a muggy afternoon.

"I'm glad we spoke to the grocer, Mr. Joe. That was a good idea you had."

"It's always a good idea to clear up misunderstandings."

"Yes sir. I see that." As they approach the Phipps Estate, Earl notices an old truck parked by the house. He grips Mr. Joe's arm. "The robbers are back!"

The man squints up the driveway. “I don’t think so.”

“That truck is jus’ like the one the robbers drove, like an old paint truck. You wasn’t here, Mr. Joe. It’s just like that old black truck.”

“Slow down, Earl. There’s no call jumping to conclusions. Lots of folks drive black trucks. Let’s go around back and see what Cook says.”

As they reach the corner of the house, the front door opens. Cook steps onto the porch, a funny expression on her face. “Earl, you have a visitor.”

THIRTY-THREE

Earl steps into the quiet darkness of the front hall. Tugging the ends of his hair and the tail of his grubby shirt, he tries to straighten himself out. He sticks close to Cook as she walks ahead of him, wishing Mr. Joe had come inside to keep him company.

When Cook pauses at a doorway, Earl recognizes the pretty sitting room. A ruddy-faced man in overalls perches on one end of the flowered sofa. Next to him sits a girl in a long dark skirt and sweater. A plate of oatmeal cookies and a pitcher of iced tea with glasses occupy the center of a low coffee table. He turns to look at Mrs. Phipps, standing beside the hearth.

"Ma'am?"

"Earl..."

It's his name, a word he hears every day, but something inside him uncurls at the sound of it. He shifts his gaze to the sofa, to the girl who's spoken.

"Don't you recognize your own sister?" Her voice is barely a whisper.

He takes a hesitant step forward. "Lucy?"

As the girl nods, her features click into place. She's changed, but it's Lucy, sure enough. He hastens to the sofa and plops down on the cushion beside her.

"Look at you," he says, awed by her altered appearance. She's thinner than he remembers. And she's wearing a heavy skirt and dark sweater. He's never seen her wear anything like it. Her long hair has been gathered at the back of her head in a tight, round bun. "You changed your hair."

"I wear it pulled back now."

Mrs. Phipps comes closer, gestures to the man sitting next to Lucy. "This gentleman is Mr. Ingold from Zebulon. Lucy lives in his home," she explains. "He has a proposal for you."

Earl inspects his sister's face. Her eyes seem to be sending a message, but he can't make it out. He marks the paleness of her skin, this girl who's always been brown as a nut from playing outdoors. She appears different from his memory of her – smaller, quieter. Where's the girl he chased through acres of tabacca fields, hiccupping with laughter? Hesitantly, he touches her hand, reassured by its warmth.

"Earl, did you hear me?"

He glances up at Mrs. Phipps. "I'm sorry, ma'am. Were you sayin' something?"

"Mr. Ingold would like to speak with you."

He turns his attention to the man who's come with Lucy. Heavy-lidded eyes study him right back. The man's lined face reveals a lifetime spent toiling under the sun. An iron-gray mustache covers the top part of his mouth. It's a good mustache. He rubs his finger over his lip. Maybe someday, he'll have a proper mustache and not this pale fuzz sprinkling his upper lip.

"Earl, Mrs. Phipps says you've been a help to her in the garden." Mr. Ingold speaks with a gravelly voice that reminds him of Mr. Spivey from the Baptist Church. Mr. Spivey sung in the choir and played fiddle on special occasions.

"Do you sing?" Earl asks.

"What? No, boy. I don't sing." The man looks at Mrs. Phipps, confusion on his face.

"Earl, why don't you tell Mr. Ingold about the work you do with Mr. Joe."

"Mr. Joe and I take care of the plants," he says, pleased to explain his duties. "We do nearly everything together in the garden, plantin' and weedin' and trimmin'. But the mowin', I do that by myself. And the pruning up high, I do that 'cause Mr. Joe doesn't like to climb the ladders on account of his balance. But he oversees."

"That's good to hear," says the man. "You see, this little girl here has been missing her kin something fierce and it put an idea into my head." He sends another quick glance to his hostess, speaking to her now. "I contacted the Salvation Army. They informed me where I could find Earl. Till recent, it's been just me and the missus with our sons on the farm." He looks down at the girl sitting beside him. "We had a house full of boys but no daughter. That's why Lucy has been such a blessing. I don't know what the missus would do without her. She's been a real help with the cooking and pitching in with the housework."

Lucy keeps her eyes cast down, not reacting to the compliment.

"When I realized I was going to be out this way, I figured I could look y'all up whilst I was here. My wife's suffering from a toxic goiter. They're treating her at Rex Hospital. Lucy will have more chores when we return to the farm, tending to my wife while she recuperates."

"I'm sorry to hear your wife's been unwell. It sounds like Lucy's had to shoulder a lot of responsibility." Mrs. Phipps looks at Lucy as she speaks, but Earl's sister keeps her eyes lowered.

"Children have to grow up fast in the country," the man says, an edge to his voice. "I'll say one thing for the girl. She's a quick learner. Why, I wasn't more than eight myself when I started helping my daddy in the fields. With my wife ailing, it's placed a strain on things. I can't afford to take more time away. My boys help out, of course. But the eldest has gone and got himself a sweetheart, says he wants to work for the railroad. All my life I've been training him to take over the farm when I pass." He clears his throat. "Anyway, that's what got me thinking." He directs a tight smile toward Mrs. Phipps. "Since she arrived, Lucy's been after me to visit Earl. I can see he's a strapping fellow. Knowin' how he's been tending to your place here, he might have skills that would be useful to me on the farm now that my eldest is leaving."

Earl leans forward. Lucy said she wouldn't forget him and she hadn't, not one bit. "Do you have mules?" he asks.

"I have four mules, plus a few dairy cows. Mostly, I raise hogs. The missus looks after the chickens… well, that's Lucy's job now. I keep a few fields of sweet potatoes and soybeans. I used to carry cotton and barley, but the end of the war killed cotton prices and Prohibition dried up the market for barley. I'm not complaining, mind you. It's hard for lots of folks. We get by."

"Exactly what kind of work would Earl be doing for you?" Mrs. Phipps takes the plate from the table and moves in front of the sofa. She offers a cookie to Lucy. The girl peeks at Mrs. Phipps then at the man beside her. Tentatively, she reaches toward the plate. The sleeve of her sweater hitches up, and she pulls the fabric to her wrist before sitting back with a cookie held carefully in one hand. Mrs. Phipps hands her a napkin then takes a seat across from the sofa.

"He'd tend to the hogs. And I'd need him to help plow and plant in the spring. He'd remove stumps and rocks when I'm clearing new fields," explains the man. "Harvest season is when we work the hardest. Sunup to sundown. But when Earl comes of age, I could stake him a little place on the property in exchange for his labor."

"I'd get to drive the team?" he asks, his tone wary.

"My boys can show you what to do."

"Do you have tabacca? I helped Farmer Tate barn tabacca."

"Zebulon has a thriving tobacco market. The missus disapproves, but several farms in the area are doing well with their crop. I've yet to try my hand."

Mrs. Phipps shifts in her chair. "Mr. Ingold, you've presented an interesting proposal to Earl. I'm sure he'd like to give this careful thought. We'd be sad to see him leave, of course. But we want what's best for him." She looks at Earl as she says this, then returns her attention to the other man. "Would you consider letting Lucy stay with us tonight? I'm sure the two young people have a lot of catching up to do. My husband can return Lucy to you tomorrow. He goes by the hospital on his way to the office."

Earl bounces lightly on the sofa. Yes, yes, yes. If Lucy stays overnight then he can introduce her to Mr. Joe and show her the treehouse. Harold said no girls, but Lucy's his sister and she's as good a tree climber as he is. He gives her a grin and catches the hopeful glance she sends him. She stills when the man drops a hand to her shoulder.

"I appreciate the offer, ma'am. But I need to take Lucy with me. See, my wife gets fretful in the ladies' ward. Some of the patients fuss and cry during the night. She has trouble sleeping. I made a promise this little girl would be by her side whenever she woke up. The nurses won't let men on the ward outside visiting hours. I'm sure you understand."

Mrs. Phipps is quiet for a moment then she nods, sending the girl a warm smile. "Of course. I imagine Lucy is a great comfort to her."

The man stands, helping Lucy to her feet.

"I appreciate your time, ma'am. And the refreshments. We'll be taking our leave, but we'll come back tomorrow to get the boy's answer."

Earl glances from Lucy to Mrs. Phipps. Surely they're not leaving so soon.

"Do you have to go this minute?" he asks.

He catches a hint of something that makes him frown, but the face the man turns to him is amiable. "We need to get back to the hospital. I don't want my wife to wake from her nap and wonder where we are."

For a second, his chin quivers in disappointment but he pulls himself together and steps out of the way. He follows behind the group as Mrs. Phipps walks her guests to the front door and says goodbye. Silently, he watches the burly man and his little sister make their way to the truck parked beside the house.

There's something about the way the man keeps a hand on Lucy's shoulder that Earl doesn't like. He bites his lip, glancing at Mrs. Phipps who stands beside him, eyes slightly narrowed.

Mr. Ingold gives Lucy a push toward the passenger side of the truck. Then he strides to the driver's side and slides behind the steering wheel. Impulsively, Earl dashes forward.

"Lucy, wait!"

His sister's head swivels to glance behind her and he's startled to see her eyes are damp with unshed tears.

He feels in his heart that what his sister needs is a hug. He needs it too, he realizes. Lucy's his whole family. She's been with him on the happiest days of his life and with him through the worst. It's been so long since he had any kin close enough to touch. He wishes that housekeeper, Miz. Fowler, was here so she could see he did too have family. He wraps his arms around Lucy's tiny frame and gives her a squeeze. She lifts herself onto her toes and clasps her arms around his shoulders, the uneaten cookie still in one hand.

"He's like Pa," she whispers, her voice urgent. Then she drops her arms and turns away, her steps wooden as she opens the passenger door and climbs into her seat.

He stands dumbly, his mind trying to process the words. He watches as Mr. Ingold says something sharp to his sister. She stares stony-faced through the windshield of the truck, her eyes never wavering from his.

THIRTY-FOUR

Mrs. Phipps stares thoughtfully after the truck making its way down the driveway. As it turns onto the road toward town, she glances at Earl.

"Was it good to see your sister again?"

"Yes ma'am." He watches her carefully.

"Has she changed much?"

He presses his lips together, unsure how to answer.

"It was sweet of you to give her a hug goodbye. It looked like she was saying something to you."

Just three words. Earl isn't sure he understood. He's pretty sure he cannot explain the words to Mrs. Phipps. Pa always said, *"Never rat on family."* Is it ratting to repeat Lucy's words to this woman? It's easy to misunderstand a thing. Is his sister telling him that this man, Mr. Ingold, has a temper? Does he get violent? Does he punch things? Has he punched her? Or is there another way in which he's like their pa?

His thoughts bump into one another, unsettling him. He wraps both arms around his waist to keep everythin' together and stares intently at the ground.

He doesn't like to be disloyal to his pa. Still, there's no denying he's a man of meanness. When he's in a temper, he strikes whoever's closest. He steals things. He destroys property. He destroys people. If his sister thinks Mr. Ingold is like Pa, then she's in harm's way. He takes a deep breath as a sliver of clear thinking cleaves through the confusion.

Lucy needs her big brother.

When he doesn't answer, Mrs. Phipps steps closer and places a hand on his shoulder. "Why don't you return to the garden and see if Mr. Joe has something for you to do? I'll check on you after supper. We'll have a chat. How's that?"

He lifts his head to gaze at his employer, unaware his stark expression reveals more than words ever could. "Yes ma'am."

Moving slowly, he makes his way around the side of the house and lets himself in through the gate. He finds Mr. Joe bent over a hedgerow near the fountain. The man stands stiffly, pressing on his side where he's prone to a hitch.

"Who was your visitor?"

"My sister, Lucy. She come with the man she was give to after Ma died. His name is Mr. Ingold. He said I could come live with them and work on his farm. He keeps hogs."

"Well, I'll be." Mr. Joe dips his handkerchief in the fountain and wipes his face.

Earl scuffs his shoe across the grass.

"You don't seem pleased. When do you have to make up your mind?"

He lifts tormented eyes to the man who's been kind to him. "I already made it."

Mr. Joe rubs a hand over his mouth, then tips his head toward a wrought-iron bench in the shade. "Come sit with me."

He takes a seat on the hard bench. A bird calls from somewhere in the trees. Another bird answers. Earl sits back, gradually settling himself as he gazes at the sky, the slips and swirls like whitewash against a bolt of blue cloth. The older man breaks the silence.

"Mrs. Phipps gave you a choice, did she?"

"Yes sir."

"What if you didn't go to this new farm? You could stay here and work with me in the garden. Would that be so bad?"

"I like working in the garden," he says softly.

"I like having you here. You've been a big help."

Earl trembles with emotion. He can see Mr. Joe is offerin' him something good, the reassurance that he has a place here. He feels that he wants to do both things. He wants to be with his sister, to look after her, but he wants to stay here, too, where he feels safe. He wants to drive a team and work with animals on a farm, but he also wants to plant flowers with Mr. Joe and spend his days inhaling the sharp, scented breath of tall trees. He's never had to make such a difficult decision in his entire life.

Mr. Joe leans forward to get a better look at his face. "Is there anything I can do to help?"

His boss's expression reflects compassion and something else that Earl doesn't fully understand but finally identifies as respect. It's not a look he's received before and it shakes him.

"Earl, did I ever tell you about my father?"

"I don't recollect that you did."

"I was born a free man but my father was not. Do you understand what I mean by this?"

"No sir."

"He didn't belong to himself, Earl. His thoughts were his own, but every other part of him belonged to another man. That man could be mean or he could be kind, depending on which way the wind blew. If he was in a dark mood, he could switch the skin from my father's back for simply looking at him crossways. From my father, I learned the physical scars that survive meanness are not the part that hurts a man; it's the scars that live in our hearts.

"Since you walked through the gate, I've seen that you carry scars. I understand wishing things was different for your sister's circumstance but there's a lot of unknown in taking a step like that. I'd hate for you to give up something good you've got right here, something that may allow you to help your sister someday in other ways." He opens his mouth to say more, then seems to reconsider. After a moment, he clears his throat. "You know, I always figured you'd take over for me when I got too old."

Earl's eyes grow wide. "You mean tend the whole garden?"

"You've learned a lot this summer. Why, it wouldn't surprise me if you could already do my job."

"I don't think so."

Mr. Joe watches him a moment, his gaze thoughtful. "You've got a lot to think about, that's for sure. Would you like to sit here and ponder a while?"

"If it's all the same to you, I'd like to cut hedges." He understands now the shrubs are square because they've been trimmed that way. The shrubs don't seem to mind. They don't wither for the cutting but stay green all year round.

"Come with me and I'll get you started."

For the remainder of the afternoon, Earl shapes and clips and measures according to Mr. Joe's instructions. The work soothes something inside him. And when he takes a step back and examines the hedgerow, the sharp corners and even sides of the bushes please him. When he considers he might not be here for even one more day, he finds it hard to breathe. All summer, all he could think about was being reunited with his sister. Now, it seems like he's gettin' what he wanted. Why don't he feel happier?

Before departing to catch the streetcar, Mr. Joe washes at the hand pump and accompanies Earl to the back patio.

"I hope you know I only want what's best for you. If there's anything I can do to help you – anything at all – you only have to say the word."

"What word?"

Mr. Joe grips his shoulder firmly. Without answering the question, he lets himself out through the gate.

Earl stands at the fence, watching him leave. He observes the tiny hitch in Mr. Joe's gait and feels a rush of affection for the man who's looked after him. A man completely different from his pa or Mr. Randolph.

Better, he realizes with dawning awareness. This is a man who chooses to *be better* every day in ways Earl is only beginning to understand.

Forlorn, he taps on the back door, accepting the plate Cook hands him. As he takes his seat at the table, he tries to picture living with Lucy. Instead of his ma or Cook preparing meals, it will be his little sister. A corner of his mouth twitches. She's barely big enough to lift a cast iron skillet. At Miss Hazel's, she had an experienced hand to help with the tricky parts of preparin' a meal. He wrinkles his nose, remembering how her biscuits and gravy never amounted to much. If Missus Ingold is too sick to look after that house full of boys, Lucy will have to manage all the housework by herself. He recalls her words. "*He's like pa.*" A grim expression steals across his face.

He's staring vacantly at nothing when the back door opens. He lifts his gaze as Mrs. Phipps approaches the table. She wraps her skirt around both legs and slides into the seat across from him.

"Earl, do you not like pork chops?"

He glances at his untouched plate. He'd forgotten it was there. "I guess I'm not hungry."

"I see." She watches him from across the table, her eyes difficult to read. "And have you thought about what you want to do?"

"I want you to know I'm grateful to you for takin' me in. You have a swell place." He searches for the right words. "You and Mr. Phipps and Harold are fine people. And Mr. Joe and Cook are my friends. That's what I think."

"I think so, too. We're all fond of you."

He drops his gaze to the table and begins to worry at a loose chip of paint. "The thing is… you see, ma'am, I figure Lucy's the only family I got left. The only family that cares about me, anyway." For a brief moment, he wonders what the other members of his family are doing. He can picture Pa in his cell, pacing like a caged animal. It's the others who give him trouble: his brothers, Welcome and Faith, his sister Rose, and little Mattie.

Mrs. Phipps shifts in her seat, pulling his gaze back to hers. "Did your sister say something to you? You can trust me, Earl. I want to help you but I can only do that if you tell me everything."

He examines the face of the woman across from him. Her expression seems clear and without any bad intent. On impulse, he decides to place his trust in her. "Mrs. Phipps, ma'am, Lucy did say somethin'. When she hugged me, she said he was like our pa."

"Mr. Ingold?"

"Yes ma'am."

"I see." She presses her lips together and stares out at the garden. It's a quiet, peaceful place but her eyes don't seem peaceful.

"I know about your father, Earl." Her voice steadies something inside him. "The Salvation Army thought it was important for me and Mr. Phipps to understand your background before you came to stay with us. If Mr. Ingold is cut from the same cloth, then I think you are better off staying with us. You're safe here."

He's sorely tempted to take what she's offering. The garden is a good place. Good smells live in the air and he likes the texture of things – loamy soil and grass and pine needles. He can't say it's better than fermented hay or the softness of cornsilk or animal odors in a barn, but working in the garden gives him satisfaction. He's surrounded by decent folks. He expects he's experienced more goodness in these past few months than his entire previous life back home. It don't matter. Not now. He can't help believin' that if Ma was here, she'd want him to look after Lucy. And he can't let his ma down.

Mrs. Phipps reaches across the table to place a hand on his arm. "Earl, honey… I need you to use your words. Tell me what's in your heart."

"Ma'am, it's a hard thing to say, but I figure I have to go. Lucy needs me to look after her."

"And what if Mr. Ingold is mean to you the way your father was?"

"I guess I can take it."

She squeezes his arm, hard, and he's startled to discover her eyes are filled with tears.

"Earl, you're breaking my heart."

They sit that way for several minutes, neither one interrupting the silence. Finally, he fills the pause with a new thought. "Ma'am, what if Lucy was to come here? She can take my bed. You heard Mr. Ingold say Lucy's a quick learner. She could help Cook in the kitchen. I know you got a lady who cleans, but Lucy can help her, too – she can dust and sweep and wipe down windows. She can even help Mr. Joe in the garden. I can sleep on the floor in the toolshed. I don't mind a bit."

Releasing his arm, she gives him a watery smile. "I would love to have Lucy with us. But just like Mr. Phipps and I signed guardianship papers for you, Mr. Ingold has signed guardianship papers for Lucy. She's his lawful ward." Something enters her eyes then, the spark of an idea. "I tell you what. I'll have Mr. Phipps stop by his attorney's office tomorrow morning. Maybe there's something that can be done. In the meantime, if you're determined to be with your sister, you have my support. I'll check on you as much as I can to make sure you're getting on in your new circumstances."

"Where's Mr. Ingold's farm?"

"Zebulon."

"Is that far? Maybe I could ride one of the mules over on Sundays and see Harold."

"I'm sorry, Earl. I'm afraid it's too far for you to walk or ride."

He nods, accepting this disappointment. "I sure am going to miss Harold. Can you tell him goodbye for me? Tell him I'm sorry we won't get to go swimming."

She gives his hand a pat and slides out of the bench. "Don't fret. I'm not prepared to give up on you. Or your sister. Once you get settled, Mr. Phipps and I will drive over and bring Harold for a visit. Would you like that?"

It warms him inside to realize Mrs. Phipps would consider bringing Harold for a visit. "That would be swell. Maybe Mr. Ingold will let me and Harold take two of his mules and go explore."

Her sudden exhalation turns into a belly laugh that sounds too big for the small woman. "Gracious, what a thought! I would pay money to see Harold on a mule."

THIRTY-FIVE

Earl awakens with a heaviness, like cold molasses has replaced all the juice in his body. He gets out of bed and does the normal things. He straightens the blanket. He removes his long johns and replaces them with a faded shirt and work britches. He washes at the hand pump, splashing cool water onto his face. With his hair slicked and his fingernails clean of garden soil, he accepts his breakfast from Cook. When he sees she has slathered a hot biscuit with raw honey, he startles her with a hug.

Flustered, she gives his shoulder a squeeze. "A little something special for your last day," she says quietly, then slips back into the kitchen.

He eats his breakfast standing beneath the pines, chewing thick slices of salty ham and saving his sweet biscuit for last. He savors every bite. After returning the plate to Cook, Earl circles back to the shed. He takes a deep breath, inhaling the room and committing it to memory. Reaching beneath the bed, he removes the travel bag Miss Hazel gave him. He hasn't touched it since the day he arrived. Peeking inside, he wipes his handkerchief around the interior to make sure there's no spiders. One by one, he places each item he owns into the bag, his shirts and trousers, his cotton long johns and underwear, plus a small pile of darned socks. He keeps the blue handkerchief in his pants pocket but places the pocketknife Mr. Joe gave him into the bag. The precious photograph of his ma he tucks into a side pocket. He gazes around the dim space that's become his home. He'll miss it. He'll miss the plants in the garden, the ones he knows and the ones he's yet to learn. He'll miss his new treehouse. He'll miss his friends.

Firming his chin, he latches the bag.

When Mr. Joe arrives, he seems to understand Earl's need to stay busy. They work in the flower beds all morning, loosening the soil and clearing debris. Soon, it will be time to put fall color into the ground. One of his favorite things is to check the flowerpots covering every available surface in the greenhouse. Pots overflow tables and barrels and stacked crates. In each pot, tight buds prepare to burst into blossoms of red and gold and purple. He won't be here to see the explosion of color.

After lunch, he carries his packed bag to the front of the house and takes a seat on the porch. Mr. Ingold promised to return in the afternoon. Once he collects Earl, the plan is to go by the hospital and fetch Missus Ingold, then drive to the farm in Zebulon.

He's full of jitters thinking about the changes comin'. Will Mr. Ingold's boys be nice to him or will they taunt him and call him names? If Mr. Ingold is a man of anger perhaps his boys are, too.

When the black truck turns up the driveway, he lifts his hand in a wave. He knows Cook is keeping an eye out. Mrs. Phipps is in the house with a gentleman who works with Mr. Phipps. Earl watched him arrive earlier, maneuvering his nice automobile beside the back gate.

When the truck parks behind it, Mr. Ingold steps from the vehicle then turns to speak to Lucy through the open window. His deep voice carries across the lawn. "Stay here. This won't take a minute."

"Mr. Ingold?" Mrs. Phipps steps through the door, holds it open with one hand. "Why don't you let Lucy stretch her legs? I'd like to invite you inside the house for a moment."

"What for?" His tone is brusque.

"I've asked our attorney to draw up a temporary agreement transferring guardianship of Earl to you. In thirty days, we'll drive over to your place and see how he's liking his new arrangement. If he's satisfied with the situation, and you're satisfied, Mr. Ingold, then my husband and I have promised Earl we'd be willing to make it permanent."

Thick brows lower over his eyes. "No one said anything about signing a paper."

Earl watches as a smile fixes itself on Mrs. Phipps' face. He wonders at it because her fingers flutter at her side like tiny hummingbird wings.

"I assure you, it's all very standard. In these situations, my husband and I find it best to lay out the terms quite clearly, so there's no misunderstanding. Our attorney is at the dining room table. This will only take a minute."

Mr. Ingold turns back to the truck, his gaze sharp on the girl inside. "Stay on the porch and behave yourself. I'll be right back."

Without another glance, he strides into the house after Mrs. Phipps. Earl flies down the steps to greet his sister. "Are you alright?"

She pushes the door closed and walks around the truck. Hands on hips, she gives him a hard stare. "Didn't you hear what I said?"

"You said Mr. Ingold's like Pa."

"So why are you coming to the farm? Don't you like it here?"

"I like it fine. But I figure you need lookin' after. You're my family." He speaks simply, surprised she doesn't understand. "Besides, we'll find a way to have fun, Lucy. Didn't we always, even when Pa was around?"

She gives him an uncertain look. "I guess."

"And you can look after me, too. You can help me know how to be helpful to Mr. Ingold so I don't get into trouble."

"I can try." She glances toward the house then back at her brother. "He's particular about how things should be done. If I'm in the house helpin' the missus, I can't look after you when you're working in the fields."

"We'll be together. That's what matters." He hesitates for a beat then says what's on his mind. "I missed you. I wasn't sure if you was comin' to get me or not."

"I missed you, too."

She tries to smile but can't seem to manage it. Her chin trembles as though she's reining in a powerful emotion. It's the same way she looked when Ma slipped to the floor.

He experiences a wave of sadness for her suffering and his part in it. He'll do whatever it takes to make things up to her. Feeling suddenly giddy with relief, he taps Lucy on the shoulder and darts away. "You're it!"

For a split second, she appears confused, almost like she doesn't remember what it means to play. She narrows her eyes at the front door, firmly closed. Then, with a muffled grunt, she leaps after him. He dodges and pivots, avoiding her reach. The sound of her quiet snickers make him grin.

He can tell the long skirt hampers her movement. After stumbling twice, she lifts the heavy fabric, bunching it into one hand as she gives chase. With a nimble turn, she finally manages to touch Earl's arm. "You're it!"

She spins out of the way as he twirls to tag her back. He reaches out, missing her but snagging the sleeve of her sweater in one hand. She continues running as he holds on, pulling the sweater off one arm.

"Missed me!" she shouts. Then she stops, breathless, her eyes wide as she meets Earl's bewildered gaze.

From where he stands, he can see dark stripe marks on her legs, exposed by the lifted hem. And the arm he's bared is visibly marked. He wraps one hand loosely around her upper arm, matching his fingers with dark bruises that encircle her skin, right where a man might grab hard and hold.

His fingers move down her arm and pass over her elbow. Gently, he touches the swollen forearm, yellow and purple as though it's been twisted in a dark rage. Tears fill his eyes. "Does it hurt?"

"Lucy!" The bellow comes from the front porch.

She gasps. In an instant, she drops her skirt and attempts to yank on the sweater, now hanging halfway off her body. She can't manage it. The sleeve's been pulled inside out. She's unable to insert her arm into the opening no matter how desperately she tries to force her way.

Earl scans the figures standing on the porch. Mr. Ingold wears a fierce expression. Mrs. Phipps has paused, one hand lifted to her mouth as though she can't quite believe what she's seen.

Lucy looks at the angry man then at the woman. Earl watches as something changes in her expression. She tugs on the other sleeve of her sweater, throwing the garment to the ground. Lifting her chin in the air, she grabs a handful of the skirt in one hand, raising the hem to her knee. Dark hatch marks crisscross both legs. Anyone can see someone has taken a switch or a cane and whipped her hard, breaking the skin in places.

Earl knows Lucy can be sassy. But she's also smart. She wouldn't make the same mistake twice. Whoever hit her took pleasure from doin' it.

"My lord," Mrs. Phipps murmurs.

He moves closer to his sister and places a protective arm around her shoulders, watching the others cautiously.

"Boy, step away."

The farmer stomps down the steps. His skin is mottled with emotion. Large hands fist at his side.

"No sir," Earl whispers.

"Mr. Ingold, stop right there. I cannot ignore the mistreatment of this child." Mrs. Phipps' voice is as stern as he's ever heard it.

"She's my responsibility. I have the right to discipline the girl how I choose." He strides toward Lucy. "Pick up your sweater, girl. We're leaving."

She glances at Earl once, eyes bleak. Then she bends to retrieve her sweater. He steps in front of her, wanting to be a shield between his sister and this man. It isn't done with conscious thought. It isn't done to provoke. It's an instinctive desire to protect what he loves. Seeing it, the man becomes more enflamed. A look steals into his eyes, hot and cunning. His open hand shoots out too fast to see. Earl swivels, stunned, as Lucy falls to the ground with a sharp cry.

His vision wavers as a wash of red sweeps across his eyes. Something violent swells within him. The man is strong, but Earl is young and quick. He rushes the man and tackles him to the ground. As if he's been doing it every day of his life, he raises a fist and slams it into the side of the man's face. It happens in less time than it takes to complete a heartbeat. If there's a single, simple thought swirling in his head, it's this – he wants to put a mark on this man for every mark he put on Lucy. He raises his fist again.

"Earl!"

He hears his name as though it's being shouted from a long way off. The sound feels muffled. He pauses, one arm reared back. He hears his breath breaking loose in deep, racking gasps. He's never in his life felt so… so… much. He's full of meanness in that moment. Like Orbry the day Ma died, he realizes. Like his pa every day.

"Earl." He feels his sister before he hears her. One slender hand rests lightly on his arm.

He glances at his balled fist. It looks like a weapon to him, like something that can do harm. He wonders at it. Lucy's hand gives a gentle squeeze. "It's okay," she says. "You don't have to hit him."

After a minute, he opens his hand and lets his arm drop loosely to his side.

"Come on now," she whispers.

He looks at his sister and finds her eyes on the other man, hard as stone. But then she turns her gaze to Earl and he knows this is his own true sister who hid beneath the house with him on warm days and chased after yellow chicks in the sunlight, her laughter trilling behind her like a rainbow of sound. She's come back to him.

He lets her help him to stand. When she takes his hand, he doesn't resist. Quietly, she leads him to the porch.

"Mr. Ingold, I believe it would be a good idea if you left now." Mrs. Phipps' voice is shaking but something about it makes Earl pay attention. There's grit in this woman. She stands on the porch step, framed on either side by Cook and Mr. Joe. Earl hadn't seen them join her, but they form a unified front around the tiny woman. Another man steps through the front door. This must be the attorney man, he realizes.

"What's going on out here?" he asks.

"We're going to need a new contract," says Mrs. Phipps. The attorney moves closer, letting the door fall shut behind him. "Mr. Ingold is going to release Lucy to our care," she continues, her voice vibrating with emotion.

The burly man rises to his feet. "I'll do no such thing," he growls. "I'm not leaving without the girl."

"You are."

Mrs. Phipps motions toward Lucy. "Come here, sweetheart."

Lucy looks at Earl. He nods reassuringly. She releases his hand and walks to the older woman.

"George, look at this." The woman turns Lucy so the attorney can clearly see the discolored welts on her arms. Then she lifts the edge of the long skirt. The man frowns when he sees the strike marks against the pale skin of her legs.

"This is a matter of child welfare," Mrs. Phipps tells him. "I'm counting on you to serve as a witness."

He faces the man, whose eyes flash angrily at the group assembled on the porch.

"Mrs. Phipps is prepared to take action on behalf of this child," the man named George says. His voice speaks calm and clear. "I suggest you get into your truck and leave at once. You will hear from my office officially before the week is out."

THIRTY-SIX

"I can't wear that." Lucy's finger points toward the swimming outfit, but her eyes never leave Cook's face.

"Honey, all the girls at the lake will be wearing this. You'll see."

"It's not proper." She casts a beseeching glance at her brother. "Earl, tell her."

Cook holds up the garment, turning it every which way. "Look here. The fabric is loose and comfortable. It's not revealing at all. And see, it comes with these long bloomers so your legs will be covered."

Lucy reminds Earl of a hunted animal, her eyes wary and defiant at the same time. "There's no sleeves on that outfit. Missus Ingold says a proper girl keeps herself modest at all times."

"There is no one more respectable than Mrs. Phipps," Cook huffs. "She would not ask you to do anything that isn't proper."

"I don't understand," Lucy says plaintively.

Cook gives Earl a poke. Evidently, she thinks he can calm his sister.

"The thing is Lucy, we've been invited to the lake, see. Harold's folks is going to take us."

"Are we catching fish for supper? I don't need no new clothes for that."

"No. It's… it's for a treat day. A special treat. It's a… well, I guess it's a city thing."

"I won't go," she insists. "Y'all go and I'll stay here."

"You can't do that, Lucy. Mr. and Mrs. Phipps left to visit friends," Cook says. "And my sister's expecting me. I'm late already."

"I'll stay here by myself. I don't need anybody to tend to me." She crosses her arms and glares as though daring someone to move her.

"Mrs. Phipps gave me strict orders before she left. I'm to get you properly outfitted to join Earl and Harold at the lake. I got to do what I'm told, same as you."

Lucy's eyes gleam with a new thought. "I don't know how to swim," she says smugly. "So I don't need no swimming outfit."

"Now, miss…"

Earl looks up when the back door opens and Harold's mother walks to the patio. She's a pretty lady, slender and pale. He can tell she doesn't get out much. The younger Mrs. Phipps – she tells him to call her Miss Nora – glances directly at him with her full attention. "I must have misunderstood. Didn't Harold tell me your father taught all his children how to swim?"

"He taught me and my brothers, ma'am."

"Pa had different rules for girls," says Lucy warily.

The woman looks thoughtful. "There's a lot of that going around. But now women have the vote and we've got to stick together."

"I vote no swimming suits," Lucy grumbles.

"I tell you what. You and I are going to help each other today. As the only two females in our party, we'll look after one another." She holds out her hand and waits patiently until Lucy slips hers into it. Then Miss Nora accepts the garments from Cook.

"Cook, you've been very patient with us. You go on to your sister's now. I think we can manage from here." She looks at the little girl beside her. "I'm going to go upstairs and Lucy is going to keep me company while I get into my swimming attire. Then I'll make sure she's outfitted properly for our excursion."

"I'm confused," Lucy whispers.

"Of course you are. Anyone in your shoes would be confused. You've bounced from one place to the other all summer and I bet every place has a different set of rules."

She nods vigorously, looking relieved someone is finally trying to understand her.

Miss Nora glances up as her son bursts through the back door. "Harold, Lucy and I are going into the house to get ready. Can you make sure Earl knows how to put on his suit?"

"Wait, what?" Earl stares at the swimming outfit in Miss Nora's hand. "I'm s'posed to wear clothes like that to go into the lake? What do I need a suit for?"

"Because proper young men do not swim buck naked in a public lake." She turns to her son. "Harold, explain it to him."

As she leads Lucy away, Harold holds up a pair of short pants and a shirt with no sleeves. In his other hand, he carries a thin, rubber belt. Immediately, Earl shakes his head.

"This is what the fellas wear. Look at me." Harold turns a complete circle.

Earl's not sure what to think. He's used to swimmin' without a stitch. But after working so hard to get Lucy to see reason, it hardly seems fittin' to disagree now that it's his turn. It's a good thing he has these folks to set him straight about things.

"I like the stripes," he decides finally, admiring the blue and white bars alternating on Harold's tank top.

His friend hands him the outfit. "Here, get dressed." He peers around like he doesn't want to be overheard. "Does your sister have to come?"

Earl holds back a sigh. It's taking Harold awhile to warm up to Lucy.

"You only just met her, Harold. You got to give her time. She's real fun. I promise."

He looks unconvinced. "If you say so."

Moving quickly now, he dresses in the swimming garments his friend passes to him one by one. "Do I need to put my trousers over top of this?"

"Nah. It's too warm for that. Just dump everything on your bed. Father brought the touring car. We'll sit on towels so we don't mess up the upholstery."

With a shrug, Earl does as he's told, then returns to the table to wait until it's time to go.

"Your ma seems nice," he says, after a minute.

"Yes. She's… she's trying to make this a nice day for Father."

When Harold's ma had returned from church with the family and was introduced to Earl, he noticed she didn't seem entirely present. It troubled him. Even when she was standin' right beside him, it felt like he was somehow alone. She'd start a sentence and then her eyes would get a sort of lost look. Her son didn't seem to notice. Or maybe he was used to it.

He hears a horn beep.

"Let's go," says Harold.

Earl's never seen a vehicle so fine. Painted a deep burgundy, the long motorcar gleams in the sun. Miss Nora settles Lucy in the center of the back seat as he and Harold squeeze in on either side. It's a cozy fit but that's okay with him. Lucy keeps her eyes on Harold's ma the whole drive. Or maybe she's eying the picnic basket Miss Nora holds in her lap. Earl isn't entirely sure.

When they reach the lake, Harold's father parks alongside a long row of shiny motorcars of every color. Earl stares in fascination, giving a slight whistle beneath his breath. He counts two yellow ones, and a blue one, and…

Harold pokes him and shoves a towel into his arms. "Come on. This way."

Earl checks that Lucy's following along and behaving herself. They make their way to a sandy spot near the water where other folks have laid out blankets and picnic baskets. A nearby stand provides folding chairs and umbrellas. Harold's father brings them a blue-and-white-striped umbrella that matches the boys' tank tops. He stabs it into the ground to create a shady spot. Wood folding chairs are opened to face the lake. Miss Nora sets the picnic basket and towels nearby.

"Who are all these folks?" Earl whispers to Harold. He hadn't realized there'd be so many people.

His friend frowns at the question. "Lots of people come on the weekend, Earl. It's a popular place."

"Oh." He watches a group of young people roughhousing on a spit of land that juts into the water. "Do you know these folks? Are they nice?"

The boy shrugs. "I don't see anyone I know." He observes as his father crosses to a group of men and begins shaking hands. "I guess Father does."

Harold turns to his mother, who's settled into a chair and closed her eyes. He appears unsure of himself. Earl takes note because it's not an expression he's used to seeing.

"Mother, would you like us to keep you company? I could sit with you a bit… if you want."

"I'm fine, dear. Y'all don't need to worry about me." She flutters her fingers toward the water. "Run along."

There's something in her voice, Earl thinks, that doesn't match the lightly spoken words or the carefree wave. He doesn't know Miss Nora. Yet for some reason, he does feel worried. A thread of emotion in her voice scratches at him. He gazes uncertainly toward the others, biting his lip. Had they heard it, too?

"You've suffered," his sister says softly. "You must feel like you're all alone."

Harold inhales audibly and Earl glances to make sure his friend is alright before turning his attention to Lucy.

Taking one of the towels from the stack, his sister lays it on the ground next to the chair where Miss Nora sits. Harold's ma has become frozen.

Earl worries Lucy's words are impertinent. She's new to city ways. If she upset Harold's ma, then Mrs. Phipps might not let Lucy stay. Keeping his arm close to his body, he motions sharply with his hand for his sister to come away from Miss Nora and join them.

She ignores him.

After a long moment, the woman opens her eyes. She looks guardedly at Lucy sitting cross-legged on the ground. "You lost your mother," she says, her voice tentative. "You lost your sister. You lost your home. Until two days ago, you lived with a man who struck you, repeatedly."

Lucy's expression never wavers. "Yes ma'am. What you say is true. But I expect everyone at this here lake has suffered. On really bad days, I like to pretend I'm gettin' all my suffering in early so I can be happy later on."

Miss Nora appears to contemplate the lakeshore and Earl follows her gaze. He mostly sees people laughin' and talkin' real loud.

"I know it don't look like it on the outside," Lucy says. "Same as you sittin' here under this pretty umbrella like you don't have a care. No one would see that your heart is broke. Everyone I know hides their pain. Ma and all us kids had to suffer Pa. And Miss Hazel from the Salvation Army, she lost her husband to the influenza and then she lost her home. And Mrs. Ingold, too, who has a bad man for a husband and selfish sons. I would hear her crying in the afternoon when she thought she was by herself." Lucy clasps her hands in her lap and gives her head a small shake. "I only just met you, Miss Nora, but I can see your sore heart. I thought it might help if you knew you wasn't alone."

Miss Nora's fingers tremble as she reaches into a small bag at her side and retrieves a pair of sun cheaters. Without looking at the children, she slips them onto her face. Lucy and Earl exchange a swift glance. He's aware how this simple action separates her from them. He wonders if maybe they should step away and leave Miss Nora to her thoughts, but after a moment, she leans toward the girl at her side.

"Lucy, my mother-in-law, Mrs. Phipps… she explained your situation. She told me about your sister, Rose – and about what happened to your other sister…"

"Frieda."

"Frieda, yes. I'm suddenly finding it difficult to dwell on my own loss when I consider what you and your sisters have already experienced in your young lives."

Lucy nods, seeming older than her years. "Frieda's a sad case, that's for sure. And Rose… well, I guess her outlook is better now 'cause she's working for Mr. and Mrs. Edwards." She glances at Earl then back to the wounded woman at her side. "Miss Hazel, she was the lady trying to find a home for me and Earl. She told me the Salvation Army folks used to ask all the girls that come through social services whether they'd been, um, tampered with, you see, by a family member mostly. Like a pa or brother or uncle. The numbers got so high, the aid ladies stopped asking. There weren't no point. Miss Hazel says it's 'cause we're poor mostly, and girls, of course."

Harold's ma watches Lucy through her cheaters. "You're an unusual child."

"I don't know about that." She stares absently at her hands, clasping and unclasping them in her lap. "Ma said something to me before she passed. She said every person suffers. And every person dies. And the only thing she could figure was that we was s'posed to have compassion in our hearts for one another. 'Cause we was all in this together, whether we knew it or not."

"It's a hard thing," Miss Nora whispers.

"Yes ma'am. It is. And if you see something easy, I'd like to know."

Earl glances at Harold still standing next to the blanket. His friend's eyes gaze vacantly toward the water, but his head tilts toward his mother's conversation.

Lucy shifts the picnic basket within reach of Miss Nora. "I guess I'll walk down to the water with these boys. But I'll come back and check on you after a while. I moved this basket close in case you want to nibble something. Cook packed a bowl of sliced melon. It looked real fresh."

She stands and waves for the fellas to join her. Carefully, she makes her way toward the lake, watching for loose stones underfoot. Earl follows close behind, slightly in awe of his sister, of how she's able to talk to Harold's ma so directly. He notices his friend is silent for a change. Once, Harold glances back to where his ma sits beneath the large umbrella, but he doesn't say a word.

Of one accord, they enter the water, assessing the temperature as they move into the depths. Smooth rocks crowd the edge where water breaks against the shore then ripples away. A chitter of insects erupts from the woods and something iridescent flies close to Earl's ear then darts away. He scrunches his toes, enjoying the way the lakebed feels against the soles of his feet. He can see why Harold's pa wanted to bring Miss Nora here. The water stretches into the distance, as clear as picture glass. Tall pines tower on every side. He studies his sister. Despite her fuss earlier, she looks nice in her swimming outfit. Pale blue ruffles make her seem softer somehow. Harold's ma brushed Lucy's long, dark hair until it shone, tying it back with a ribbon. Earl can still see faint bruises along her arms, but they aren't near as noticeable as they had been.

"Lucy?"

He slips closer to her in the water, gives her shoulder a tap so she'll look at him.

"What?"

"When did Ma say that to you, what you told Miss Nora?"

She rubs her nose and stays silent for such a long moment, he's not sure she's going to answer. "It was when you run over to Farmer Tate's," she says finally.

"Was she angry? I mean, did she look angry or sound angry when she said it?"

"Ma wasn't angry. I think she was worried for us – for what might happen if she wasn't there to look after us."

It hurts to think about his ma. It hurts him to think of her worry and pain. It breaks his heart. "Lucy..." His voice cracks and he starts again. "Lucy, I never tole you how sorry I am for what happened. It was awful what I done."

Dark eyes gaze intently into his and he has a sudden thought that maybe she's changed. She's still Lucy. But she's more. Or she's different. He's not sure. After a minute, she places a hand on his arm and he's grateful for it.

"She knew it was an accident, Earl. I do, too. No one loved Ma more than you did."

He wonders if this is true but thinks maybe it is. The word 'love' was rarely spoken in their home, but he misses his ma every single day.

"Earl?"

"What?"

She turns to watch Harold's pa where he stands with a bunch of men, laughing. Someone has passed out cigars and they smoke with their heads back, enjoying the day. Lucy shifts her gaze toward deeper water where Harold waits, swallowed up to his waist. He gazes back at them, not impatiently. "You go be with Harold. I'm going to sit with Miss Nora."

"Are you sure?"

"I'm sure."

He watches as she makes her way back to the blanket and drops to the ground next to Harold's ma. Absently, cupping the lake water with both hands, he waits to see what will happen. Maybe Lucy tells a joke because Miss Nora smiles, really smiles, for the first time since Earl met her.

He turns and starts pushing his way through the water to where Harold has ducked himself to get wet all over. He emerges with a grin and tips his head back and forth to shake his ears dry.

The water feels nice. Earl always liked bein' in the river back home. He likes the way the cool slip of liquid feels against his skin. In the center of the lake, a large floating platform bobs on the surface. Boys and girls cluster on the solid wood or splash in the water nearby.

"Do you think you can swim to that platform?" Harold asks.

"Sure."

"Want to race?"

He gauges the distance, then looks at the boy by his side. "I'll beat you," he says matter-of-factly.

"I know. That's why you're going to let me have a head start."

"I am?"

"It's only fair. You're older and taller. So, count to… ten. Don't count fast. Count normal." He demonstrates. "One. Two. Three… just like that. When you reach ten, that's when you start swimming. Understand?"

"Count to ten. Normal, not fast. I understand."

Harold moves forward until he's at the perfect depth to take his first stroke. "Okay. Start."

Earl watches as Harold lifts both arms over his head and propels himself forward. For a moment, he forgets what he's supposed to do, then starts counting under his breath. He observes Harold pull away, each slice of his arms cutting rhythmically through the water. When he reaches ten, Earl strikes out after his friend, swimming with long, easy strokes.

THIRTY-SEVEN

Earl has no idea what to do with his swimming clothes now that the swimming is done. It's been a fun day. He swam and swam. He and Harold raced and sometimes they floated on top of the water. He'd been nervous about the other kids at the lake but nobody said a mean word to him.

"Do you think I should lay these things on the patio table?" he asks Lucy. "Mrs. Phipps ain't got no clothes line."

"Cook says Mrs. Phipps sends out her laundry. But there's an airing cupboard in the mudroom. Give me your swimming outfit. I'll take it in when I go."

"Okay. Wait here." He goes to the shed and changes into his clothes then returns with the swimming suit. He finds Lucy seated at the table. Her eyes move slowly, taking in the whole garden.

"This is about the prettiest place I've ever seen," she says softly.

He sits on top of the table next to her and gazes with pleasure at the view. He's glad she likes it. He hoped she would. "I expect it's one of my favorite places," he says. He peers down at his sister. Her hair has fallen to one side and he can see a pale bruise on the back of her neck. "Why do you think Mr. Ingold hurt you?" he asks.

"He liked hittin', I think. And he didn't like me much." She turns the words back at him. "Why do you think Pa hurt you?"

He shrugs. He's wondered the same thing.

"But you don't get hit here?"

"Oh, no. Not even when I do something dumb." Reaching down with his finger, he lightly touches the back of her neck. "What was that one for?"

She presses her fingers to the spot. "Mr. Ingold grabbed me 'cause I reached for a biscuit without saying please."

He points toward a stripe mark on her leg, barely visible below her bloomers. "And that one?"

"I was takin' sheets off the line barefoot. He told me I was slovenly and dishonored his home."

"Why'd he twist your arm?" he asks, relieved to see the yellow and purple bruises have begun to fade.

"I refused to hold his boy's hand when we was sayin' a blessing around the table. His boy was mean and he would crush his hand around mine to try and make me cry."

"Did you?"

"Not once."

He nods, unsurprised. Lucy could have a big heart, as big as Ma's. But she could also be a tough nut.

"I know it was selfish of me to bring Mr. Ingold here."

Lucy peeks sideways at him. "It's 'cause I was gettin' scared. I had to do something."

"You was scared he'd hurt you too bad?"

"No," she whispers, barely loud enough for him to hear. "I was scared I would hurt him."

Earl leans closer to make sure he's hearin' correctly.

"I used to think about it all the time," she says, no longer meetin' his eyes. "I'd think about him sleeping and how I could tiptoe into the room so silent he'd never know I was there. And even if the missus saw me, she'd watch and let me inch closer, conk him in the head with a shovel. Then things would be better, like they was when Pa left for prison. Wasn't that a good time, Earl?"

It had been a good time. Except for Orbry. But him and Ma and Lucy and the baby. That had been nice.

"I think this is going to be a good time, too," he says.

Her lips lift. It makes him happy to see it. The dimple that only pops out on special occasions flashes, then is gone.

"Lucy..."

"What?"

"That first day you was here, you said Mr. Ingold was like Pa. Was..." He hesitates. "Was there another way he's like Pa?"

She's quiet for a long moment. "I know what you're thinkin'. I worried about it. The missus gave me a pallet to sleep on in the pantry. One night, the middle boy came to the kitchen to get buttermilk. I could hear him. I heard him move to the pantry door, stop outside. I heard him breathing."

Fear clutches at his heart. "Did he hurt you, Lucy?"

"He tried. Mr. Ingold caught him before… well… before." She rubs both hands over her face, drops them into her lap. "He thrashed that boy good. I was glad to see it. The next day, he told his sons if anyone touched me before my woman's flow started, they'd answer to him. I don't know if he would have kept me safe or not. He looked at me, too… I didn't like it." She puffs out a breath. "Anyway, I expect all them boys would have had their way with me eventually." She lifts her eyes to his, her expression solemn. "If you hadn't saved me."

At the sound of the back door opening, he and Lucy swivel to find Cook heading their way. She halts in front of the two of them and crosses her arms, her gaze meeting Earl's with great seriousness.

"Now that you're back from your big day, I need to talk to you."

Earl's heart takes off. He must've done something terrible. Even though he told Lucy they didn't hit folks here, that didn't mean they wouldn't scold him. He'll feel terrible if he's done something to upset Cook. He grabs hold of his legs and squeezes them to stay put.

For a minute, her eyes bore into his, then her face collapses into laughter. "Oh, Earl. I'm just having fun. Then I see the look on your face and I feel bad for making you worry."

He looks at Lucy and her eyes dance like she's in on some tomfoolery.

"Lucy and I have decided to prepare your favorite meal," Cook says.

He's still unsure it's okay to smile. "My favorite meal?"

"Think about the food you love more than anything in the world. You give me your choice, and we'll make it for supper tomorrow night."

His mouth drops open as her words sink in. "I can have anything I want?"

She slaps her hip, enjoying his reaction. "It's the least I can do after what you done."

"For rescuing me from Mr. Ingold," adds Lucy. "In case it wasn't clear."

"We look after each other."

"Tomorrow morning, I'll need your decision," says Cook.

"I know now," he says.

Earl doesn't usually make swift decisions, but this one is easy. He sees the look of surprise on her face.

"You already know what you want?"

"I want buttermilk fried chicken. Can you make that?"

"Every woman what stands at a stove can make buttermilk fried chicken, Earl. Ain't I served that to you yet?"

"No ma'am."

"Alright, what do you want to go with it?"

He sucks on his bottom lip before sending her a hopeful look. "Cake?" he whispers.

"What did you say? Cake?"

"Yellow cake. Round, yellow cake." He clasps his hands together with excitement. "Two pieces!"

"Two pieces of cake! I never heard such a thing. Two pieces of cake at one meal? You'll get sick."

"I won't get sick."

She lets out a sigh, shaking her head. "If that's what you want, I'll make you fried chicken and cake."

"Buttermilk fried chicken."

"Yes, yes. I've got it." She gives him a long look. "Is there anything else?"

"And yellow cake."

"Lord have mercy, yes – and yellow cake." She lifts her hands briefly to Heaven, then turns away, mumbling to herself. She wears a funny expression as she opens the back door and heads inside.

Mrs. Phipps grabs the screen door before it can close. She glances at Lucy. "Young lady, it's time for you to get ready for bed. You've had a long day."

"Yes ma'am. G'night, Earl." She gathers the swimming clothes and hops down from the table.

As his sister goes to enter the house, Mrs. Phipps lays a hand on her shoulder, holding her gently in place. "Lucy, you showed a kindness to my daughter-in-law today. It meant a lot to her. It means a lot to me. Thank you."

Lucy nods somberly then continues inside.

Mrs. Phipps lets the door close then walks to the table. She motions for Earl to shift down and sit properly.

Eyes wide, he drops into his seat and faces her.

She reaches into her pocket and pulls out a cloth napkin. When she opens it, inside is a warm cookie. She gestures for him to accept it.

He looks at the cookie, looks at her.

"It's okay for you to have a cookie. They're fresh-baked. After all the swimming you kids did today, I thought you'd have more appetite. Harold's already eaten two."

"Thank you, ma'am." He accepts the cookie and takes a bite.

"My grandson tells me you boys have been constructing a treehouse in the woods."

"He said it was okay," he mumbles, mouth full of oatmeal raisin.

"Yes, it's okay. I suppose every boy should have a treehouse."

"It's lookin' real good," he says, swallowing. He takes another bite. "You could climb up if you had a mind to. Harold said we shouldn't allow girls – absolutely no girls. But he let Lucy visit. I bet he'd let you visit, too."

"I think my tree-climbing days are over, Earl, but I appreciate the thought." She crosses her arms on the table, looks him in the eye. "It's been an eventful summer for you, hasn't it?"

He freezes, forgetting to chew.

"Go ahead and swallow, Earl." She hands him the napkin. "Now that things have settled down a bit, do you find you still enjoy your work in the garden?"

He swallows, using the napkin to wipe his mouth. "Yes ma'am. I like the garden. I like it fine."

"Mr. Phipps and I had a conversation about you."

"You did?"

"We've had a nice, long summer to get to know you. Hopefully, you feel like you've had time to get to know us." She watches him quietly. He watches her back. "How do you like working with Mr. Joe? You two seem to get along."

"He's a good teacher."

"I'm glad to hear that. I happen to know he finds you to be a good worker. That's why Mr. Phipps and I would like to start paying you a wage."

He rubs his mouth, unsure how to respond.

"Do you understand, Earl? You're going to get paid."

"Money?"

"Yes, Earl, money."

"What for?"

"For tending to the garden, Earl, for doing all the things you're doing now. You're going to be fourteen soon and Mr. Phipps and I would be permitted to list you as a household employee. If you wanted, we could even give you an official title."

"What's that?"

"A title? Well, you could be our junior gardener. And if anyone asks what you do, you tell them, 'I'm the junior gardener.' And Mr. Joe, he'd be the senior gardener. See?"

He considers this information. "I like that."

"The salary won't be much to start. I'll open a new account in both our names at the First National Bank. They know me there and they'll take good care of your money. One afternoon this week, I'll show you how to fill out a withdrawal slip. I'll help you keep a record of your deposits and withdrawals, unless you think you'd like to learn to do that?"

"Mrs. Phipps, I don't know about keeping track of money."

"That's understandable, Earl. But I'd like to help you with that if you don't mind. The weather's going to turn cool soon and there won't be as much work to do in the garden. Once your chores are done, I can work with you for an hour in the afternoon. We'll sit at the kitchen table and work on your sums. That way, someday, you'll be able to take care of your own money. I can also help with reading and writing. Nothing hard, we'll go at your pace.

Maybe include the occasional lesson on grammar and vocabulary. If a man has the right words at his disposal, he doesn't need to rely on his fists." She searches his eyes. "What do you say?"

He wipes one hand slowly down the side of his leg, thinking about his answer. "Thank you, ma'am. You've treated me real good – you and Mr. Phipps and Mr. Joe and Cook – and you took in Lucy when you didn't have to. I won't ever forget it." He drops his gaze to the table.

"Is something wrong?"

He struggles to find the words for what's in his heart. "Mrs. Phipps, I have to tell you somethin'. It's not an easy thing to say."

"It's alright. You can tell me anything."

Gathering his gumption, he looks her straight in the eye. "Mrs. Phipps, I appreciate you offerin' to teach me and all. But I might never be bright like Lucy. It's jus'... I'll make mistakes. I won't mean to, but I will. So, you might not want to pay me a wage. If I can keep sleepin' in the shed and bein' a help to Mr. Joe, I'll be grateful."

"Earl, honey, I am well aware you're going to make mistakes."

His eyes widen in surprise. "You are?"

"Yes. And I know I'm going to make mistakes too. It's what people do."

"But you're smart."

She makes a dismissive sound. "Earl, there's all kinds of smart. I know people who are book-smart and other folks who are people-smart and folks who are machine-smart. Mr. Joe is just about the smartest man I know at growing things. From what I've observed, you might be, too. And

Earl, every kind of person makes every kind of mistake. No one is so smart they don't make mistakes. How else would we learn how to do things better the next time?"

He cocks his head, pondering this idea. "I never thought of it like that."

She gives his hand a pat. "The world needs all our gifts."

"Even mine?"

"Even yours."

THIRTY-EIGHT

When the screen door closes behind Mrs. Phipps, Earl places both hands where he believes his heart to be.

"I'm gonna get a wage." He whispers the words, pressing against his chest and the pain that lives inside him. He's come to terms with the pain and what it means. He understands it's the hole in his heart that used to be filled by his ma. It has the shape of her. It has the feel of her and the smell of her, but it isn't her. She's gone and it's on account of him. The pain of that will be with him till he draws his last breath. "Lucy's here now and we're going to look after each other," he tells his ma. "Mrs. Phipps is gonna teach me how to be better."

Be better. He's still figurin' out what that means, but he knows he wants it.

From the patio, he can hear rustles in the hedge behind the house. Something small creeps among the leaves. He peers in that direction and watches silently as a small pink petal slips loose from its blossom and floats to the ground.

Through the open windows, he can hear Cook giving Lucy instructions for breakfast the next morning. There's a clatter of cookware as Cook explains the purpose of each pot and pan. He expects his food might be a little undercooked for the next few weeks until Lucy gets the hang of things but she's sharp, his sister. She'll catch on in no time. She'll be a big help in the house. And if Mrs. Phipps is going to teach him, as slow as he is, for sure Lucy will get school, too. There's no tellin' what she can amount to. Someday, maybe she'll work for Mr. Phipps in one of his factories. She'd be good at bossin' people.

Rising from the patio table, he takes the cloth napkin with him and places it on a workbench inside the shed. He'll return it to Cook in the morning.

Darkness inches its way across the garden but there's still a bit of light left in the day, so he makes his way to the greenhouse. He stands in the doorway, admiring the pots of flowers. The buds bulge, allowing colorful petals to peek through. Tomorrow, he and Mr. Joe will finally move them into the ground. It will be something to see when everything's in bloom.

He considers Mrs. Phipps' words, about the world needing everyone's gifts. Feeling thoughtful, he closes the greenhouse door and returns to the toolshed, sitting cross-legged on the ground. He rests his head against the wall, waiting to feel tired. Releasing a slow breath, he peels away the blinders from his eyes and peeks into the past. Searching for something pleasant, he finally finds the memory he's seeking. He's standing in the doorway of his ma's bedroom, the baby tucked into her cradle and Ma singing something soft in words he doesn't understand.

He remembers the strength of her hand, how it could lift a full stock pot, but rest lightly on his brow – a tender touch after a harsh blow from his pa.

He misses his ma the most when night descends upon the garden and he's alone. Eyes closed, he remembers listening for Ma's voice calling him to dinner as he hid among the rustling stalks of Farmer Tate's cornfield. He can see her clearly, backlit in the doorway by the glow of a kerosene lamp. Eyes on her silhouette, he calls in the darkness. "Coming, Ma!"

A drop hits his hand. For a moment, he thinks it's rainin'. Then he realizes it comes from him. His eyes have filled with tears. They streak his face, run into his mouth, trickle down his neck. He gazes around the garden and it's as if he's staring through fabric, something sheer and gauzy for ladies. It distorts his view, imbuing the landscape with weight and magic. When he's empty, he wipes a sleeve across his wet face and releases a shuddering sigh.

Suddenly weary, he rises to his feet and enters the shed. He changes into his long johns and climbs into bed. With a muffled yawn, he pulls the blanket to his chin and turns onto his side. He imagines he can hear the garden breathing heavy around him like a living thing. Inhale. Exhale. He pictures his ma kneeling at his side, one hand pressed against his cheek, the way she used to calm him goodnight. As his eyes drift shut, her voice reaches his ears, whisper-light in the darkness. "Earl, honey, you did good."

A smile tugs at his lips. Maybe somewhere in Heaven, his ma is thinking sweet thoughts. She is missing him. He is missing her.

And tomorrow, there will be cake.

AUTHOR'S NOTE

My great-grandfather was sentenced to fifteen years in prison for the crime of incest. The trial was documented with a full-page article in the local newspaper. His crime and ultimate incarceration set in motion a chain of events – the transfer of two daughters to live with a childless, retired couple, the anticipated birthday visit to see their mother and the subsequent need to kill a chicken for their celebratory supper. The real Earl was my grandmother's brother. Once he arrived at the home of his benefactor, he never left. Eventually, the family built him a small, two-room house at the back of the property. He continued as caretaker there until his passing in 1983. He's buried in North Carolina, next to the mother he loved, and accidentally killed.

ACKNOWLEDGEMENTS

The seeds of this story were planted thirty years ago when I shared a hotel room with my grandmother. I used the opportunity to interview her about her life and recorded her answers. As a child, I'd been a prodigious eavesdropper. I hovered in shadows as my parents played cards with aunts and uncles. I put my ear to bedroom walls to hear private conversations. I discovered family skeletons – crimes inflicted by my great-grandfather against his wife and children. The psychological damage rippled through generations. I knew there was a rape and a trial. I knew there was an accidental killing. It was years before I'd gathered sufficient details to connect the dots. Even then, there were critical gaps in the narrative.

As members of my parents' generation passed away, snippets of family history emerged from shoeboxes and file drawers – a photocopy of a 1921 newspaper article covering my great-grandfather's trial for incest plus autobiographical notes from an uncle who'd been dissuaded from publishing by family members uncomfortable with the history he unearthed. I used what I learned about Earl as the framework then fictionalized "in-between the lines" to craft the finished work.

I'm grateful to individuals who reviewed early chapters: Sharilyn, Meg, Ben and Zachary. In addition, I'm indebted to Ann Howard Creel and Marlene Adelstein for developmental editing during critical phases of the novel's evolution. Debra Howell was an essential partner for questions about grammar and style. Beta readers provided by The Spun Yarn shared invaluable feedback.

Finally, I'd like to thank collaborators and associates of Matador Publishing who saw potential in this project and gave it their time and attention: Hannah Dakin, Fern Bushnell, Andrea Johnson, Jack Wedgbury, Chelsea Taylor & Rosie Lowe, Meera Vithlani, Megan Ofoegbu, along with Sam, Gary and everyone else who provided support along each stage of the book's journey.

I might have abandoned this project ages ago if not for a conversation with my friend Elaine. She asked questions, expressed disbelief, then urged me to put everything down on paper. Over the next few years, she provided the encouragement I needed to keep going.

It's important to reiterate that this work is loosely inspired by actual events but it is not biography. I took creative liberties. Dates were changed and identifying details removed to protect the privacy of individuals connected to Earl's life.

I remember meeting Earl only once. I found him to be quiet and humble. He did not like to talk about his past.

This book is printed on paper from sustainable sources managed under the Forest Stewardship Council (FSC) scheme.

It has been printed in the UK to reduce transportation miles and their impact upon the environment.

For every new title that Matador publishes, we plant a tree to offset CO_2, partnering with the More Trees scheme.

For more about how Matador offsets its environmental impact, see www.troubador.co.uk/about/